LIGHT OF THE MOON

Light of the Moon

the Moon

By David James

A

LEGEND OF THE DREAMER

NOVEL

First Edition
First paperback printing, November 2012
First e-format, November 2012

Cover design by Keary Taylor
Edited by Helen Boswell

The characters and events portrayed in this book are fictitious. Any similarity to real persons, living or dead, is coincidental and not intended by the author.

Knapp, David, 1986-
Light of the Moon (Legend of the Dreamer #1)/ by David James. - 1st ed.

ISBN-13: 978-1480082564

Printed in the United States of America

For my parents and sisters-
because they have always believed in me.
If not for them,
my dreams would be only dreams.

"A DREAMER IS ONE WHO CAN ONLY
FIND HIS WAY BY MOONLIGHT,
AND HIS PUNISHMENT
IS THAT HE SEES THE
DAWN BEFORE THE REST OF THE WORLD."
OSCAR WILDE

"THERE IS SOMETHING HAUNTING IN THE
LIGHT OF THE MOON;
IT HAS ALL THE DISPASSIONATENESS
OF A DISEMBODIED SOUL,
AND SOMETHING OF ITS INCONCEIVABLE
MYSTERY."
JOSEPH CONRAD

~

"She closed her eyes, nervous.
She had not sung for nearly twenty years.
To sing was to remember,
and she could barely even live.
But now was not the time for fear.
It rarely ever was."

~

PROLOGUE
THE CHILD OF SHADOW AND LIGHT

THE DEEP SOUTH, LOUISIANA
1804

HER SKIN WAS BLACKER THAN THE SHADOWED sky above her, a mark of the memory of her ancestors. She was a descendant of the most powerful kind of people, those of hope and song, changed by the cruel binds of slavery. On the lone hilltop where only a macabre willow tree grew, she stood blended with the night. Her wild, dark hair rose up and away from her vernal face and eyes the color of wilted wisteria, reaching toward the shining stars and moon. The air near the Singing Tree was still, but the girl shivered as though a storm was rising.

Beside the girl was an older woman with skin that matched her own but reflected a much larger piece of history. The woman's eyes were white clouds in a dark sky, covered by a mist so fine many often forgot she was blind. Her eyes were a mark of the life she lived, of the sights she had seen and the songs she had sung to hide endless emotions. They were the result of hope, a moment in her history when she had found her voice, her song, and then, abruptly, the blade of a whip.

Still, the woman saw more than most.

"Daughter," she said in a voice that was nothing more than a whisper, but because the night was so still and quiet it moved swiftly to the girl's ears. She smiled down, teeth pearls against everything black, hugged herself and ran both hands down the backs of her arms feeling the raised puckers of skin forever damaged. She hoped her daughter would never have to live in slavery, but knew it was already too late. Her daughter had lost her ring finger on her left hand only weeks earlier. A punishment for loving someone she shouldn't. "Are you listening, child? Are you ready? Is your soul, your *ti bon agne* awake?"

"Yes, Momma," the young child said, her voice threaded with apprehension.

The girl had never been to the Singing Tree, had never seen her Momma even look its way. Children of the Night, as her Amma called them, were punished for wandering too close to the Singing Tree. Amma said it gave them too much hope to sing, so they didn't anymore.

But her Momma, the Woman of Prophecy, always had belief in her milky eyes, and this night was different from any other. This night was filled with secrets waiting to be told. It was filled with hope. With magic.

"Close your eyes, child, and let me sing you a legend," the woman breathed. She closed her eyes, nervous. She had not sung for nearly twenty years. To sing was to remember, and she could barely even live. But now was not the time for fear. It rarely ever was.

The woman turned to look at the girl beside her. So young, so not ready to take on the world.

Yet, the woman thought, *she will have to be. This is the end and the beginning, and no one has any way to stop it. It is life and death, this prophecy, shivering through time like poison. When will it end?*

This was how it had been since the time of the first seer, Mryddin; legend passed from mother to daughter and back again. They had called him Mryddin the Merciful when she was a child, the only man strong and kind enough to love the witches. But now there was no time for mercy. If her child was not ready the legend would vanish, taking the world with it.

So because the choice was made for her, the woman raised her hands to the heavens and began to hum the ancient melody her mother taught her; a steady, deep song, as if drums lived inside her. She planted her feet firmly against the ground, exhaled, and as if her breath was caught on wind, her voice lifted up toward the heavens and punctured a hole in the sky, sending a beam of light to shine on mother and daughter. The moon's silver hand hugged them and the legend began, though she was careful to say only what was needed and not what was important. Truth needed to be kept quiet; the world was listening, and it was changing ever more.

"It starts," the woman said, "like so many stories do, with a boy, a girl, and a love that doomed the world. This however, dear child, is not like the stories you know. This is not a happy story with a happy ending. It ends just like it begins, in fire and blood and death. You see, child, this is the story of an angel who fell in love with the Devil, and the forbidden love that destroyed them both; their child of shadow and light."

The girl listened as her Momma told her the story of a beautiful angel and the love that scorned her. Of the child that began to grow inside her, killing her from the inside out.

Soon, the girl's throat began to feel dry and coarse, as though she had tasted the fires of Hell. She swallowed the bittersweet words of life and death when her Momma explained that for the child to live, the mother, the angel, had to die.

"Why?" the daughter asked. "If she was an angel, couldn't she live forever?"

Momma just smiled and said, "There is a price for everything, even life and death and love. When love runs rampant in the depths of Hell, nothing is what it seems. Death was her price to pay for love."

The girl felt her heart clench, but didn't know exactly why. She became silent, her voice gone completely, and did not speak again until the story had left her mother and played in the air around them both once more.

Momma's voice grew quieter as she continued. She told of the child, who was banished from Hell, Heaven, and Earth to live in the limbo of the sky. "With him went the rest of the children who were not meant to be, the offspring of angels and those of their fallen kin, demons. They were cursed to stay trapped in the sky forever. Except, of course, there was a twist. Because of the child's bloodline, he could not be trapped in the sky like the rest; the child of shadow and light is the only son born to the Devil himself. Instead of a life in limbo, the child fell to Earth and lived in secrecy through time. Though the Devil still searches, his son is protected by the blood of his mother, the beautiful and powerful angel, Gabriella. You see, the blood of the Devil is pure hatred, and the blood of an angel is pure love. Though cursed, the son can only be found when he falls in true love. Until then, the world is safe.

"This," Momma continued, "is where the prophecy begins. When the boy, the Dreamer we call him as he is free to walk through his memories by stepping through his dreams but never able to remember them completely, falls in love, *true* love, the Devil will find him."

The mother took a deep breath, and sang the poem that was the *Legend of the Dreamer*. She whispered the story of the boy who was reborn after every death, and of the three hands of the Devil that ran after him in each life. She cried sounds of despair as the boy fell in true love and the Devil came to find him. She sang a song of hope as one boy and one girl became lost in battle and in love.

When the woman was done she looked years older. She had been warned against this, the way the prophecy ate you alive once you told it. It was written in the soul of every woman who kept it and, once spoken, was forever gone.

"You must remember, child," the woman said, "that there is always hope. The boy *will* fall in love. The Devil and his three hands will come for him and war will ravage the world. But in the end, there is only one question that we can ask ourselves."

"What question, Momma?" the girl asked in a cracked whisper.

The mother smiled and turned to her daughter. Though she was blind, the woman imagined what the girl must look like: Nervous, wild, and almost free.

"In the end, everything comes down to love. And so, we must ask ourselves this: Is love enough to save us all?"

"Is it?"

The woman smiled. "We can only hope."

The night was cold, but the daughter was so warm that she hardly needed the tattered shawl her mother had brought for her.

"Momma," she said through a smile, "Is it real, that story?"

For a second, when she closed her eyes to wish the

story true, she smelled the sea-salt air of her ancestors when they traveled across oceans for new land. It felt like a hug, the kiss of air against her cheek, and she knew that it must be true.

"Do you think it so, child?"

"Yes," she breathed, her eyes still closed.

"This air around us has been alive much longer than we, and in it are hints of history and death and life. In the breeze is our lifeline, our lines of blood spread through the ages. Not many can see this, however. Only a Woman of Prophecy has the sight to see the legend. Most think the air is just a wind, a wisp of nothing on a summer's day. Most cannot see our stories."

The daughter could still smell the sea-salt air and she knew it was not a coincidence but a memory of her history, her family's past.

Was this magic? Her Momma had told her the magic tales since she could remember. Could they be real?

"See who we are," Momma urged her. "Embrace your past to see your future."

The girl felt the gusting wind rush around her like a swirling blanket of whispers. The air grew cold as images suddenly appeared before her, dancing in the moonlight. Tightness threatened to enclose mother and daughter as they began to see the past as it was so many years before, so far in the past that the air smelled as sweet as sugar and burned as menacingly as fire.

"Momma! Momma!" her daughter screamed, though her voice was lost to a blinding windstorm that had just picked up. "Momma, what's wrong?"

"Child..." she spoke, her hand clutching her heart, weak after giving an almighty truth so freely. "It is time for me to leave this world and move on to the next. It is time for you to become what you must be, who you are."

"But I don't know what you mean, Momma! Don't leave me!" Pain seeped through her body. Agony like she never knew filled her soul.

"You are the protector, child. All around you is the history of us, of our truths. Follow your heart and protect the prophecy, and when the time is right, share it with your own daughters. You are the Woman of Prophecy. You must save the world by saving the one who is the Dreamer. Without this prophecy the world will be under the spell of the three demons and the Devil himself. When Doomsday is certain, the Dreamer will find us. Let fate be your guide. We keep our secrets in the stars. Blanket the Dreamer in our sacred word so that he may save us all. Help him understand his destiny."

Just as the daughter shouted and a tear rolled down her night-lit face, a breath of wind escaped the starry night and carried her mother away as if on wings.

Calm strength filled the daughter's soul; a new beginning had taken hold.

That night, the new Woman of Prophecy began to understand her obligation, her curse. She was the one who was entrusted with the poem. She would be the one to pass the legend down from mother to daughter until the Dreamer came and salvation was harvested once again.

And so she waits until the voices of evil, of cold, corrupted greed become too loud to hear the warmth of those of truth and virtue. It is then that the Dreamer will come to save the world and fulfill the legend that the Woman of Prophecy keeps so guarded in the night among the stars. For they hold secrets, the stars; dark truths of beautiful and dangerous magic.

PART ONE

The Cruel Hands of Autumn

Murder hits small town

JEFFERSON COUNTY - Murder has hit the small town community of Lakewood Hollow, Colorado. Mayor John White was found murdered in his home late Sunday evening.

After this highly publicized death, Sheriff Morgan of the Lakewood Hollow Police Department has stated "the horrific death of our beloved mayor is certainly linked to our high missing persons count."

Police officials across Jefferson County are stating that the count is up to 28 missing, and locals are calling this "the most perverse and sickening death spree Colorado has ever seen." Morgan, however, has urged the public to consider that "aside from the death of Mayor White, there is no substantial evidence that the 28 missing people were, in fact, murdered. As of now, White is an anomaly in the current case, and possibly the victim of a copy cat."

While police have yet to locate any bodies other than White, all missing persons (including the circumstances surrounding the mayor) have left behind vast pools of blood. Morgan confirmed that blood at every crime scene "has been tested and each has confirmed who that missing person is."

The Bloodletter, as the media has named the rogue abductor, has taken to painting what look to be song lyrics on walls of each victim's home in blood. Although unidentifiable to authorities, experts are working on deciphering the words and the message behind the Bloodletter.

Morgan has stated that local units are "holding additional information until further notice while we work to solve the investigation with departments throughout Jefferson County." Communities are being told to keep calm and act normally while authorities unravel the tragic mystery of the Bloodletter.

CHAPTER ONE
OF MIST AND NIGHTMARES

-CALUM-

THE TREES TOWERED ABOVE, CAGING ME IN *the clearing. A thick mist of fog crawled across the forest floor, rising and falling in heavy waves of dark gray as if breathing.*

Down on my knees, I was shaking.

Hands pressed to the ground, I was afraid.

Pain broke my throat as I screamed. The mist grabbed my fingers and pulled, digging them deep into the dirt. I felt it crawl up my arms and down my throat; stealing my voice, it searched for my heart. It burned, this mist of nightmares. Sitting like ash in my lungs, it stole my breath.

A howl broke through the mist and shivered towards me; the cry of this lone wolf made time beat half as fast. For that moment, the mist listened too, and I could breathe.

My eyes searched the hollow for a way out, but found none.

The trees clung to an amber glow that seemed to live and die around the jagged edges of their branches. With every breath I took, I could see the eerie color burst with life, subside with every exhale. One hundred tiny thorns reached for me, branches waving in the wary light.

I looked up to see a sky of shadows mixed with the vestige of a few faint stars.

In this nightmare, even the stars were trapped.

Then, as the tops of the trees turned a bleeding red in the dark, the mist began to pull again. Leaves began to rip from branches, dancing with the wind in a circle over my head, covering all but a single patch of moonlight. Catching red on its way down, the light of the moon bathed the clearing in a bloody glow. Leaves dripped down with the light, falling slow as death.

Suddenly, a burst of wind reached across the clearing and brushed the leaves next to me back and forth and back again. The movements were slow, measured, and left no mark in the cloudy mist that rose in sudden swirls around me. Still, I felt the frigid air surround me, touch my neck with a cold kiss, and when my hand pulled a drop of sweat from my nose, the wetness looked like blood.

As the wolf howled again, my heart beat so quickly it screamed. My pulse raced toward my heart and crashed into it in an explosion of rampant fury.

I squeezed my eyes shut, tighter and tighter, until I couldn't see anything but a world spotted black and white with darkness. Against my swiftly beating heart, I watched the spots dance in my mind. I tried to forget the crimson forest, forget the mist and nightmares and blood.

I tried to remember the stars.

The mist ran a finger down my back, reminding me what was beyond. Solid waves of it tickled leaves, shaking to the rhythm of the wolf's lament, that sorrowful lullaby calling to my heart.

Lost in a chaotic symphony, I could not forget the sounds.

My stomach burned. I wanted to scream. I had to.

No. No! *My throat exploded in silent pain. My mind screamed at me from somewhere deep within, a place hidden from the dark.*

Wake up! *I could feel blisters pop; blood and sadness oozed down my throat.*

The entire forest screamed, but I was choking. I clung desperately to the wolf's cry and felt my face burn red with tears. No breath, no hope, no sound. I had nothing but the wolf to help me scream.

Hope was lost to red, all blood and mist.

I threw my hands to the ground, coughing as the wind shoved me forward.

I couldn't breathe.

I tried to inhale, to suck in the cold air around me, but it was no use. With every half breath I sputtered and coughed, spitting red onto the ground. The mist twined gray; shadowed fingers around my lungs, my heart.

No! Wake up! *My fingers clawed at the dirt as the mist and leaves erupted in a storm of red. The wind punched the trees until they were bruised and broken, their branches hung in the light of the blood sky, dead and disfigured. Leaves shot to the ground, crashing madly like bombs. I could hear the sound of them ripping through the wind, wailing in pain, until finally they hit the ground and burst into flames.*

Tears flew down my face. I grabbed my throat, but it was too slippery to hold.

And then, the forest was suddenly silent.

Silent, but not still.

The dead trees were dark and wilted. The wind attacked them with such force that branches flew into me, cutting my arms and face. The world tilted, and in that war I saw my fate. Somehow I knew this was a twisted version of my future.

This was how I was going to die.

I watched the chaos. The world of amber and red grew hazy. The mist turned black at the edges of my mind, and soon covered my vision, killing the swift speed of time.

Then, slowly, the blackness turned into a very faint white light. It was beautiful, comforting; all around me was blinding. The forest was gone.

I closed my eyes and let hope linger.

Whispers seemed to surround me, haunting melodies of quiet voices. Though I couldn't make out what was being said, the song lingered in me until even the tips of my fingers tingled.

My veins pumped hotter, the blood flowed faster. A heat started to fill my body and soul, and I felt myself lift off the ground and into the warm white. The air was thick, wrapping itself around me and pushing into my lungs

I opened my eyes and, for a moment, thought I saw a flash of purple. A face in the mist.

Save me, *I thought.*

At once the sky erupted in a storm of lightning, so bright and blinding I held a hand up to my face to shield my eyes, turning my face to blink.

I gasped. In the divine light my skin looked almost black, tiny dots of light flickering within it.

A voice in the night, cracked with desperation, filled the world around me until it was everything: "Awake, Caeles. Awake! The time has come for you to embrace your destiny. You must join us again, brother. Look in your heart and see the past as it was and will be.*

"Awake, Caeles...

"Look to the stars for guidance..."

~

Heart crashing against my ribs, I awoke with sweat rolling down my face.

Breathing rapidly. Eyes searching. Mouth open.

Cold. *Freezing.* Shivers crawling like snakes on my skin.

I grabbed at the sheets around me.

It was over. I was really awake.

I lay back against my pillow. My heart slowed, and I breathed easier. I let the sheets go, closed my eyes, and tried to find myself.

Rain tapped against my window. Soft pings against glass sang slowly, and then faster and louder until I knew I could not fall back asleep. Like the rain, confusion pounded at my mind.

I ground my teeth together. Who was Caeles? Would I ever wake to a peaceful morning? Or be plagued forever by wuthering dreams.

Outside, dawn was breaking. I could see the dim, hesitant colors of it trying to cut through the storm.

"Calum!" I heard Mom yell from down the hall. "I hope you're awake. You'll be late for school and I am not waiting an hour to drive you like last time."

A burst of air escaped my mouth. I ran a hand through my hair and said, "Yeah, Mom. Just waking up." My voice tasted like gravel, as though the mist had been real.

I threw the covers back but stayed in bed. My hand moved over the clustered birthmark on my upper arm. I had hardly any freckles on my body, but the ones I did have were brown, normal. This birthmark, though, had always been a dirty black, as if midnight had kissed each spot.

Since I was small, I'd wondered what the mark meant, and for a while I thought it meant I was special. Sometimes still, when morning or night came too early and I was alone, I would wish on each of the twenty-five dots and pretend they were wishing stars.

I closed my eyes and pressed into the mark.

A wish. Just one.

That's all I needed.

I let go and let my heart race against everything my mind said shouldn't be.

A wish. *Love.* Just one.

CHAPTER TWO
BEAUTIFUL MONSTER

-CALUM-

SEPTEMBER WAS A LINGERING BLACK IN Colorado, and the sleepy city of Lakewood Hollow was forever wet this month; not even the mountains could keep the storms away. Clouds rolled in, bringing thunder and lightning, and rain dropped from the sky as if it never would again. The air was sweet. Every breath I took was filled with a shaking crash, every exhale a boom.

"Any big plans today after school?" Mom asked as we stopped at the light on the corner of Misery and Joy, about a block away from school. The *swish, squeak, swish* of wiper blades against glass made her voice a trill of quavering notes.

"No, not really," I said. I could still taste the mist.

She was putting on lipstick, Desperately Red, and smacked her lips just as we jolted forward on Misery.

Smack. "Well, let me know if anything changes."

Like an old habit, she touched the space below her right eye that, up until this past year, had been continuously black and blue.

"I will."

Blood red nails brushed through her tawny hair,

twisting the ends and letting the pieces fall around her shoulders.

Smack. "You know you'll never meet anyone if you just sit at home all weekend writing those silly songs no one sings. I think you need to really put yourself out there. It's on all the television shows. You can't expect to be happy if you just..."

I sighed. She wasn't talking to me anymore.

Take your own advice, Mom, I used to say. Now nothing and no one can touch her. My silence says more than anything.

So many things I used to do with her: Laugh, smile, love. When things were colored black and blue, I knew how to live. Now, in a world as gray as the sky outside, I was just as lost as the sunlight.

I touched a finger to the window. I could almost feel the rain if not for the glass, almost feel the wind push back against me. I pressed harder, harder until I heard the window scream *no*. I felt it move. My finger turned red, the nail white, and so, so cold.

I pulled away, and a shiver ran up my arm and crashed into my heart.

The day Dad left was the day Mom stopped loving me. I remember the door slamming, screams breaking glass. I remember looking out my window to see him driving away. Mom broken and bleeding on the floor, all tears and pain. I remember reaching down to brush glass from her face, and the look in her eyes that said she would never love me, never see *me*, again.

Mom looked at me from the side, her right eyebrow arched. "You okay?" I could smell the whiskey on her breath. "You look a little pale. Those disappearances on the news last night didn't scare you did they? All that blood...

The police will figure it out. They know what to do." She reached a hand across the console to brush a crop of my dark hair back behind my ear, but stopped before she got too close. "You really need to do something about that hair. I don't know what you kids see in looking like you live on the streets these days."

"I'm fine, Mom," I whispered, shrugging away, ignoring the way she wouldn't touch me. I tugged the sleeves of my charcoal hoodie down to cover my hands. "Fine."

She smiled and said, "I know."

Mom smiled a lot more since that day. She moved as if dancing, as if each day broke and set in song. Every morning I would hear her singing in the shower, every night laughing herself to sleep. People said they saw a sparkle in her eyes, one that hadn't been there before.

If not for the whiskey I might have believed them, but I hadn't seen her eyes directly in almost a year. Every now and then, however, when she thought I couldn't see, I would catch her looking up at the sky in memory of something that made her eyes wet. It was then that I remembered her eyes were gray, light and dark like rain at dusk.

I'm fine, I thought as I breathed in and out.

I'm fine, but-

I am my father's son.

I moved my hand to my birthmark. My skin was always warm, as if my blood burned fire; even through my hoodie I could feel the heat of it against my palm. In that, I found a small comfort.

All around me the world was changing. The leaves committed graceful suicide one by one with each gust of wind, dancing to the ground in piles. One day soon I would look up and see that every tree was barren, alone and dead.

I couldn't help but think: *Am I dying? Is she?*

"Calum? Hello, Calum? *Hello?*"

I jumped. "Sorry, Mom. What?"

She sighed, and the scent of oak and old raisins filled the car. I wondered if she would ever stop now that he was gone, but I knew she wouldn't; he was easier to forget at the bottom of a bottle. "Remember I'll be at the office a little later than normal tonight. You're on your own for dinner. That'll be okay, right?"

"Yeah. I think I'll probably end up going to Tyler's after school, anyway. I'll see what he says."

"I'm just so overwhelmed with this new account. I swear, if we don't get a new business plan together soon they'll move on to another marketing firm."

"I'm sure you'll be fine."

She smiled. *Smack.* "I know. Just nerves."

Her eyes focused on the road for a while, but every now and then I saw them glance at me, lingering on a subject she found better left unsaid. Until, "Are you sure you'll be all right?"

I am dead to her.

"Yeah, Mom. I'll be okay, really." I rolled my head to the right so I could watch the scenery roll by. Rays of sun tried to push through the barrier of dark clouds with little hope. My breath made foggy circles on the window. My hands brushed my jeans. "I was just thinking about Dad."

"Well, as long as you're okay."

In the window, I could see her reflection, see the way her skin paled white and her lips thinned. I saw the way her eyes screamed: *Smile like a mother should. Pretend. Smile and he'll stop talking.*

Everything would be okay if we just forgot *him*.

I wanted to but I couldn't. Every day I grew more angry; each was a dark tunnel and I couldn't see a light at the end. Even though I never went over the edge, my toes hung over and I was afraid hope had already fallen off the cliff.

In my reflection I saw what Mom did; my father's nose and jaw, his lips and hair. His scowl. His anger. Only my eyes were my own.

When had I become this monster?

When had I truly become the son of Luke Wade?

My hands balled together, turning red and white.

This, I thought. *This is because of him, this madness I feel day after day, like I can't trust anyone. This constant shiver of regret is* his *fault.*

My teeth were clenched, eyebrows bent. With every breath I took I felt my heart race a little faster, every second my reflection more my father's.

Would I ever be myself again?

"And you know you can call me whenever, even during school. I'm here for you whenever you need me," she said, her voice hovering over a single, dark note much too high. Her eyes glued to the road, never blinking.

"Thanks, Mom," I said to my reflection.

I saw her eyes flicker at me, then down, and then back up to the visor mirror; what she was about to say would be easier with me as a shadow of myself.

I knew what was coming; I felt the familiar feeling run toward me, hurtling itself at me just as fiercely as the rain against the car.

The past. *Him.* Memories.

Mom's voice was numb and fearful, a lament of graceless agony, and I could feel the mist rising like waves in my throat.

She spoke quickly, her words almost slurring together. "You look *so* much like him, Calum. But your eyes... I remember the first time I saw your eyes I thought to myself that someone had found a way to trap moonlight reflected on the bluest sea in each of them. So bright they seemed to glow. I thought for sure I could see my soul inside your eyes, like mirrors looking deep inside me. Every time you look at me..."

Her voice grew quiet. "I can't look anymore. I just... I sometimes wonder if you would have... If you'll end up like..."

Her knuckles were white, shaking against the steering wheel. She whispered, "I just want to be happy."

I am nothing.

My eyes found a water mark on the windshield. In seconds I would vomit.

You look so much like him.

Her words cut deep.

I felt sick; a fever of hot and cold touching me all over.

All I could think was this: *I am my father's son.*

I felt screaming fury build inside me. If I could destroy my reflection, I could kill what was left of my father. I could get rid of these monsters forever: Anger, sorrow, guilt. My hands balled themselves into tight fists, turning white.

I stopped breathing until all I heard was my heart, and thought, *Don't give in. Don't become him.*

Mom and I fell into silence, and I let my mind drift hopelessly away. The sounds of the radio filled my voids. The bittersweet symphony of autumn, the season of life and death, drummed against my conscience.

When we pulled into the school's parking lot, Mom leaned back in her seat and the clean smell of lemongrass filled the car. I wondered what she smelled like before perfume covered her, but I couldn't recall a memory without it. I loved the sharp, sweet smell, so comforting and homelike. Somehow, it made me feel better even though she didn't.

Suddenly, like a wave being pulled back by an unforgiving tide, Mom said, "I know he still loves me."

I couldn't stop the anger from crashing against me then; I felt myself being pulled down, down until I couldn't breathe and the world became dark and cold. This was a quiet kind of rage. The kind that made no noise before it pounced. Before it ate your heart and left you shaking, all dust and bone and nothing.

"Don't say that, Mom," I whispered.

I turned away from my shadow and closed my eyes but Dad was everywhere.

I wondered if I still loved him, or her.

I thought about those things always; I had never seen love, true love. I wasn't even sure it existed, or if I believed.

"He still loves me. Us. I can feel it right before I fall asleep at night..."

You feel the whiskey in your blood.

"...and I see him in the shadows of my candles..."

You see him in the glare of an empty bottle.

"... When I sit by the fire, I can feel him and I know he still loves me. Us."

He will never love us. You will never be the same.

I looked hard at the windshield, noticing a bug the color of rust crawling across the surface, fighting against raindrops. It was something to focus on, but all I could think of was *Dad, Dad, Dad.*

Am I so like him that she won't look at me for more than a second?

"And I -"

I am nothing!

"All right, Mom! I'm late so I'll see you later."

"Oh," she breathed. She ran both hands down the front of her black blazer and shook her head slightly. "Right. Do you need a note or anything?" Her hand flew to her purse, and I could see the scraps of paper filling the inside, waiting: To be taken, to be touched, to hold an excuse. She had so many the papers spilled onto her lap.

"I'll be okay," I said. And then, thinking of the missing people I'd heard of on the news and the Bloodletter, "Be safe, Mom."

I shot her a quick smile and started to get out of the car, the door squeaking as I opened it.

"Bye!" she called already pulling away.

I felt light, a shiver of relief.

A smile slowly grabbed my lips and curved them up as I walked toward the school. I let the rain fall on me, let the cool droplets burst hard against my skin. In those few moments alone, I began to feel something I lost and found each morning; purpose was in the air around me, and I breathed as deeply as I could.

I looked up at the two story brick building, its gleaming blue-black windows glaring down and catching rare flickers of sunlight. The ominous Lakewood Hollow High School name plate was fixed above the main doors, its iron letters flanked by tall trees the color of autumn. Leaves cluttered the school's lawn, the reds, yellows, and oranges making the grass carpet look dusted with dead fireflies.

The air was stale, filled with the scent of decaying

things, but the rain from the mountains added a crisp edge that lingered in the wind.

With each step I felt my anger fade.

Here, I knew who I was, and the thrilling confidence of knowing pushed a rare energy through my veins. A rhythm of words found the beat of my heart, pushed out, and crashed in the air around me:

> *So the sun breaks the day*
> *So am I who breaks-*
> *The day is a shadow*
> *And I am the sun.*

Here, I had my best friend, Tyler. I had friends - faces that smiled, and those that didn't. Still, they looked. They saw me.

Here, I was someone.

Suddenly, I tripped on a piece of concrete that hadn't been set right in the sidewalk. Out of the corner of my eye, I thought I saw a shadow of something familiar.

My heart beat in time to *Dad, Dad, Dad.*

I thought I heard a whisper on the wind. A voice deep with a mysterious delirium of pain and need that sent an anxious chill crawling up my spine.

> *Calum.*
> *You are your father's son.*

But when I looked back I saw only a tree, blazing red with dying leaves.

~

Mr. Brandt didn't leave much room for people to

like him. He was brash and harsh, and always smelled of disdain. He never smiled, never laughed. Mr. Brandt was crooked and morose, his edges pained with age and misery.

He reminded me of home.

"Pass?" he muttered, not looking at me.

I handed him the office slip, then made my way to a seat near the back. Mr. Brandt faced the board and went back to scratching a complicated problem in the blackness. The room was quiet and sleepy, though every other second carried chills: Dry chalk against the board like grinding bones. I felt eyes upon eyes bore into me as I moved deeper into the room, until none could see me except one.

"You know if you ever make it to school on time no one will know what to do," Tyler whispered, his voice low.

I stepped over his leg to sit down; he was keeping it in an air cast after he twisted his ankle during the last football game.

He leaned close. "Everything okay? You look like you've seen a ghost."

"Just more of the usual," I said, sitting down.

He stared at me. His smile began to fade, his dark green eyes narrowed. "I don't buy that. What's up, really?"

My voice caught in my throat; a whisper exploding up and breaking open my lips. In one word, the mist came back as though it never left: "Nightmares."

Tyler leaned closer, the muscles in his arms rippling as he moved. This close, I could see thirty shades of green in his eyes.

Thirty shades of concern.

He breathed, "Still? I thought those stopped a year ago after... Well, *after*."

After he left.

So many good things happened after, but for some

reason my nightmares made me remember the before.

Before, when his anger choked me.

I felt Tyler's hand poke mine. "It doesn't mean anything if you don't want it to. Remember that."

My chest hurt. I hadn't realized I was holding my breath. "Sometimes you don't have a choice in what things mean to you."

A beat. A breath. "Sometimes you do."

Brandt faced us again, gathering papers on his desk. He shifted them, stacked and re-stacked, so that when he was done they looked exactly the same. As much as I hated Brandt, I understood. He was stalling. Buying extra time before he had to face reality.

But one thing Brandt didn't understand was this: Sometimes reality was far better than the world of nightmares, its familiarity easier than inconstant dreams.

Brandt adjusted his tie. Chin up, his brown, bored eyes glanced around the room focusing on nothing. "After you copy down the problem on the board, try solving for the solution." He sighed. "This is only Junior Algebra, people. If you can't do this I suggest you adjust your schedule for your senior year so we can see each other again. Remember, there is only one correct solution but multiple ways to solve for it. Stay quiet."

Tyler tapped his pencil on his desk. His lips puffed out as he exhaled and breathed, "Turn around."

"What?" I asked.

"What happened in your nightmares?"

"Quiet!" Brandt's eyes narrowed, his yellow teeth bared behind thin lips. "No talking."

For the next ten minutes I pretended: To be interested, to copy notes, to solve problems. In the quiet room surrounded by normality, I pretended to be normal, too.

I pretended to forget.

When Brandt revealed the solution and the possible ways to get it, Tyler swore and I knew we had the same problem; our answers were wrong, no matter which way we took to find them.

As Brandt started to explain what was right and wrong, I searched my notebook for a blank page to take notes on. The entire thing was filled with doodles and words and silly songs. I stopped when I found one nearly blank, except for one word, one question: *Love?*

"Even though adding the numerators together after finding the lowest common denominator seems right, the sum would not give you the correct overall answer in the end. In fact," Brandt said as he crossed off a wrong number on the board, "you should have realized the only way to get the correct answer here is to subtract."

I understood.

I drew a single line on the page, subtracting what needed to go: ~~Love?~~

I smiled and looked up to see Tyler, eyebrow raised, looking at me. He shook his head and looked down. His hand moved across his paper in fury as he muttered, "Stupid, stupid, stupid."

"I don't get it either," I whispered to him.

He didn't look up. "You shouldn't just give up, though."

"I haven't," I said, confused. "Brandt's not even going to put this on the test."

When he looked at me I saw concern behind the green. His voice was a sharp hiss. "C'mon, Calum. I see you giving up, and you can't anymore. I won't let you. What exactly were your nightmares about that you're acting like this?"

"Like what?"

He looked down at my paper. "Like you've given up on everything but being miserable."

I looked down too, and realized I'd been filling in the page with pictures. A boy with large hands sat in the middle of the page, surrounded by lines and lines of trees. I had pressed so hard with my pencil that breaths of gray ash flew across the surface in dark shadows; the ~~Love?~~ was impossible to see.

"Explain," Tyler said quietly, like he cared. Like always.

I exhaled and watched the pencil ash dance and die; pieces of gray running across the desk and jumping off.

At his desk, Brandt was lost in his newspaper. I saw the headline: *Bloodletter: What Nightmares Are Made Of.*

I shivered. I breathed, "It was so real this time, so real I could still taste it this morning. I was in a forest surrounded by all these dying things. It was like there were a thousand ghosts around me; mist was everywhere, alive and breathing and suffocating me. I almost died. I almost...

"Then there was this light that was everywhere at once. It pulled me up, hugged me and I was finally able to breathe. And my skin... It was black and shiny and filled with tiny lights as bright as the moon."

There was Tyler and nothing else but the memories I wanted so badly gone. "I almost died again."

"But you didn't," he said as I thought, *Like always.*

"How do you know your dreams are *supposed* to have meaning anyway?" Tyler continued. "Sometimes a dream is just a dream."

"I don't know, Tyler. This dream, especially, was

just intense. They have to mean something. I can feel it. I just wish I knew what they were telling me."

Tyler moved closer to me. His eyes found mine and for a moment it felt as though he was trying to look beyond the blue. His eyes, like clouds before a tornado, moved back and forth, searching.

I hoped he would find some truth inside.

"Calum," he said. "You are not your father."

I expected this: Mist in my throat, eating me alive again until memories of my father made me scream. Instead I felt relief, a calm warmth of familiarity, of always.

"Thanks," I said.

"Well, you aren't him. You forget that sometimes."

I almost laughed. "I wish I could forget so much more."

"Nah," he said. "No one should forget the past. Just maybe not dwell on it as much. You have to know where you came from to know where you're going."

Still, as we fell into silence, I tried.

Underneath the other, I wrote a new word in my notebook: *Hope*.

Then, for the first time in years, my thoughts were not of what was, but what could be. They were desperate and vivid thoughts, clinging to my every breath and falling onto my paper in words: *Family, friends, future*.

My lips tugged up at the sides and Tyler said, "Better, Calum. Better."

And then I felt the air being sucked from the room, and whispers like bees cut through the quiet.

I looked up. A shiver tickled my chest when I saw her. Invisible hands wrapped themselves around my heart and squeezed.

"Who is that?" Tyler asked.

I shook my head. She was a stranger, a mystery, but one thought choked me until I couldn't breathe: *I know her.*

Brandt had his arm around her shoulders; even from my desk I could see the way she leaned away. His smile didn't fit his face, the lines mapped in discourse. Every other second he would look down at the seating chart in his hand as he introduced us one by one.

She was beautiful.

Her dark brown curls fell in loose waves past her shoulders, and they seemed to move in a heavy tide with every turn of her head. Her face was shaped like a heart. Her skin was a dark, liquid gold, dotted with tiny freckles that looked like stars upon it. With every name, her lips opened, slightly smiling; they were full and shining and red as blood on snow. As she brushed a curl away from her lips, I saw the faint outline of a tattoo on her right pointer finger, though I couldn't make out what is was.

How do I know you? I thought.

My heart *boomed* so hard against my ribs until:

I can't breathe.

"And this is Calum Wade."

Too much, too fast.

Our eyes met.

I'm dying.

One moment lingered forever.

Hope.

Blue against eyes so dark they looked violet.

~~*Love?*~~.

Her eyes narrowed into this: *I hate you.*

I can't breathe.

"Do you know her?" Tyler asked when she turned away.

Those eyes, I thought. *I know those eyes.*

44

"No," I whispered. My hands were palm down on my desk, fingers spread out like branches, digging hard into the fake wood. "I've never seen her in my life."

The bell sounded and Tyler said, "Well, Kate looked like she really knew you. Wonder what that was about."

Kate. Her name was ash in my mouth, more bitter than mist, and thoughts of her filled my mind.

I hurried toward the hall with my head down, avoiding Kate as much as possible. As I rushed past her though, my eyes couldn't look away. When they locked with hers, helpless against the violet, the world dissolved into a ballad of quiet rage, whispered words like daggers in the air.

-Kate-

"Welcome to your nightmare, Calum Wade," I whispered so only he could hear. "You have three days."

I knew it was him the moment our eyes met; it was though the air smoldered in agony around me. Made everything too hot. Made anger shiver through my body.

His eyes: *As blue as though they were filled with cold, dead bodies...*

Made me forget how to breathe.

Finally, after so long we found him.

Relief burned around my heart and made way for more anger. For revenge.

I would have to tell Marcus soon, but until then Calum was mine. Until then I was stuck in this school, this Hell. Every second here made me glad we didn't have school in the Order. Only training, which was fine with me; I got to kill things.

I balled my fists tightly.

Three days.

There, in the tiny, sickly-illuminated classroom, I began the countdown that meant his death.

Three days, I repeated silently.

My heart began an unsteady cadence, burning and beating like fire.

Days now instead of months separated Calum from the world of the living and the land of the dead. Maybe I should have been sympathetic, but all I could think was this: He would die and I would finally live. Be free, happy.

If I wouldn't have found him the countdown would have been my own. I would have run until I couldn't, and life was not nearly as fun if you were the one running away.

I never ran away.

I ran toward the kill, one foot after the other, racing against the wind, nothing stopping me until I delivered the final death blow.

And Calum? I could kill him in one beat of my heart.

I was going to enjoy this game.

I just couldn't let the Orieno get him first.

CHAPTER THREE
BLACK KEYS

-CALUM-

LAKEWOOD WAS UNDER A DOME, IT FELT like; a dreamquake where time tilted on its side and hours became slowly moving figments of reality. For the rest of the day classes went by in blurs, muted and hollow. Lifeless. Each moment bled into the next until I felt more alive inside my mind than out of it. The world there was electric; it was life laced with question and possibility.

An unrelenting whisper like poison: *Three days.*

That one decaying thought made my pulse race every time someone spoke to me. No more was my sense of here and now, but rather what might be. Around every corner, I jumped, thinking it was her; living between life and reality I felt my energy wither, haunted by the memory of Kate.

"I see nothing. Again," Tyler said looking around.

I pointed down the hall. "She was just there."

He sighed. "That's what you said the last five times you thought you saw her. There *are* other people in the hall, Calum. The lunch bell just rang."

"I swear I'm not making this up. She's following me!"

"Maybe." Tyler put his hand on my shoulder. "But I'm pretty sure she wasn't in the guy's bathroom."

A smile flickered. "I told you I wasn't sure about that."

"Though if she was," he continued, "I might have to rethink why we're avoiding her."

I punched him in the arm.

"What?" he laughed. "All I'm saying is that if she likes you enough to stalk you in the bathroom, she can't be all that bad."

I shook my head and opened my mouth but nothing came out. Tyler was wrong. This felt different, serious.

Bodies pushed against me, rising in waves too close.

When I spoke, my voice surprised me. It shook and warbled through the air, sounding flat. "I can't get what she said out of my head."

"What did she say again?" Tyler asked, his voice softer. Our steps marked time together as we walked down the hall. "You have three days?"

I nodded as my shoulder jerked up, waves upon waves elbowing back. "Yeah, but I have no idea what that means. I mean three days to *what*? Live?"

Tyler laughed again but I couldn't. Those times I saw her the world became cold and slow, too slow. Our eyes would lock and I could see nothing else but her: Shaking fists, shoulders pushed forward, teeth grinding, and eyes that could make the warmest heart grow cold.

Too many waves closing in. Soon, I would drown in this sea. I could feel the air begin to thin as the scent of sweat and perfume took over.

Tyler and I turned the corner closest to the cafeteria and I felt the wrothy waves crash against me in one final blow until all the air was gone and I was left alone, suffocating on the floor.

"Watch where you're walking," Kate said as she shoved past us. Then, a whisper of shattered glass hidden against a crash of thunder: "Calum Wade, I will *kill* you."

"Watch it yourself," Tyler said, helping me up. "Okay, I take back what I said. No way you want anything to do with her even if she likes hanging out in bathrooms. You all right?"

Those eyes.

"Yeah, I'm fine. Thanks."

I am always fine.

"Okay." He grabbed at his navy and white LET'S GO ALL THE WAY AT HOMECOMING football shirt. The entire team was wearing them today. "I need to go see Nurse Anne real fast to see if I'm cleared to play at the Homecoming game next week. Coach will kill me if my leg isn't better."

"See you at lunch."

"Grab me a piece of pizza if you beat me?"

I nodded. "No problem."

Before he left, Tyler grabbed my shoulder and silence fell between us. The hall was quiet, a deathlike expanse of sea free of movement. In the distance I heard the roar of lunch like thunder.

One

Two

Three

Three seconds before someone opened the cafeteria door and the thunder boomed louder.

One

Two

Three

Tyler's voice cracked through the dead hall. "Don't

sweat the small stuff, Calum. Kate's clearly someone neither of us should be hanging around. I mean, if you don't know her and she already made some threat toward you after only being at Lakewood a few minutes, she can't be good. If you've never seen her before, there's no way she has anything against you. Don't even think about her, just let it go."

"I know," I said but all I could think was a panicked thought: *I know those eyes from somewhere. Purple rain falling down in sheets; I am caught in this storm. There's only this, only her. That's all I can see, and all I can think is: I must have seen her before.*

And then, for a terrifying moment, my thoughts boomed and bent into feelings strong enough to paralyze: *Will Dad come back? Will he kill this time?*

I breathed in...

This is too much, this storm of him and her.

...and tried to forget.

Tyler smiled as he walked away calling, "Seriously. Let this go, otherwise it'll eat you alive."

But, as I turned and walked through the cafeteria doors and the thunder crashed against me, my eyes hit two hundred others forcing one thought to rise above the rest: *They could be anywhere.*

Tyler was right; I could feel those thoughts sinking their teeth into my heart until I had no choice but to live them all over again.

I tried to push it all away, but couldn't.

Then, instead of thinking about what was, I found myself focusing on what wasn't.

I am not breathing.

I am not living.

I am not me.

I could not forget.

As I walked to where my friends sat, I lost myself in the sounds of the screams of teenage dreams, hoping I could find a way to breathe again. And, in the middle of the wonderland that no one really understood because it never seemed long enough to let you, I remembered.

Mom and I stood shaking in the icy October night, wind screaming at us as though it never would again. The whole night was like that: Loud and angry. Even the moon, full and infinitely bright, seemed to shiver with quiet rage like an old enemy. And as the moon lit up the sky, so did our house burning orange in the darkness.

"Stupid kid," my father said to the police. He rubbed his thumb against the back of his head. "He's only five. Must have knocked a candle over in his sleep."

I hadn't.

It had been the anger.

The moon. Always when the moon was full, bursting.

Mom squeezed against me, but I could feel her pulling away as though the wind was pushing her back. She had a rule, I knew: Never be close enough for it to mean something.

"Let's go sit in the car, Calum," she said. "It's too cold to stand out here."

It was even colder in the car, the wind somehow finding its way in through the cracks and thin windows. In the back seat, I could see Dad still talking to the police, see the way he pointed at me, his lips forming words: Stupid, idiot, worthless, nothing. I could see the fire reflected in his eyes.

That's when I first thought this: I am nothing.

And when I felt anger rise again, felt rage burn inside and destroy me like flames to our house, I thought this: I am my father's son.

"*Calum?*" *Mom said, her voice tense and afraid.* "*Don't do it again. Get out of the car!*"

But I couldn't move.

I could hear him scream louder than the wind. "*I'm not paying for what that stupid kid did. I didn't even want him.*"

I closed my eyes. I could feel the familiar rush of tormented hate as it coursed through me like acid.

Stop. Stop. Why couldn't this stop?

I heard a car door slam and mine open and Mom was pulling me out of the car but it was too late. I felt the car explode, felt the heat as the burst of metal and plastic and fire threw us across the yard.

I heard Mom land next to me, heard bone crunch and heavy breathing and "*I'm okay. It's just my wrist.*"

"*See! The boy's a freak!*" *Dad shouted.*

He was right.

I felt more anger, but pushed it away.

I promised myself I'd never feel angry again.

I'd hide it somewhere deep inside so I could never find it, push it far away so it would never find me, until it disappeared forever and I was free. Until I could live and breathe and be me without destroying things I loved.

I didn't know how it happened, this secret power only my parents knew of but never spoke about, but I knew anger was the reason. What else could it be?

Like a fist against my face: "*Damn kid is a freak.*"

He was the reason, too.

I opened my eyes and saw the stars, how they blinked and lit the sky in close clusters. Saw how they made beautiful shapes. Somehow, even though they were all different sizes and colors, they came together as though they always had. As if it was normal to be that close.

That was the first time I noticed the stars.

The last time I cried.

I picked out a star, the brightest one, and made a wish.

~

"Nothing is how it's supposed to be," said Annabelle Lee. Her body moved like an ebony worm as I sat down, her eyes struggled to find a safe place on me, like always; I was a topic better left unsaid.

"Hi, Calum," Annabelle said smiling cold.

An unspoken rule: If they were to really look at me, they wouldn't like what they saw; a boy filled with a dark past no one really wanted to understand. Secrets everyone suspected but no one dared question. So they smiled and waved and said they were happy to see me, their eyes never meeting mine.

I was more ghost than boy; they saw me, but didn't.

No one but Tyler ever really did.

But I had something unspoken, too: I liked it that way. If they didn't have to look, neither did I. These were the hours I could pretend to be normal.

Pretend to forget that *I am not me.*

"Homecoming is next week and they haven't even started putting up the decorations I made," Annabelle complained. "Everything is so wrong."

"So you've said for the past three days, Annabelle," said Tyler. Somehow he managed to beat me to the table. He took a huge bite of pizza and said, "Hey, Calum."

"*Sick*, Tyler," Annabelle said, her long black hair, straight as arrows flying, tossing back. "Swallow before you speak. We don't need to see what you're chewing, thanks."

I cringed. She always said his name like *Ty-luh*, with a shrill lift at the end as though she were singing, which might have been nice had her voice sounded any less deviant.

"You say that everyday, babe," Chad told her as he reached his hand farther down her arm, brushing it up and down and up again. Annabelle and Chad Glass had been dating on and off since middle school; they had matching rings to prove it. "And the school can go to Hell if they don't like your decorations."

Annabelle rolled her eyes. "Shut up, Chad. They just haven't put them up yet. They will like tomorrow or something."

"Then why are you making such a big deal about it?"

"Because it is a big deal! You have no idea what I went through making those decorations."

"I just defended you!" Chad shouted, throwing his arms out in confusion.

"You just don't get it." She sighed. "You don't know me at all."

I don't know me, either, I thought.

"I used to," Chad said under his breath.

"Yeah," I whispered. No one heard over the noise.

Jason Miles, wearing his shirt that matched Tyler and Chad's, slammed into the table when he sat down. "What's up guys?"

Annabelle slid closer to him. "Chad's being a dick."

"So, nothing new?" Jason laughed, and shoved a

handful of fries in his mouth.

"Shut up, man," Chad said, but he smiled at Jason. They started talking about next week's game just as Annabelle's friend Michelle sat down next to her.

Tyler leaned in close so only I could hear. "Think they'll last?"

"Chad and Annabelle?" I laughed. "This time or the next seven times they break up and get back together?"

"Good point. Hey, cast is off! Nurse Anne said I'm good to go. I just have to watch myself during the next few games. Make sure I don't play too rough."

"You? Play rough? *No*," I joked.

He punched me lightly in the arm. I was just about to punch him back when Chad slammed his hands on the table in a crash that forced silence.

"So, Jason," Chad said slowly, his teeth clenched. He cleared his throat. "You getting pumped for the game next week?"

He nodded. "Sure." And then, "Hey Annabelle? You're in British History third period, right? You think you could help me with my homework later tonight? I have to write this paper on World War Something and I could really use you."

"Yeah." Annabelle blushed. "I'll come over your house at like nine."

Chad gritted his teeth. "Actually, we already had plans, Jason, so I guess-"

"No, we didn't," Annabelle said. Her voice was high, hanging in the air like temptation. She looked at Jason and said, "We didn't have plans. Chad doesn't know what he's talking about."

"Yes, we did!" Chad said, his words falling frantically. He stood up, and his hands gripped the table, turning white. "Why are you doing this again, Annabelle?"

Annabelle ignored him. "So, Jason, I'll see you later tonight. I have some stuff you can help me with, too."

"What, Anatomy?" Tyler muttered.

Jason smiled at Annabelle, and I could see them turn toward each other. Annabelle inched away from Chad, moving slowly closer to Jason until they were almost touching.

Chad fell into his seat. "You know what? I'll come over, too. I'm in British History sixth period and could use the extra help. That won't be a problem, will it guys?"

"What?" Annabelle whispered.

Jason coughed and sputtered, "Oh. What? Yes. I mean, no, that won't be a problem."

"Great!" Chad smiled. He winked at Tyler. "See you both at nine."

Tyler cleared his throat and the table seemed to shift back to normal. Michelle and Annabelle began discussing their Homecoming dresses, turning away from Jason and Chad.

"You have a date for the dance yet?" Tyler asked me.

"Nah," I shrugged. "Not yet."

Jason poked me, as if he didn't think I was real. "You should ask that new girl!"

I shook my head. I had just been starting to forget.

Jason turned to Tyler. "What's her name?"

I opened my mouth to change the subject, hoping against everything that someone would interrupt Jason.

"Kate!" Jason exclaimed. "That's it. You should go for her. Rumor has it she's been checking you out all day, lucky bastard."

Chills up my spine. I could hear the waves as they

ran toward me again, and I knew it was only a matter of time before I drowned.

Tyler glanced at me and said, "No way. I heard she was some sort of crazy chick. I'd stay clear."

I remembered her voice: *Three days.*

"Not her," I said quietly.

"No? She's hot though," Chad said. "And the crazy one's are always the best at-"

"At *what*, Chad?" Annabelle's voice was cold, hard.

"Uh, nothing."

"Exactly." She looked at me. "She *is* crazy. I heard some weird stuff about her when I was in the office this morning."

"Me too!" Michelle squealed. "There are rumors going around that she transferred here from Maine because she was in this coven of witches."

Annabelle nodded seriously. "And they killed people."

Chad snorted. "Yeah, I'm sure they did."

Annabelle glared at him, but didn't say anything else.

"I heard something like that too, actually," Jason said. He leaned in like he was about to tell a secret. "Except I heard she was part of some cult in Detroit that worships the devil. I heard she's only here to find her next sacrifice."

Annabelle gasped. "No!"

"I knew she was too pretty," Michelle said, pulling a finger through her mess of strawberry curls. "She probably takes baths in blood to keep her skin so perfect, like some vampire."

Annabelle nearly screamed. "What if she's the Bloodletter?"

"A girl? Right," Jason laughed. "You think she's

related to Elizabeth Bathory, that serial killer countess that took baths in the blood of her victims?"

Michelle put her hand over her mouth. She slowly brought it down and, as her eyes moved rapidly from side to side, she said, "*Ohmygod.* Isn't Kate's last name Bathory?"

Tyler waved his hands in the air, mocking. He rolled his eyes and said in a high-pitched squeal, "Isn't her last name Bloodletter?"

Michelle gasped. Her hand was shaking. "Ohmygod, is it really?"

"No, it's Black," Chad said. He smiled and tilted his head at Jason. "You need help with your history, huh?"

"Shut up, Chad," Annabelle said, her lips pursed. "And how do *you* know her last name, anyway?"

He grinned and took a sip of his water. "Oh, you know."

Annabelle threw her hands on the table and stood up. "No, I do not know! How do you know her name?"

"I just do," he said.

"You tell me right now!"

"Calm down, Annabelle. I'll tell you tonight at Jason's. I have a feeling we won't have much history to talk about."

Annabelle grabbed Michelle's arm and said, "I need to go to the bathroom."

After they left, Chad couldn't stop smiling.

"So, do you have a date for Homecoming?" he asked Jason. "Maybe whoever you're taking can double with me and Annabelle."

"I haven't asked anyone yet," Jason muttered. He picked at his food as Chad continued to tell him about his plans for his Homecoming night with Annabelle.

Tyler whispered to me, "Annabelle and Chad really are perfect for each other aren't they?"

I nodded. "I'm just glad the conversation always goes right back to them."

"Yeah, sorry. I figured you wouldn't want to talk about Kate."

I shrugged. "It's just after everything she's said today I'd rather not think about it."

"I get that, but you can't ignore stuff forever."

I sighed. "I know. This is different."

The loud, metallic sound of the bell rang through the noise. In one swift motion, everyone moved toward the doors.

"Is it different?" Tyler asked when we stood up. "Or is it just more of the same."

My storm: *Kate. Dad.* "I don't know."

Tyler gripped my shoulder. "Well, hey. Do you want to come over for dinner tonight? No practice today. We can pretend to do that review packet for Brandt's class."

"Eh," I started. I didn't want to think about Monday's quiz, either.

I knew I needed to think, to try and understand *why* my heart seemed to live and die with three thoughts: The pain of Dad, the mystery of Kate, the confusion of me. I just couldn't seem to find a place to start. There was no middle ground, only high and low.

"C'mon," Tyler urged. "We have to start sometime. I have practice on Saturday mornings so I can't tomorrow."

"All right. That sounds good."

"Good! Meet me at my locker after school and we can just ride to my house together."

"Sounds good," I said, not really paying attention.

My eyes were searching the crowd, looking, wondering.

Is she close?

She could be anywhere.

Tyler's voice in my ear: "She's not here."

I tripped on nothing. "What? Who?" I said as he steadied me. My lips were dry with a taste of the memory of Kate. My tongue ran across them. I needed air.

"When I was in the office I heard Nurse Anne say that Kate went home sick," he said. "Must have been right after we saw her in the hall. You don't have to worry. She's not here today."

"Good," I said.

Still, Kate's voice haunted me, and I couldn't help thinking about how the freckles on her face reminded me of the stars I once wished upon.

I gripped my arm, felt the warmth of my skin where my birthmark forever was, and let the wave of students carry me into the hall.

You don't have to worry.

Let them pull me under.

She's not here today.

Let the feelings drift away.

-KATE-

"HE'S THE ONE. I'M SURE OF IT."

A snarl. *How do you know?*

I said, "I saw it in his eyes like you warned."

If you are sure, he barked, *then bring him to us. Tell him what you must to get him to the compound, nothing more and nothing less.*

Even over the phone Marcus' voice begged me to obey.

I nodded. "I'll have him to you in three days."

Good. Three days will be enough. We cannot wait any longer than that. Is the binding spell real? Did those treasonous fools speak the truth? The boy knows nothing of what he is?

"The binding was real," I said, choking on the words and what they meant to me. What they made me remember. Then the lie came easily: "No. I've said nothing to him."

He must know what he is, Marcus said. His voice rang in my ear making blood pound in my head. *Has he shown any signs of his powers?*

"None that I can see. The binding spell worked."

It's fading too quickly if the Orieno have found him as well. Keep watching. Do what you must. Don't let them get him. We need him.

"Yes, Marcus."

His voice spilled out in anger. *The Orieno grows stronger each day you and the others are out searching.*

"Yes, I know."

You know what will happen if we're too late then.

I whispered, "Yes."

I cannot protect you if you fail. You'll be no better than them.

"I won't fail."

No hesitation: *Do not come back if you do.*

Silence.

I heard the phone's screen crack under my grip.

Three days, I thought. *Three days until I'm free.*

When I was sure Marcus was gone-

I finally breathed: *You are mine Calum Wade.*

-Calum-

Some blurry class periods later I found myself in the last hour of the day: Newspaper with Mr. Knight. Relief painted the room in light; outside in the courtyard, the sun broke through the dark clouds and fell into the room in three beams of gold.

Light to dark and back again.

Even though I felt my thoughts poke and prod in the back of my mind, reminding me of three worries on repeat, I felt the weight of the day fade. As the class came to life, so did I. Here, I felt as close to myself as I ever could, lost in the chaos of deadlines and gossip and words that had nothing to do with me. Working on *The Hollow*, the real me meant nothing, and that meant everything.

The room buzzed with quiet whispers, clicked as computer keys pounded down, as the bell rang. No one looked up; *The Hollow's* Homecoming issue deadline was yesterday.

When the smell of cotton candy hit my nose, I ducked my head close to my desk pretending I was correcting an article.

Not today, I thought. *I don't have the energy for this.*

"Hey, Calum," a voice said, as sickly sweet as her perfume.

I didn't look up. "Hi, Tanya. I'm actually in the middle of this article for Knight. Sorry."

There were too many people noticing me today, too many moments that made me remember why I didn't want to be noticed.

I thought, *Just let me be a ghost for one more day.*

"Oh," she said. She must have leaned close because suddenly I could barely breathe. She tapped a highlighter-pink finger on my desk, slow like her words. "I was hoping you could, like, maybe help me with my article."

I shook my head. "Sorry. You know how Knight gets. I really need to finish this."

She whispered, "Too bad."

Sighing, I said, "I don't think I'd be much help with the gossip column anyway." I looked up to see her pouting.

Her lips stuck together in shades of pink, strings of gloss hanging down like prison bars. She twirled a finger in her hair, leaned back, and giggled. "I think you'd be good at anything. By the way, do you like my new lipstick?" She puffed out her lips so the gloss bubbled in the middle. "It's called *Puck*er-Me Pink."

"Calum, could you come here for a second?" Mr. Knight called from his desk, saving me.

I quickly stood up. "Sorry, Tanya. Gotta go!"

I almost laughed at the look on her face, as though her perfume had been discontinued.

What a horrible day that would be.

"What's up?" I asked Knight. "I'm almost done with setting up some interviews for the Homecoming bonfire, I just have to ask a few more people."

Knight held up a hand. "Relax, Calum. I just thought you might need some space to, ah, breathe, so to speak." He laughed under his breath, making me realize again how young he was.

I pressed my hands to a paper on his desk, feeling my body lean forward into it. "Thanks."

Knight set his pen down. "Rough day?"

It was one of those moments when a whisper

wouldn't do, but speaking normally was too much.

So I nodded, breathed deeply, and felt words fill my lungs like paper breaths: *Yes. It's been a day I want to forget. Too much is running through my mind. My heart is beating so fast because I'm afraid my Dad is going to come back and finish what he started, come back for my mother and me. I'm afraid* ~~I am just like~~ *I'll become him because sometimes I get so angry I can't control it and then I can't see and I explode in rage. And then there's Kate. I don't know why* ~~I'm afraid of her~~ *she's all I can think about.*

He ran a hand through his thick, straw-colored hair, his eyes blinking beneath his black-framed glasses. He sighed, "I see. Me too. My girlfriend's been getting really nervous about these Bloodletter attacks; one of her coworkers has gone missing. No body, just blood and *gone* like the rest. It's been rough, to say the least."

A chill ran down my back.

Blood and gone.

"Do you think we should run a story?" I asked.

Our eyes met. "No," he said. "Not when it's like this. We don't run stories about this kind of thing, Calum."

"What do we do?"

He drummed his fingers on his desk. "We think about the good things and pray the rest sorts itself out."

Words thick with the poison of sadness caught in my throat and fell out in a burning whisper. "But what if there are no good things?"

Knight looked at me. He said, "There are always good things to see if you want them badly enough."

His eyes, deep and dark brown, said, *I'm sorry.*

He knew just as much as me that the good things were not so easy to find, even if you wanted them with all your heart.

He leaned close. Moments like this he reminded me of Tyler, of a friend. Maybe even of a father. "If you ever need to talk..."

I cleared my throat. "I know," I said. "Thanks."

Thanks for being there, I didn't.

He winked and said loudly, "And speaking of your article, good job on it so far. Just make sure you get those interviews done."

I smiled, *breathed*, and started to turn away.

"Not so fast," Knight said, waving me back. "I really did have something to talk to you about."

"Shoot."

"*The Hollow* is getting a new staffer and I wanted you to kind of show her around. You know, answer questions and whatnot. She's a junior like you, and was on the paper at her old school. Her transcripts said she's pretty decent, but you can never be sure."

"Yeah, no problem. When does she get here?"

A knock.

A laugh. "She gets here now, apparently."

My heart.

My stomach.

No.

And then, "Calum Wade, this is our new student, Kate Black. Kate, Calum will be showing you around for the next few days until you feel comfortable. Okay? Okay! Now, get to work both of you. If we don't get this issue out by Monday, we won't have it in time for Homecoming."

Maybe it was because I hadn't seen it before, but when she smiled at Knight the air around me seemed to shiver, making anger impossible.

Making breathing impossible.

"Thanks," she said, eyes smiling purple. When she smiled it was something like the first light of day, or a melody played only with the black keys of a piano; panged with inconceivable mystery. The melody of her voice as she spoke reverberated off every bone in my body, making my heart quake, hurt. "I'll be sure to let you know if I need anything, Mr. Knight, though I don't think it'll take more than three days to fit in."

I felt those words attack me: *Three days.*

"Three days, huh?" Knight raised an eyebrow. He grinned. "That's confident of you. I like it! Now go work."

Kate smiled. "Yes, sir." She turned to me, her smile set like stone against her sunset skin. "Let's go, Calum. Time is ticking away."

We walked to the back of the room and sat. I could see Tanya looking daggers at us, and I couldn't help feeling thankful Kate didn't smell like candy. That girls like Tanya wanted nothing to do with ones like Kate. Instead, Kate smelled like a rainstorm and, as I looked at her, I realized she was probably just as dangerous.

"Stop looking at me," she said as she flipped open her notebook and started writing.

"Okay, sorry," I muttered, but couldn't look away.

As a flicker of sunlight flashed through the windows, I caught the shape of her tattoo. A deep black circle was inked on her finger in the place that a ring might hold. In it rested six lines crossing in a star, held together by a smaller circle in the middle. Several of the outer sections were filled in with ruby red ink, making it look like blood had spilled on the edges. The rest of the sections were pale, as if the blood had been there once and then was gone.

Blood and gone. I shivered.

Snap. Her pencil broke in her hands.

"Sorry," I said again, though I didn't know why.

"Pathetic," she growled and turned away.

A sad pang of Kate and *three days* and Dad washed over me beginning at my heart and destroyed what could have been. Or maybe, what never was.

I'm tired of this, I thought as I tried to write. *I'm so tired of pretending things aren't happening when they're all I can think about.*

I'm tired of being me.

Outside, falling leaves covered the grass. They kept swirling around as if being thrown by cruel, unseen hands. In the orange I saw images of my mom, and in the yellow my dad. In the red, Kate's eyes shown through. I picked a spot on the ground outside just visible from my seat, and told myself that if a leaf landed there I would start over new. I would forgive and try again.

I would become a different me.

Maybe I would even give Kate one more chance.

Fall, a thought whispered in my mind. *Fall there.*

I had another secret: I lied before.

The truth was that I *could* see the good things in my life, but they were all singed with dark, burnt edges that would never fade. All the good seemed to burn away before I had a chance to keep it.

Good and gone.

Fall.

I closed my eyes-

Fall there.

opened them, and pretended the leaves were stars.

Fall.

And then it did.

A heart-shaped leaf of brilliant red, brighter than all the rest, dropped from the sky like a star through the night, and landed in the exact spot my eyes watched. It was violently red, like blood on the green grass, except for edges that were turned up, brown and curled and dying.

CHAPTER FOUR
NEVER MORE

-CALUM-

"MOM SAYS THE NEWS JUST REPORTED TWELVE more people missing in Jefferson County," Tyler said when I got to his locker after school. His voice was dry; he'd heard this before. We all had. "She said the report was pretty graphic. Apparently 'blood flowed freely' in Jefferson today, and there were even more disappearances in Denver. Still no bodies though, aside from White. The houses were all just destroyed with bloody words, and the bodies were just-"

"Gone?" I interrupted.

He paused. His eyes flicked to me like he was remembering, or realizing something he'd forgotten. Then, quieter than usual, "Yeah. Gone. Like always."

I said nothing.

We looked at each other for a minute, maybe more. Watched each other as people rushed passed us in the hall, as they moved toward the door screaming happily.

Finally I asked, "You think we should be as worried as they say?"

"About the people gone missing?"

I shook my head. *No.* "About the blood."

Tyler's face moved back and forth. Stopped. His mouth opened and closed. Then, after too long, "I don't think so. If there was anything to worry about, really worry, everyone would be more afraid. Act more serious about it all."

I nodded. "You're right. Ready to go?"

"Yeah. After you."

As we walked out to meet the sky puckered black, I couldn't help but think: *What if that's the problem? What if they're acting okay because they're afraid? What if they're ignoring it all in hopes it'll go away?*

Like me.

Thunder boomed above.

"I saw Kate again," I said as I stepped in a puddle.

Tyler bumped into me. "I thought she went home sick?"

"Nope, guess not. She's in Newspaper with me."

He tapped my back. "Guess you can't cut a break today, huh? Just stay clear of her for a while and see what happens."

I felt a certain slant of something baneful blur inside me. Staying away from Kate would be good. Being close to her made me not know how to pretend; today I could only think of her when she was close. Always too close.

I remembered: *Three days.*

Until what?

All I could think of was that and her.

I felt my teeth grind together, felt the anger take hold of my heart and squeeze until her name beat through me like a pulse.

I wanted her gone, wished the Bloodletter would take her like the rest. Blood and gone like all of them.

I heard Tyler from a distance. "Calum? Get it

together! You're shaking."

I felt and saw and thought: *Three-*
Tyler's hand against my cheek, hard and fast
Thunder clapping, lightning breaking the sky open
Kate, so close I miss her when she's gone
-days.

"I'm back," I said.

Tyler looked nervous, afraid maybe, and the pain of that made me want to run. "You sure you want to stay away from her?"

Things I wouldn't say cut my throat, burning: *No. Today's the first day in a long time I've felt something other than sad. Today's the first day I haven't known who I'm pretending to be and I think Kate is a part of that. I can't help but think about the way she looked at me, like she knew all my secrets, ones I don't even know. One look in her eyes and I could see that she knew more about me than I ever have.*

I think I dreamed of her eyes.

But instead I said, my voice so deep and low it hurt my throat, "Yes. I want her gone."

Without warning a flash of lightning shot down from the dark sky and pierced the ground beside me, cracking a stone in three. Water from a close puddle sprayed up, soaking my jeans.

"What the..." I said jumping back.

Rain began falling in slow drops. I felt the air grow cold around me from it, thunder dropping heavy, too.

Then, as though every drop of rain was a note, I heard a voice fall from the sky:

Caeles.
Become who you are.

73

Look to us.
Give in.
Don't be afraid.
Don't give up.

Tyler's eyes were wide. "What was that?"

The voice from my dream. "You heard that too?"

He pointed at the rock. "Yeah. Wow, that almost took you out!"

My head tilted. "You heard the thunder? Saw the lightning? Nothing else?"

"Yeah. Why? What did you hear?"

I said, "Nothing. Just making sure I'm not dreaming."

He laughed. "That was way too close."

I could smell the burning stone. "Everything is these days."

Tyler stopped a few feet from his car. "You know, if you like her then I like her. She might have seemed like a piece of work today, but everyone has bad first days at new schools. You wanna just give Kate a second chance?"

I remembered the leaf.

The voice: *Don't give up.*

"Maybe," I said as I got in the car and shut the door.

Tyler opened his door and fell in. "Just let me know where we stand."

I didn't say anything.

Maybe the voice was just another me inside. Like advice from the real me I couldn't see, my subconscious.

But then who was Caeles?

Maybe I was going crazy.

I crossed my fingers: *I am not my father.*

Tyler said, "You know Homecoming is just around the corner-"

"I'm not asking her, Tyler."

"Just saying," he laughed, normal and easy like always.

~

"Thanks, Mrs. Little!" I yelled as Tyler and I ran up to his room.

"Anytime, dear!" Mrs. Little called back, a smile planted firmly on a face covered in make-up looking barely there, surrounded by curls of soft blonde hair that never moved. "Wait, Calum! Don't you boys want something to snack on?"

"We're fine, Mom," Tyler said. He gave me a push to move.

"Dinner is in a few," she said to the both of us as we disappeared up the stairs.

Tyler's room was hidden from the rest of the house in the attic of their two story home. I loved being in it, tucked away in a piece of the world that was untouchable.

I thought Tyler had his room decorated perfectly, with band and sports posters everywhere, his massive amounts of CDs and DVDs covering every other square inch of the place. Clothes were abandoned in piles. There was an abundance of football and baseball trophies covering one wall, complete with his bat and glove. His football jersey was thrown over a chair by the computer.

Tyler's room always smelled like freedom.

Here, my family didn't exist.

"I think Mom likes you more than me," Tyler laughed.

I wanted to smile.

In ways, I knew this house, this family, better than my own. Mr. Little was a doctor at the Wheat Ridge Medical Center one town over, and Mrs. Little was a teacher with the Lakewood Hollow Jump-Start program, only working half days so she could stay home for most of the afternoon with their little four year-old daughter, Kendra.

"Here," Tyler said as he handed me a stack of clothes. "These don't fit me anymore and Mom wanted me to give them to you. I promise they're still cool, Coach just has me bulking up this season."

"Thanks," I said. *Brother*, I didn't.

I wanted to smile, but couldn't.

"Careful, I don't know if Mom washed them," Tyler joked.

"Sick!" I laughed once and sat down in the chair next to his computer. "Remind me why I'm your friend again?"

He jumped to lay on his bed, threw a pillow at me, and said, "Because I know all your secrets. You'd have to kill me if we ever stopped being friends."

I leaned back in the chair and sighed as quiet comfort fell between us. Somehow, even though my mind felt heavy and tired, being in this house felt good. Relaxing, as though it really were my home.

Slowly, I let my lips curve up.

Still, a soft, steady beating sounded in the back of my mind like a drum: *Caeles. Become who you are.* The words that only I could hear. The voice I had kept a secret.

Not all my secrets, I thought. *You don't know them all.*

Tyler's voice broke my thoughts. "What was up with you today?" he asked, too loudly.

I shifted my weight. Even though I knew, I asked, "What do you mean?"

He blew a puff of air. "You were all over the place today. Eyes darting left and right. I mean, I swear I saw you twitch a few times whenever you thought you saw Kate. I know what she said to you, and I agree it's creepy, but you just weren't yourself today. You haven't been for a while."

"Honestly?"

"That would be the way to go."

I sighed. "I don't know."

Tyler rolled his eyes. "How is that being honest? I thought we didn't have secrets."

"We don't!" *We do.* "I really just *don't know.* Maybe I'm tired from not sleeping well. Lately, it's like the entire day I worry about what I'll dream about that night. And then, when I finally get to bed, I drift off hoping it will be different and it never is. Everything comes crashing down in my dreams; they're so vivid and real and there's always blood. Always nightmares and mist. Death and fire. And then I see Kate today and I'm not even safe during the day!" I felt my eyes burn. I ran my hands through my hair. "They go together, I think, Kate and the nightmares. I just wish I knew what everything meant."

I leaned back in the chair, rubbed the sweat from my hands on my jeans, and waited. I expected Tyler to talk, *wanted* him to, but he was silent.

For a moment, I was numb with waiting.

And then Tyler's voice cut me deep: "Do you think this has more to do with Kate, or that one year ago today your Dad left?"

I felt my throat close. I breathed, "What?"

Tyler gazed out the window on the wall near his bed. He looked captivated by the view, so I looked too, seeing the rain that had started to pour just as we had reached the Little's was now beginning to calm. The sky, dark gray, was pierced with the softness of an evening sunset.

I wished it would storm.

I caught my reflection in the window; all I could ever see was *him*, not me.

"I don't know," I whispered. "I'm sorry. I don't."

For a while neither of us moved. Then, without warning, Tyler sat up on his bed and leaned back on his elbows.

"Okay, Calum," he started. "I'll say this as many times as you need to hear it because I've known you since before I knew what friendship was. *You're my brother*. No one understands us when we talk and we argue all the time. So, just listen."

I opened my mouth.

"Ah!" Tyler pointed at me. "Listen."

He breathed in, slow as death, then pushed all the air out of his body. His voice became low, deeper than before so it was no more than a whisper. Still, somehow, it screamed. "You need to understand that as much as you look like your Dad, you will never be him. I'm not gonna lie and say you don't kind of look like him, but that's it. That's where you and him end. I know you get freaked out when you look in a mirror because the first person you see is him. But when anyone else does, there isn't anyone but you."

He tried to smile, but I could see the color of his eyes grow light with worry. I felt my own become pointed, could feel the anger feed my heart so it pumped through my veins.

"You don't understand! I get so angry sometimes

it's like I'm truly going to turn into his son one day." I flew up. My fingers tore through my hair, pulling the ends so some broke away. My teeth hurt, clenched tight together. Everything was raw, about to break. "Am I so like him that I don't even have a hope to be *me*? One day, I might hurt someone just like he did!"

I wanted to scream.

I opened my mouth, but suddenly caught sight of my reflection in the window again. In this light, with twilight pushing against the clouds outside and the rainwater holding on to the window, I was twisted into the man I never wanted to become. Now, I looked more like him than ever.

My shoulders sagged down, life seeping out of me until I could barely stand. I fell back into the chair. I pressed a finger against my eye so hard it hurt. So hard maybe I would never see my reflection again.

My head fell. I sniffed, felt tears run down my throat, and whispered to Tyler, *"I'm broken.* I don't even know who I am. Sometimes I have moments when I feel strong enough to be me, but other times I just see someone else. "

He didn't move, and I didn't look at him. When he spoke, his voice was a hushed breath of quiet confidence, and I found myself wondering why he cared enough to say: "I know you were hurt. I know your Mom was. But no one is coming back to hurt you again. Trust me when I say that you worrying about this, about hurting someone just like your Dad hurt you, means that you will never even get close to that temptation."

I felt chills run up and down my back, hints of one thought I could never forget: *He cares. Tyler cares about me maybe more than anyone.*

He continued, "And I know you've been worrying about all this for a while now. For a year I've seen you get slowly more anxious the closer we got to today. But I want you to know that your past can't come back to hurt you anymore, and if you don't want to, you will never become your father. You get to decide who you will be. It's your life, not anyone else's. So, let's worry about Kate instead of things we have no control over, because that crazy bitch made your day a living Hell today!"

Without wanting to, I laughed. Tyler grinned.

"Thanks," I said. "She was wasn't she?"

"A real killer," he said laughing. "You should have seen how many times she was looking at you in the halls. It was intense!"

"Seriously! Every time I looked up she was staring at me."

He raised an eyebrow. "She couldn't keep her eyes off you. And, by the way, she kept cracking her knuckles whenever you walked by. Sounded like somebody wanted some *action*!"

I frowned.

Suddenly, the whole thing wasn't so funny.

"Like *action* in a funny way." He paused when he saw my face. And then, as if it were, he asked, "Too much?"

"Too messed up," I said.

Outside a crack of thunder sounded; one final boom, shaking my heart, to make the air thick with worry. One crash to bend our laughter into doubt. Our voices sounded too loud in the room, with nothing but our hearts to beat out the noise.

Tyler said, "What was up with her threatening you? It's kind of scary when you think about it."

I didn't want to think about it.

"Let's stop talking about this, Tyler," I said.

He shook his head. "No way! I mean I kind of want to figure out what she's all about, don't you? She just comes here out of nowhere and is so cold and distant towards everyone, especially you. Someone like that has something to hide." He scratched his chin. "I bet she has a secret past. Maybe she was kicked out of her old school. Maybe she faked all her records and really *is* the Bloodletter like everyone thinks."

I asked, "How is it possible that you and Tanya have never gotten together?"

He gasped. "What if Kate's a spy?"

"Maybe she's just the new girl at a different school and doesn't know anyone," I said.

He waved his hand. "No, that's not it and you know it." He grabbed a baseball off the floor and, tossing it up at the ceiling, rolled onto his back. "Something's off. Don't you think there's something odd about her?"

I felt my throat clench. A bristle of cold fell over my head and down my back: *Is there a way to hate someone so much you can't stop thinking about them?*

I felt the words before they sounded, felt them crawl up my throat and spread like mist, uncontrollable and dangerous. True. "I think maybe she's lonely."

Nothing but the smack of the baseball against Tyler's hands sat between us. It was a moment set in perfect hesitation, like the eye of a storm.

I looked up at Tyler, and found myself overwhelmed by everything I wasn't. Tyler was in a different league than I was. Running back of the school's football team, he looked the part. He was built, buff and tall, so much so that his shirts strained under the pressure.

His short, brown hair was never done, but somehow looked perfectly styled and artfully messy. He was proud, but not overtly so; his confidence was something I was jealous of.

I asked, "Do you ever feel like you don't belong?"

"What do you mean?" he wondered.

"Do you ever feel like you just don't fit in with everyone else? Not in an unpopular kind of way... It's like I was made different, or something. Sometimes I catch myself not saying anything because I'm too buried in my head, thinking."

I took a breath and focused on my hands. "I look around and see all these couples and perfect families. Like yours. And you know I love your family, but they're so happy and mine is just... not. I mean, isn't life supposed to get better by the time you're seventeen? At school everyone is dating someone, everyone has those moments when they're in complete bliss, hand-holding and kissing and smiling, and I just haven't had that. I don't know if I ever will."

Tyler was gazing out the window when I looked up.

"That's where you're wrong, Calum" Tyler said, quietly. "Not everyone is like that. I *don't* feel like I fit in all the time. Why do you think I'm always playing football or baseball?"

I shrugged. "You're popular, Tyler. You've always done those things. They'd be lost without you."

Tyler sat up straight and threw his hands up in the air. "But that's just it! It's *me* that would be lost without *them*."

My chin lifted. "You've got the perfect life, Tyler. Don't you get that? You could have any girl you wanted. You could have anything."

The laugh that shot out of his mouth was high,

crackled. "That's exactly my problem! Every day I see my parents looking so happy, so complete with only each other. That's what I want. So I go to school and date and try to fit in. But I haven't found that right person yet, that one I want to be with forever. I have never *ever* felt butterflies when I kiss. I've never felt any kind of heart-stopping emotion, no racing pulse. Nothing. I can't feel anything. That's why I date so much; why I haven't settled down. It's because I'm *dead* inside."

He ran his fingers through his hair. "I just want to *feel*. Have a kiss that changes me, ya know? I've heard so many times before that I'll know if I love someone the moment I kiss them, that it'll feel like a million tiny sparks shooting straight to my heart. I want that, Calum."

I asked, "You think you can tell if you love someone from a kiss?"

"I think you know you love them before," Tyler said, "but I think a kiss is what seals it. You can see into someone's soul through their eyes, Calum, but you can touch their heart through a kiss."

Confusion ran through me, like shadows moving swiftly through night. How was Tyler feeling like this? How, when he had everything I wanted, did he make it sound like he had nothing at all?

"Just because you haven't found the right person yet doesn't mean they won't come around," I said, though I didn't know if I believed it. "Your parents are lucky. You can't let yourself down now because you haven't fallen in love yet. We're in *high school*. I mean, c'mon."

He sighed letting his hands fall. "Yeah, I know. *I know.* I just want it."

For a moment, silence was the only noise.

"I know," he repeated quietly. "I just feel pressure

sometimes, from everyone."

"Me too," I said. "It feels impossible to be who everyone thinks I am when I can't even figure out who I am alone. Like I'm living day by day, right where they want me to be, but lost and unsure as to where I'm going or who I am."

On his bed, Tyler smiled. "Exactly."

He picked up the baseball again and tossed it to me. I caught it, one handed.

"You know," he said. "Maybe we just need time to let it all work out."

I sighed. "I know. It's not that easy, though."

"Maybe that's why we want it so badly."

~

I breathed in the aroma of family as Tyler and I walked down the stairs; the air smelled as though even it had been made from scratch.

"Tyler, could you grab the napkins from the kitchen? And Calum, the ketchup's in the fridge," Mrs. Little called to us from the dining room.

"Honey?" Mr. Little asked his wife. "Do we have any pepper, by chance?"

"Calum! Pepper, please," she called to me.

"Thanks, dear," I heard Mr. Little say.

"Don't thank me, thank Calum. And tomorrow you're cooking dinner. I don't recall having a name tag on my apron that says 'Betty Little: Chef, Maid, Slave'."

I laughed just as Tyler rolled his eyes. I put the pepper and ketchup on the table and sat down next to Tyler.

Mr. Little smiled at me. "Thanks, Calum."

"Welcome," I said. "Everything looks great, Mrs. Little."

Tyler elbowed me, snorting. "Suck up."

"Thank *you*, Calum," Mrs. Little said. Her eyes slanted down, but she smiled as she said, "It's nice that someone appreciates this."

Mr. Little reached over to squeeze her hand. "I do, dear. I was just testing you."

She kissed him, cupping his face with her hands. Her wedding ring glinted in the false light of the room, the gold band making the diamonds shine with yellow verve. "Sure you were."

"So, should we leave you two alone or what?" Tyler said as he passed me a napkin.

"You always were funny," said Mr. Little.

"Funny looking!" Kendra erupted when she came into the room. She was wearing a pink ballet tutu and a gold crown. Red lines streaked from her lips, covering her face in broken lines of lipstick.

Mrs. Little covered her mouth. Her eyes laughed, but she held her voice steady. "Honey! What happened?"

Tyler couldn't keep it in. "You look like you got in a fight with a drag queen and lost."

I kicked him.

"Tyler," warned his dad.

"She does!" he laughed.

"What's a dwag qween?" Kendra asked as Mrs. Little dipped a napkin in her glass of water and wiped the lipstick off.

"Nothing," Mrs. Little said, looking at Tyler. "You look very pretty."

"Yeah," I said. "I love your crown, Kendra. Are you a princess today?"

She beamed. Her face was still lined pink, but Mrs. Little had let her go. "I'm a pwincess. Will you be my pwince?"

Tyler groaned. "Oh, man."

"Of course," I said, trying to keep from laughing. "But why don't we play after dinner. I'm starved!"

Kendra nodded again, her face falling to serious. "Mom! Hungwy!"

Mrs. Little rolled her eyes, and I saw a bit of Tyler there. "Was there a memo sent out that I forgot to read? Something about treating your mother like a slave?"

"You didn't get it?" Tyler asked.

"I read it last Tuesday, I think," Mr. Little said, rubbing his finger on his chin, pretending to think.

"*No*," said Mrs. Little. "I must have missed it."

Mr. Little passed me the rolls and grinned. "It was a gem of a memo."

"I learned a lot," Tyler said, breaking his roll in two. "Did you know that you're also supposed to make us dessert?"

"Is that so?" Mrs. Little said.

Tyler shrugged. "And there was something in there about giving the oldest child extra allowance."

"And the best friend," I said quickly.

Mrs. Little put her hands on her hips and threw her mouth open in mock horror. "Calum Wade! I expected better from you!"

Kendra giggled. "Pwince Calum!"

The table burst into laughter.

Then, as though a cold breeze had blown in from the living room, we heard the news report from the television:

...more than yesterday. It seems as though the

Bloodletter is not slowing down, and his nightly attacks are becoming more common than ever. Although the Lakewood Hollow Police Department is not willing to give any new information, our sources say that as many as twenty new victims have been abducted since last night. Of course, no bodies have been found, and because the LHPD is not allowed to file a missing persons report for twenty-four hours, the community is at a loss. Still, we are being told not to panic as nothing has been confirmed as murder. The LHPD is urging citizens to maintain a normal lifestyle...

My throat burned dry. I reached for my glass of water too quickly and it fell, sending a river across the table and over the edge.

In my mind, the water turned red. And as it disappeared off the table I could only think of one thing: *Blood and gone.*

Mrs. Little cleared her throat. "Okay. Let's forget about all that and be grateful we're together for the moment."

I wished I knew how to forget-
anything.

"Calum, sweetie. How is it?" she asked as she blotted away the spilled water. "Do you have enough to eat?"

My voice cracked. "Yes, thanks."

A melody of classical music peddled its way into the dining area from somewhere beyond.

"Mom," Tyler sputtered through a mouthful of salad. "Do we have to listen to this stuff?"

"Atmosphere makes the meal, Tyler," she replied. "Besides, you used to love Chopin."

"You did," agreed Mr. Little. "I remember you used

to take those piano lessons. They were all you could talk about."

"No way," said Tyler. "I don't remember that at all."

"I remember you did!" I said, laughing. "You used to sing all your classical songs when you came over. You even tried to get me to take lessons. Something about forming a band called the 'C and T Piano Posse.' I was supposed to write the lyrics for our songs. You would not let up about that."

"And I still agree with myself. You should have taken those lessons with me," he said. "And you always are writing in one notebook or another. The 'Piano Posse' could have been awesome."

"Posse," Kendra giggled.

"Those were the days," Tyler said.

"Oh, please," said Mrs. Little. "We had to bribe you to go. Candy, chips, anything to get you to the studio. That was back when we thought we were helping you out by getting you involved in something musical. It was supposed to help with your learning skills, math and whatnot. It was in all the books."

"That was until we saw you throw a ball," Mr. Little said, and stuck his fork out to make a point. "That, and when we heard you sing all bets were off."

"I could sing a mean version of *Twinkle, Twinkle,*" Tyler said. "Even my teachers said so."

"Uh..." I started.

"I'm going to have to go with you on this one, Calum," Mr. Little said, chuckling. "You son, like myself, were not blessed with the gift of song."

We all laughed, even little Kendra.

I smiled at the way we ate together, the Littles and

I. It felt so consoling, so real and not at the same time. Time flew swiftly by, as always.

For a moment, all was well.

CHAPTER FIVE
COLD MEMORY

-CALUM-

THE NIGHT WAS COOL AND CALM AS I MADE MY way back towards my tiny home just after midnight. Mrs. Little hadn't wanted me to walk home, but I convinced her that I was getting picked up by my Mom the next block over. I needed to walk, to have a little more time all to myself.

I needed to be alone, even though I didn't want to be.

The sky moved like ink alit with a gray, foggy darkness, and even though there was a chill in the air, I felt warm. The edges of my mouth felt sore from smiling too hard.

I felt light.

For the first time in days, I felt like writing a song, and I thought of the words I might string together to make something beautiful:

Happiness like a bittersweet lament cried-
by a thunderstorm in the middle of a furious sea.
A fallen tree in the middle of a forest sleeping-
on a bed of wild roses.

So cold the river, so fast-
that the stones polish to gems-
a thousand of them glistening under a sun-
so yellow it's gold. The sun falling down-
painting the trees orange-red.

I walked slowly with my hands shoved deep in my pockets, my backpack slung firmly over my shoulder. A brush of wind licked at my face and then went on to touch the leaves of the trees beside me. Even though it was autumn, I felt the warmth of summer; everything was light beneath the shadows.

I looked down and focused my eyes on the sidewalk, looked at the many cracks and uplifted stones molded in the pavement.

Interesting, I thought. *Nothing is ever perfect, always cracked around the edges somewhere.*

Maybe that's what perfection is: Flawed.

Suddenly, a breeze carried an uneasy feeling my way, but I pushed it away before it meant anything.

I reached down to stroke the jagged leaf of a weed, finding it to be much softer than I anticipated. The bristles woven tightly into the vein of the leaf felt prickly, and they seemed to shock me when I touched them.

The night was electric. I could feel it like the beginnings of a storm, the way the air ebbed and pulsed around me like a liquid current. I felt powerful, like I always did days before a full moon. When I was young, I used to think I was a superhero, someone made real by belief. But, no. Still, my walk was stronger, my stance more firm. Out of the corner of my eye I could almost see flickers of electricity dance on wind.

I was deep in thought when a voice called out from

behind a tall bush to my right, making me jump and drop my backpack from my shoulder.

Just when I thought I could forget, a memory came back as cold and real as before; a raspy voice twisting like dark shadows in the night: "Hello, Calum. *Calum!* My little boy."

My feet froze, taking my whole body with them into an icy, unmoving coma. I knew the voice so well, it crushed against me like a brick wall.

Dad.

"How have you been, little boy? You look well."

The wind gushed against his voice, slamming into it in steaming puffs of fog in the black night air.

His voice was higher than I remembered, different. No matter how much the wind howled, I couldn't erase the memories I had of that voice screaming at me all night long.

In a second I was five years old again.

"Dad... Get away," I breathed.

A sharp shiver ran up my spine.

I found my feet and forced them to step back.

I stumbled. My hand reached down and grabbed at the cement. I felt the tiny, loose stones dig themselves deep into my palm and pull blood out.

I needed to stand.

I needed to run.

Move! my mind screamed, but I did nothing. *He shouldn't be here. Why is he here?*

He reached out a hand but pulled back almost at once. He looked away and down, as if he was listening to something.

I tried to breathe but choked.

My bloody hand was still glued to the sidewalk, the salt-like pebble tears of cement burning through my nerves.

He stepped forward with his arms open like he expected me to run into them for a hug. His tongue reached out, licking his lips.

I dug my hand further into the ground and pain shot up my arm. Then, as fast as I could, I stood.

He smiled. "Calum."

Even though the autumn air flooded around me, I could not take a breath from it.

His eyes were glazed over and there was a red fire in them, a burning that looked like hunger. His face was calm, but his wicked grin was both painful and sweet to look at. It was too wide for his face. He was pale, nearly white against the moonlight. His tongue continued to caress his lips as if they were covered with an endless amount of sugar.

Suddenly his entire face twitched. His fingers clawed at his scalp and dug deep. He let out a high-pitched bark. "No! Go away!"

I tripped on a fallen branch and stumbled back. He grabbed my arm and his touch felt cold, frozen. The icy feeling matched the fire in his eyes perfectly, as though rage lived there instead of a soul.

"I'm doing this for you," he said, his voice deranged and mad. His head snapped back as his mouth fell open. "Don't you hear that song I'm singing? Didn't you see the words I wrote for you?"

Red liquid dripped from his lips as he sang:

One, two, I see you.
Three, four, kill some more.
Five, six, bones like sticks.
Seven, eight, blood to taste.
Nine, ten, do it again.

One, two, I'm coming for you...

Beads of sweat moved down my scalp.

I saw my words, red as blood, blaring in my mind: *The sun falling down, painting the trees red.*

Burning lights flared in his black eyes. His hand became tight on my arm.

"Let go!" I shouted, trying to pull my arm back in a weak attempt that only made him grip harder.

My strength vanished, my emotions gone.

His other hand shot to my throat and grew tight around it. His head twitched from side to side rapidly, turning nearly full circle like an owl's. I heard his neck crack, *break.*

At once his voice was calm and too steady, monotone, different.

A new voice, as if he was not what he had been: "I won't stop until you're dead, and you have two days left."

My heart caught in my throat. "*What?*"

Time froze.

The wind stopped blowing.

My heart was about to explode when suddenly the half-moon seemed to shine brighter, framing us in a second of light. That was all I needed to make a move. I didn't think. I grabbed my arm back and ran toward where I knew Mom would be.

"Two days!" Dad screamed after me as I ran, his voice a growl.

The words ran after me, speeding down the street trying to catch me.

"I'm coming for you..." I heard him hiss.

I didn't stop running until I reached my front porch.

I looked behind me.

No one.

A headache was starting to form deep in my head, warning me of my impending nightmares. Dizzy static, tinted blue, threatened me.

I grabbed the door handle, turned, and pushed.

The house was dark, mimicking the blackness of the night, though it felt much different. It smelled familiar, like home. I instantly locked the door and felt better.

Kate.

Dad.

Kate.

Dad.

My thoughts rushed together in a sea of something terrible.

I didn't even bother taking my shoes off as I lay down on my bed. A ghostly wind beat harshly against my closed window. I heard a *crack* like someone's neck was being broken.

I jumped.

My fingers ran over my birthmark. Then, almost instantly, I was asleep.

I dreamt a lament that night, a horrid song of lingering misery of moments I could never leave behind.

Black night shivers.
Cold memory lingers.
Red eyes burn.
One thousand beautiful reasons to live,
And I can only think of one to die.
Father.
Shadow around every corner,
False warmth in every smile.
Black.

The whole world becomes black with him.
It is a nightmare.
Horror.

When I awoke during night's chorus, shivering, hands like ice, I had forgotten it completely. My only thoughts were cold memories of Dad and Kate.

I tried to forget.

I fell back to sleep hoping-

ignorance would be my complete bliss.

-KATE-

HE WAS IN PAIN. I COULD TELL.

As he dreamt, horror traced his face in jagged lines. Sweat poured down from his hairline, rolling right over his closed blue eyes.

Those eyes, I thought, swearing. *Those eyes are dangerous.*

He was pretending to be innocent, but I knew he understood the game he was playing. How could he not? I knew since I was twelve he would be the one to die.

I am so close to victory.

I whispered for him to trust me. My voice was so quiet it was nothing more than a lingering thought on a breeze, floating in through his window from below. It was inception, the smallest of ideas planted so it would grow and burst into a want, a need, a desire so fierce it would eat him alive. Anything painful.

I knew, after all. His secret was no more.

He was dangerous, just like his father.

I reached down and brushed a finger against the snake that was curling around my leg. It was a gardener, harmless, so I killed it, twisting it into a knot until it split in two.

Pop.

"The devil is here," I whispered. "If there's only two days until the Orieno execute Calum's capture, I have to do this soon. I have to get him first. I *have* to."

I could see Calum's power pulse around him. Hints of blue light played in the air around his body, and even with his eyes closed I could see them glow like two stars in the night.

Everyone around him acted like Calum was normal. How did they not know? Even with the binding spell, how was he keeping this a secret?

He was smart, but I was smarter.

The Orieno would not get him first.

Hell had no place for the damned like Calum Wade.

CHAPTER SIX
NIGHT OF SHADOW AND RAIN

-CALUM-

NIGHT DEMISED IN ICE.

Morning was born in inferno.

Sun beat through my window, waking me in an ocean of warm sweat. At once I smelled hints of burnt air, the fragrance raw, influencing my headache like gasoline on fire.

Lying face up on my bed, the ceiling of my bedroom seemed to rush towards me, falling as if to crush my memories. Only for once I didn't want to forget, not this dream. There was something about it, something that made me want to remember it in detail as though it held secrets and whispered truths.

I tried to remember.

My head jolted up, bringing my body forward so that I was sitting on the damp bed, hair pushed forward, and mouth dropped open so that breathy shots of hot air escaped. Sitting up so fast, blackness threatened to take over my world and tinges of blue colored the gritty edges of my vision.

I wondered about the downcast light, feared that because I was beginning to see it more and more, there was something wrong.

A candle on my bedside table flared, saturating the entire room in a yellow glow, shining brightly even as the sun beat it senseless; I caught the flare from the corner of my eye. I didn't remember lighting it.

I blew against the flame until it left the wick and ran, fading to smoke.

My heart was beating so fast I didn't care about anything but my dream. My dirty hair was chunked into thick, wet pieces and I could feel my eyes bulge out from my pale face, searching the room for a shadow of the man I had seen in my dreams.

Black, everywhere.
Sounds of breath, of fear.
I was in a place full of smoke, gray and bleak, the air heavy around me. It was cold, too cold to be a dream, but it was. It could have been nothing else.

I was shivering, rubbing my hands on my crossed arms to warm myself. My eyes darted around the place searching for a sign of something familiar, anything at all, but nothing formed out of the vapor.

"Hello?" I yelled. My voice wavered slightly and seemed to only carry a few feet as if it had been sucked up by the gray.

At the sound of my voice the smoke shifted, its hazy tendrils reaching toward me like fingers, curling in anticipation.

I tried to run but my feet were stuck to the ground with such conviction that I could not make them budge.

The fingers came closer, moving toward me like the hair of ghosts.

My mouth opened to scream for help, for anyone

that might hear me. My voice shivered again, mimicking my shaking body, and just as my cry for help escalated to a level beyond wavering, one twist of gray reached completely forward and placed itself against my lips, blocking any sound from escaping. Instead, the sound exploded in my ears, ringing as though the dead were living in my mind.

I was frozen, unable to move, to speak. Only my eyes darted back and forth, seeing gray murkiness and ghostly lines.

"Sssoo..." an obscure voice echoed. The sound was like glass breaking, like a thousand nails being dragged down a dusted chalkboard.

The voice poked a nerve deep inside me, telling me to run, forcing me to think of only death. It was horror beyond horror. I could smell the demise in the air, feel the hot pulse of annihilation on my lips and hear the shattered sound of death in the voice.

"You..." the voice echoed again, resounding. "You have found a way to fight me. You... You think you can defeat me? You... You're hidden from me... You have no idea..."

My finger twitched as I tried to run away.

It was no use.

"You see, Dreamer?" the voice said, the darkness echoing like laughter. "You are no match for me. You think you are an equal to me? You... You are nothing. You... are nothing... to anyone. They can only keep you safe for so long."

And with that a solid shape rose from somewhere deep within the smokiness. Loud, cackling laughter crackled in the death-filled air, making my head spin. The gray swirled around the mass like a tornado, rotating up in a spiral. And as the haze cleared, the dark laughter grew louder and more sinister. The laugh had two tones intermixing: Deep base, high shriek.

"You will be nothing, Dreamer," *the man said, if it could be called such a thing. The form that had emerged from the haze looked like death, happy death. His pale face was tilted back in hysterical laughter, his yellowed teeth showing sharp as fangs, and his arms tilted up to an unshowing sky.*

He leaned forward, smiling, and leveled his eyes on me. They were the color of blood. They glowed red with fire, crimson flames flickering within them.

"Dad?" *I asked.*

Laughter like nails grinding slowly down a chalkboard screamed back. "I am not the man you think I am."

"Who are you?"

"Fool! I am one of three and none of the sssame. It isss time," *he said, the blood in his eyes matching his voice.*

Slowly, he extended one hand and pointed a gray finger at my face. It reached farther and farther until it was right between my eyes, nearly touching my skin.

A wicked grin lit up the man's face and a burst of fire exploded in his eyes.

The finger reached out the few more inches it needed to touch me and I felt the hot, blinding contact of the thing as it licked my bare skin.

"No!" *the man shouted, the fire in his eyes blazing like an erupting volcano.*

Light exploded through the haze in fierce, blue heat.

The man was gone in a howl.

Hastily, I rolled out of bed and made my way

downstairs, rubbing my eyes until they felt sore, raw and awake. As alive as I wanted to be. I reached slowly up and touched the spot in between, wondering.

Could Dad be the Bloodletter?

I thought, *What does that make me?*

I stopped in the hallway next to a mirror. I wanted more than anything in that moment to keep walking, but I had to see. I had to know if I was the same. I held my breath, closed my eyes, and turned to face my reflection.

Two days, he'd said last night, while Kate had given me three.

How many did I have left?

When my eyes opened, I saw me. Just me, with the shadow of my past looking back.

~

"No more, Mom," I said, my mouth full with warm eggs. "Seriously, I'm stuffed."

"Oh, come on," she said, spooning more on my plate. "If you don't eat it'll just go to waste."

I puffed a drone of tight air onto my plate and the eggs quivered. This had become our Saturday morning ritual; Mom making breakfast, usually scrambled eggs or omelets with a side of bacon and burnt toast, me eating most of it and her settling for a bowl of bran-something, scowling with each bite.

"So, how is Tanner?" she questioned me. "How is everything going at school? I feel like we haven't talked in a long time."

"*Tyler*, Mom," I said, ignoring the fact that she couldn't remember my best friend's name. "He's good. Same old."

She set her mug of coffee on the table, the liquid splashing out in drops too light to be only coffee. Looking out the window, she said, "Are you sure? Nothing new?"

My mind raced. *Dad. Kate.*

"Mom, there's something..."

I touched my neck in the spot where it was still tender from the night before. Every time I mentioned Dad's name it was like someone threw a blanket of cold unease over the house.

"What is it?"

She wanted nothing, her eyes spoke that much. I could see the way they shone, dull and gray, and knew my secret would break her completely. She was already crying.

Last night would be another secret untold.

"Everything is pretty good," I said, smiling wide. I felt her look away. "I'm sure, Mom. Nothing new."

I could see it in her eyes whenever I spoke: *Luke.*

This conversation was killing her.

My heart: *I am killing her.*

I turned to look down at my plate.

I wanted to say this: *Tyler is right. I will never be what he is. I know that now. There is nothing to worry about.*

But I couldn't.

Still, I worried for Mom more. Her eyes were sunken so that a deep blackness encircled each, and her skin had become sallow and tight. Even her lips seemed thinner, as if her breaths came less frequently. As if she weren't breathing at all.

"So," I started, not knowing where I was going. "I went over Tyler's last night to have dinner with his family. Mrs. Little wishes you her best."

She grabbed the newspaper next to her, turning it to

the Lifestyles section. "Hmmm. Sounds nice."

"You know, Mom," I tried, "you should really think about coming over to the Littles one day. I know they would really love to have the both of us over."

"We'll see," she replied, her face buried in the newspaper. "Twenty more gone from Jefferson County. They say the count is up to a few hundred in Detroit and Memphis. Two more missing since yesterday from Lakewood Hollow. I wonder why they didn't mention any names. Have you heard anything?"

"Not a thing," I sighed and took another sip of my bitter coffee.

She wrinkled the paper and moved it closer. "They're saying everyone should act normal, that because nothing is confirmed we shouldn't worry."

I couldn't help it. "Mayor White is dead. The whole state is basically red with blood and you agree we should ignore it?"

She didn't answer.

We sat in the kitchen for a few more minutes, quietly sipping our coffee and enjoying the silence of company. It was the perfect Saturday morning, except that Mom wasn't really reading the paper, and I wasn't really enjoying the silence.

"So, what are your plans for the rest of the day?" Mom said, brushing the paper softly with her hand to smooth the permanent wrinkles.

"The Homecoming bonfire is tonight," I told her. "If they don't cancel it because of the missing people."

"Sounds good," she said.

"Are you sure? We could hang out instead, I went to the bonfire last year so I pretty much know how it goes."

"No, no. It's really okay," she said, smiling and shaking her head. "I actually have some work I need to finish for a board meeting on Monday, so that will give me some extra time to work in the quiet house."

"Okay," I said.

She got up from the table, gripping her mug tightly. "I think I'm going to go rest for a while. I'll see you in a bit. Remember to wear a sweatshirt tonight. Your green one's clean."

Perfect, I thought.

~

Every year Homecoming made the air thick with hope and anticipation. And every year that feeling reached a crescendo on the night of the Homecoming bonfire. Students gathered from all crowds to feel the warmth for all different reasons. There were those hoping they might meet their true love, and those anticipating a night with one already found. Hope for popularity and anticipation of rejection. The bonfire was a night of moments; some screamed out loud and some better left unsaid. Tonight, though, the quiet moments were framed in a circle of officers, armed and ready.

I looked at the police in their blue uniforms, the orange light from the bonfire making their black holsters shine. They were safety.

For tonight-

I'm safe.

Though I couldn't help but wonder: If Lakewood Hollow was supposed to be living normally, why were we surrounded like this?

I made my way through bodies that moved like

flames afraid to burn out, each of them kissing another, intertwined. I always loved the way the air smelled on this night: burnt and alive. It reminded me of everything good about my childhood, all the happy memories of camping trips and s'mores before the downfall. There was something about a bonfire that made it magical, a beacon in the night signaling that anything could happen.

I saw Annabelle and Chad kissing feverishly in the darkness just beyond the firelight, ignoring the officer glaring at them. Their rings glinted against the fire and, bright as the flames were, the night seemed to embrace them in shadow. I wondered if they were cold, or if their love was keeping them warm. With their hands linked together, dark and light, I wondered if they were happy.

The shadows dancing off the fire felt like warnings; somewhere out there was my father, his heart beating for one more drop of blood.

I moved slow, cautious. Looking around, I found Tyler standing with a few guys from the football team. Brett, Justin, and Charlie; they always included me in anything the group did. Or tried to. I tried to be polite about turning them down most of the time; I couldn't stand around for hours talking about grunts and burps. Together Tyler and I were different, but with this group I knew I didn't fit. I tugged my green hood on and walked over.

"Hey guys," I said, pulling my hoodie tighter around me. "What's going on?"

Charlie grunted.

"Not much, Wade," Justin said, slapping my back. "What's up?"

"Nothing," I shrugged, feeling my shoulders shake.

Tyler walked up next to me and whispered, "You okay? You seem upset."

I sighed. "You know, sometimes I hate that you've known me for so long."

His lips tilted to a smile, but in the soft light I could see his emerald eyes dark as night wanting more. "Spill it. Come on, let's walk."

The crowd shifted around us as we moved, waving to people we knew and those we didn't. For every step we took, a pop of burning log sounded, sparking bright moments of light into the night.

I breathed deeply, inhaling the smoky air as if autumn would be gone tomorrow. I whispered, "I saw my Dad last night on the way back from your house."

Tyler stopped but said nothing. His eyes, now an orange color from the light of the fire, were wide. Was even he afraid of my father?

"He was just there, out of nowhere," I continued. "He was crazy and he grabbed my arm and my neck and his eyes were so angry."

"You okay?" Tyler's voice was barely audible. "Did he hurt you?"

I shook my head. "I'm okay, but he told me I have two more days left."

"Two days? But Kate said you had three. Does that mean they know each other?"

I felt my face grow pale. "I don't know. But I don't want to think about it now, Tyler. What happens to me tomorrow or the day after? I don't want to think about it."

He nodded. "Okay."

For a while we stood there, both silent. The sounds of the bonfire popped around us, but somehow we stayed untouched.

And then words I couldn't stop escaped: "You should have seen the way he looked, Tyler." I was shaking now. "His eyes so sunken-in like he was nearly dead. He was so pale. But he was so *excited* to see me. It was like he was possessed by someone that wanted me dead."

Tyler just smiled. "I don't know what's going on," he said and patted my shoulder, "but I do know that at least for tonight we should forget this. Like you said, let's not think about it right now. We're as safe as we can be here; there are like twenty cops walking around. Forget Kate. Forget your Dad. Forget everything that has ever made us anything less. Maybe it's what we both need. It'll be like magic. Tonight will solve everything if we just let it."

"Yeah," I said, though my entire body shivered. Even so, I thought of the night before, of Dad. With so many people around, surely one more night couldn't hurt anything. "Maybe you're right. Let's just have fun."

"And tomorrow we can figure everything out."

Tyler shouted at his friends and we walked back over to where they were standing, waiting for magic to happen.

Charlie grunted.

"Whoa! You're right, Charlie," Justin said. "Check it out guys. Across the fire. Smokin'!"

The three of them grunted back as Tyler elbowed me in the shoulder. "It's her. It's Kate."

She was standing across the fire, the flames flickering across her face, sheltering her from me. Sparks seemed to fall from the sky, reminding me of the single red leaf that fell the day before, burned like the ash from the fire.

"Go talk to her," Tyler said, pushing me forward. "Maybe this is the sign you were waiting for. Go confront her and ask her what the hell is going on."

But I couldn't. I was frozen. "No."

"Do it," he urged. "Ask her what she meant when she told you 'three days'. You deserve an answer."

I didn't even realize I was moving until I was right in front of her, beyond the fire. Had I walked through the flames, or around them?

I stood there, unsure, hands in my pockets.

"What?" she asked, arms crossed, a frown etched deep in her face. The light from the fire made the tattoo on her finger blaze like a tiny flame itself. Her eyes were locked on the fire, looking a beautiful shade of yellow-purple.

Talk.

"Hi," I said.

Like lightning she turned to face me, her hand reaching forward, finger poking me in the chest. So close, her face glowed, the firelight shining like a hundred soft candles. I almost fell backwards.

"I don't know how you hide it so well. You think you're so great, so in control of everything but you have no idea." Her lips bent and she shook her head.

"Uh. Okay," I started, ignoring the way her touch made me dizzy. "I have no idea what you're talking about, Kate. I've done nothing to you. I barely even know you. *You're* the one who threatened me. Tell me what's happening in a few days. Tell me what's going on!"

She crossed her arms again and spat, "Oh, shut up. You know exactly what's going on and who I am. You are sick and pathetic going around like you are trying to blend in. All these innocent people missing and you don't even blink!"

Cold.

"What? I have nothing to do with the missing

people. Do you know anything about what's going on?"

"I know more than you think." She scowled. "The Bloodletter is the least of your worries. The Orieno is gaining strength and you sit in school and do nothing like you have no idea what's been happening all around you. That you don't know *you're* the one they want and all these people would be alive if not for you." She shook her head. "Marcus warned me that this would happen, that you would play the fool, but don't think your little act here tricked me for one second. I'll give you tonight; there are too many cops. But if you leave I *will* kill you no matter what the Order says. No matter what the consequence."

I felt so cold.

My entire body felt dead, as cold and lifeless as a corpse. Still, my heart beat fast, so rapidly it seemed to stop. My vision tilted and, my lips dry and crack, I whispered, "Kate. What are you talking about?"

Her eyes met mine for the first time all night and I could have sworn the fire burned brighter, more blue and purple and angry. The other world faded to black around us and it was just her and I.

One moment lasted forever.

One dark, infinite inferno.

"Oh my god," she breathed, bringing a hand to her mouth. She took a step back. "Why do you look... How... You have no idea do you?"

Fear burned in her eyes, and I found myself being more afraid because of it.

"Kate," I said stepping forward. "Explain this to me so I can understand. What are you talking about?"

"Don't," she said, and moved further back. "Don't you dare come near me!"

She reached out and punched me in the stomach. It

was like nothing else I'd ever felt; not even Tyler could punch that hard. I fell to the ground in a heap just as rain began to fall from blackness. The world burned around me. Rain poured down, for a moment looking like mirrored droplets of tiny flames, reflecting the fire before killing it. Smoke lifted into the dark sky.

From across the extinguished fire I could see Kate, running away through the crowd. I was sure she had made it rain. Who else but a beautiful monster could have killed such a beautiful night?

CHAPTER SEVEN
HEARTS ON FIRE

-CALUM-

Hearts falling from the sky,
Twisting like bodies in the air.
Burning.
Hearts on fire.
Red and orange and green turned black.
Life falling all around me,
My world burning.
Cruel hands, black and gray,
Moving toward me.
Wanting.
Needing.
Branches of autumn's rage,
Spiked daggers of decay.
Moving closer.
Everything moving closer.
Always closer.

Then, in the second before I drifted back to the real world and away from the cruel dream, I heard a voice; the same lyrical timbre I'd heard in the parking lot two days before. Though perhaps it was me, my mind, dreaming a warning I couldn't understand.

> *"Walk away from trouble.*
> *Rise with your brother moon.*
> *Follow the light of it, a road.*
> *Listen.*
> *It is time, for darkness is close.*
> *Become who you will always be, Caeles,*
> *Who you have been born to be*
> *One thousand times before, and always."*

The voice played over and over in my mind, but it made no sense. Nothing did. Like razor blades stuck deep underneath my tongue, my world felt uncomfortable to live in. Last night's dream left me in disarray. Only when I woke did I realize the hearts had been *real* hearts, burning bright as they fell as madly as torn leaves. Realizing that made my own shake with fury.

And as I lay listening to my heartbeat, barely breathing, I could only think of Kate.

Today is the day, I thought, sucking in air through my nose. Sunday had come and gone without a thought, and I still smelled like fire, dark and smoky. *Last Friday I met Kate and Dad tried to kill me. Today must bring something, some kind of truth to help me understand.*

As much as I feared what was to come, one thought, bright as the sun rising red outside, raced through my mind: *Today I will have an answer.* One way or another I knew today was a day that would bleed truth. I could feel it.

I kept my eyes closed. Time went by so slowly when you were half asleep and half awake; it was the perfect time to daydream. Hoping, of course, that you didn't actually fall back into a nightmare. My alarm was still safely set though, so I didn't worry. No way did I want to be at school early. Not today.

I rolled over so that I could see out the window, resting both hands, as if praying, under my cheek. The sun was already high in the sky and its rays beat down, warming my room and making it too hot to be under the comforter. It was such a strange sight to see first thing in the early morning, before school, before my world actually started. Lately, the darkness of autumn had become prominent, overflowing the atmosphere with its feeling of chilled comings. But today was different. Today was light.

Maybe it won't be so bad.

With a big sigh, I ripped off my comforter and felt a breath of relief as the cool bedroom air hit my naked calves, skipped over my boxers, and ran up my stomach and chest. I rolled out of bed. My feet crunched on crumpled pieces of paper inked black and blue with words. I bent down and picked up a piece so scratched with ink, scars ran up and down where I had crossed through words.

This I ~~wonder~~ can feel:
I am ~~nothing~~ my dreams.
I am ~~afraid of~~ haunted by them.
~~They tell me secrets.~~ They are whispers of truths.
I can feel my soul screaming at me ~~to open up and believe~~.
Still, ~~there isn't~~ I can't find a truth to believe in.
I am ~~nothing without truth~~ someone

more than this.

I am someone.

~~*Am I even alive?*~~ *Who am I?*

The words shook in my hand, tiny letters shattering me. I had written this months ago. My dreams then were so haunted and real. I remembered the mist taking me each night. I remembered the light, my savage, saving grace. I remembered so much about my dreams, but I still didn't know the truth about my reality.

Still my dreams were like that.

Still I had no truth.

I threw the paper to the floor and pushed my shoulders back. Today would be different than my dreams; it would be real. Answers were powerful things. That was enough.

I walked to the mirror on the back of my door and locked eyes with my reflection. Even if I didn't know who I was today, I knew who I wouldn't be.

I remembered his words: *I'm doing this for you...*

"I am not my father," I whispered.

For a moment, he was all I could see. His eyes looked back. His hair lay matted on mine. His lips smiled as he drank me in.

I closed my eyes, willing that singing voice to fill my head again. I knew it wasn't anything real, but lately, aside from Tyler, it was the only thing that believed in me.

Then, like the light in my dreams: *Become who you will always be...*

When I opened them, my eyes shone as bright as the moon, ever blue, and I was me.

I was *me.*

I had black bags under my eyes, and my hair, looking more messy than normal, was thrown every which way. I still had on my hoodie from yesterday and somehow it was half on and half off, one arm in and one arm exposed.

But I was me.

I was not my father's son today.

I smiled-

let him fade to dust.

~

The hot water felt so good, soothing my muscles and burning my skin red; and within ten minutes I was showered and back in my room. I grabbed a clean pair of dark jeans from my dresser, almost fell over into a pile of paper as I was putting them on, and tugged a gray sweater over my head. I rubbed my eyes a little, trying to get the blackness out of them, but it was no use.

I made my way over to my desk. Sat, clicking the keys of my computer, searching. Somehow, I found myself looking at pictures in my photo album. I was amazed at how much I had grown over the past year, into someone more than the scrawny guy I had been when I started high school. I surfed through pictures and came to one of me and Tyler at our kindergarten graduation. His mom had forwarded it to me years ago. In it we were small, tiny compared to everything else. We were smiling. I didn't remember that day, but I remembered being that age. That's when the problems had started. Funny, how some people change and some stay the same.

My eyes drifted toward the bottom of the screen. The clock blinked neon: 10:02 AM.

I froze.

My breath caught in my throat.

School started two hours ago.

I moved so quickly that I knocked over my desk chair and fell onto the floor.

Why didn't my alarm go off?

With a thud of regret washing over me, I realized I had fallen asleep without setting the clock. I must have.

Where's Mom?

10:03 AM.

No time to think. Time was rushing forward without me, not waiting.

I grabbed my phone off the dresser, my backpack from the floor, and flung my door open, making it hit the wall, probably leaving a dent in the soft frame.

Mom would have my head for that one.

My legs couldn't carry me fast enough as I flew down the hallway and then down the stairs, only touching three of them. In a crash I landed, fell to my knees on the floor, and looked around.

"Mom?" I called, hoping she had just fallen asleep on the couch. "Mom? Where are you?" I tried to shout, but my words came out as a cry. "I need a ride to school."

I ran into the living room, found it empty and shouted, "Mom! You here?"

No answer.

No Mom.

It was as if the world had slowed and died, and silence upon silence was living inside the house; I knew something was wrong. I could feel it everywhere; in the quiet, thick air of unease around me. I could see it in the pictures nailed to the walls, hanging crooked and dreadful and wrong.

I stepped into the kitchen.

Nothing.

I ran around the house in a desperate frenzy hoping to see some sign of her, anything that would tell me where she was but I found nothing.

I dug my phone out of my pocket and dialed her cell phone number.

I jogged around the house one more time as I listened to the sound of metallic ringing in my ear.

The call went to voicemail.

My thoughts were interrupted by the *ding* of the doorbell, too heavy and false in this hush. I walked to the window and peeked out from behind the curtains.

Harsh, loud: *Ding.*

My heart fluttered and then dropped past my feet and into the floor below. The air was sucked out of me with a malicious intensity; I was never going to get it back and, for a second frozen in time, I was helpless against the fear.

Dad.

Ding.

"Ca-lum!" I heard him call, his voice sardonic and wild. "I know you're in there. Hello. *Hello!* Come out, come out and talk to me."

His words, like an evil song, cut through the air with anxious rhythm. His face wore a sinister smile looking of blood lust as if he were smelling the sweetest perfume and wanting nothing more than to bathe in it. His eyes were on fire with a redness that I was quickly beginning to recognize as twisted fury. He was sick.

Ding.

I didn't know what to do. My mind raced with nothing, running faster and faster on empty.

Ding.

His face twitched, like before, the spasm running

through his body like rage. *"Calum! Calum!"*

And faster: *Ding.*

Ding.

"Calum!"

Ding.

He began to whistle in time to the doorbell, his lips barely puckered together against his smile, and then words took shape as he sang:

"One, two, I see you.
Three, four, kill some more..."

Somewhere deep inside me my adrenaline kicked in and I ran. I ran out the back door and away from the man I didn't know and from the house I didn't feel safe in. I didn't know where I was running to and I couldn't see clearly, but I knew that I needed to get away. I needed to be somewhere safe where there would be people, lots of people.

Gone was the time to be alone.

As I ran I could hear my Dad scream behind me and then not at all; I couldn't shake the feeling that I'd been here before.

Screaming.

There was nothing but screaming.

Chapter Eight
Blood and Truth

-Calum-

The wind howled around me. My legs moved without my help, propelling me forward. I arrived at the school in a matter of minutes, slowed to a walk when I was in the parking lot, and stopped to catch my breath. My adrenaline was still pumping hard through my body, but I could see my surroundings now. The sky was darkening, the gloomy clouds extended outward in wisps like gray fingers. Singular drops of rain fell, warning but doing little more. A storm was just beyond the horizon, past the mountains, waiting.

Dad.

Another burst of panic sent a wave of dizzying blue fog, hitting my senses with blunt force. I blinked, threw my hands to my knees and bent forward. My head began to pound, throb.

I don't know what to do, I thought. *What do I do?*

Somewhere deep within the ache, I thought I heard my named being called. *Calum.* It sounded like angels singing. *Calum, embrace who you are, what you can do. Embrace it.* But then, like so many times before, blue threatened and the voice became a memory.

I walked toward the ominous letters of the high school. All I wanted right now was to talk to Tyler. I pushed open the doors of the school, walking full force, and ran into what felt like a brick wall.

"Stay back!" I heard someone shout.

Chaos had taken Lakewood High. People were everywhere, running this way and that, limbs tangled. The common area was so packed with bodies that I couldn't see any space between them.

I jumped as an arm grabbed me from my left.

"Calum!" Annabelle screamed at me. "What are you doing here? We thought you died! Have you seen Jason?"

"What's going on?" I shouted above the noise. "What are you talking about?"

Her eyes grew wide. "Chad's dead," she whimpered, "and Jason's gone. I know he is!"

Suddenly, Tyler exploded behind her and, when he saw who Annabelle was talking to, grabbed me and shoved me down behind a bench.

"What are you doing here?" he whispered. He was sweating, his voice shaking. I had never seen him so afraid. "Go! You have to leave right now before he knows you're here."

I pushed his hand off me. "Before who knows I'm here? What is everyone running around for?"

Before Tyler could answer I heard the first scream. It started loud, earsplitting, and then leveled off to a sob before it became a wet gurgle. I had never heard death before, and the sound of it made my skin crawl.

"He's here," Tyler whispered. "We thought it was all about Kate but we were wrong. He's come for you. He keeps saying your name."

I couldn't breath. "Who?"

Tyler leaned in close. "Your Dad."

Annabelle choked, "The Bloodletter."

Slowly, without even realizing I was doing it, I was up, standing amidst the students that filled the wide open area. Looking around, I saw what I had not seen before. Blood was everywhere. Students had been tossed in heaps of bloody bodies at random. I saw Chad's hand sticking out from beneath the nearest one, the ring on his finger too familiar to be a mistake.

"Chad..." I breathed as I stepped toward what was left of him.

"Don't," Tyler said grabbing my arm and pulling me back. I heard Annabelle sob. "We have to get out of here."

"But all these people," I started, shaking my head back and forth. "How did he get here so fast?"

"I don't know," Tyler said. "A few minutes ago he ran out of the school and we thought it was safe, but he's back. I've never seen anyone move as fast."

I reached for my phone to call the police but Tyler knocked it out of my hand.

"There's no time for that," he said while his eyes pleaded in warning. "It's no use. People are saying he got the police first. There's hardly anyone left in town; your Dad's been going at it all morning. No police. No teachers. Mayor White was already gone. He targeted everyone that would be able to help us, and crowded the rest in school."

"But why would he do that?"

Annabelle shivered next to me. "Because," she said in a small, hollow voice that I could barely hear above the screaming. "If everyone is dead there's no one left to tell the story."

My hands ran through my hair. I whirled around in circles, trying to understand what was happening. If no one was left, who would help?

I caught my reflection in the window behind me and stopped. I was smiling, a wicked grin on my face. Blood was dripping from my mouth down my chin and I was licking my lips as if I actually liked the taste. I waved, my hand moving at an odd angle.

"Hello, Calum. I told you today was the day. It has to be this way. Are you ready to die?"

A horrible panic raced through me as I heard Annabelle scream. Tyler pulled me close and then reached for her. Together we were three, a wall against what was. Together, we let out a collective shudder that made my father twitch, his eyes blinking in pleasure.

Still, the three of us were breathing.

"Why are you doing this?" I screamed, my voice too loud then too quiet.

"There is no other way." He smiled, and bits of flesh and blood spattered his lips. "Because if you don't die, then *I* will, and I want to live more than anything in this world."

He lunged at me. Tyler pushed me to the floor and I landed on top of Mr. Brandt, his eyes disconnected from his face. I heard a pop.

"Run, Calum!" Tyler screamed. He picked up a chair and threw it at my Dad, but he had changed directions and went for Annabelle instead. The second he touched her she screamed. He sunk his teeth deep in her neck and ripped and a chuck of meaty flesh flew across the room and hit the window with an echoing thud. A streak of red falling down kept time to the slow fall of Annabelle's body as she collapsed on the floor. Dead.

"No!" I screamed, just as Dad turned to Tyler. "You don't have to do this, Dad! Stop!"

But no one heard me. All around was the sound of the wounded dying. There were too many moans, too many screams and sobs to hear anything but the blood beat viciously in my ears.

Tyler and Dad ran at each other. I tried to move but a hand grabbed me. My legs kicked out, hopelessly making contact with nothing. I screamed, punching the air around me because I couldn't see who it was.

"Shut up and follow me," a voice said.

Kate.

I shouted, "Let me go!"

Her lips were wet with blood. "No! We have to get out of here! This wasn't supposed to happen! Can't you see?"

She had a grip like iron, but I managed to get away and started to run to where Tyler and Dad were fighting. I couldn't tell who was winning, but the sounds of skin ripping were loud enough.

"Let's go!" Kate yelled and grabbed my leg hard, pulling it back.

I fell, my head hit the floor and blackness erupted around me like death.

"It is not in the stars to hold our destiny but in ourselves."
- William Shakespeare

PART TWO

A RISING HEART

~

"WE WALK OUR DAYS AS HOLLOW MEN,
NEVER TRULY REALIZING THIS DAY
MIGHT BE OUR LAST. THIS DAY MIGHT
CHANGE EVERYTHING."

~

CHAPTER NINE
RED TEARS

-CALUM-

IN MY DREAM I COULD STILL SMELL THE blood, still see the bodies twisted and cut and dead. I could still hear the screams as my father stole lives and broke hearts.

I was flying.

"Calum," the voice said, the one I'd grown to know. "You must realize that this is the way it's supposed to be. You were meant for this life."

A shape of a man emerged from the night, shadow upon shadow of blackness. Stars filled the spaces where lips might be, blinked in place of his eyes.

I opened my mouth to speak, but I was frozen. I couldn't move, couldn't speak; in this sky I was barely living. I could feel my heart slow, until it was nothing and all was silent except the voice.

"I cannot stay long," the man said, all shadows and stars. "It is not time for me to interfere just yet, but know we are always watching. In your dreams we are watching. When it is time, you will know it. For now you must become who you were born to be, who you have been born to be

thousands of times before."

Stars like sparks of fire dotted his face, shooting across it. "I cannot say more. Accept your powers. Accept who you are. Don't let fear hold you back.

"Become who you are, Caeles..."

At once, as though death had taken me, the stars faded and nothing but darkness was seen.

~

Blue.
Violet.
Always blue and violet.
Blue and violet against one another.
Together, blue and violet.
Blue.
Violet.
Always.

-Kate-

CALUM WAS SUPPOSED TO DIE TODAY.

I could feel my heart screaming loud as I drove away from the town dressed in blood. Like the tall, white peaked mountains dotted in the distance, I could see cars littering the road, empty and painted red.

The Bloodletter wasted no time.

That meant one thing: Calum's father was under the Orieno's control. Rage now raced through his veins like blood; he was surviving on the power of the Orieno. Possessed and damned. Killing without remorse. But he was able to walk during the day, and wasn't trapped in the night like other Orieno victims.

How?

Did Calum know so many people wanted him dead?

I felt myself drive into a frenzy, my foot pushing hard on the gas. The tires squealed against the rain. Faster, always faster, I drove, until the small town of Lakewood Hollow was no more than a memory. A bloody mess of a memory so far gone it was no more.

Those possessed, sleeping souls caught by the Orieno demons would soon rise from the ashes of that town burned, as would the moon lift from the skyline and provide me a blanket of darkness.

-CALUM-

IMMEDIATELY, AS IF SLEEP HAD ONLY subsided it, my head exploded with pain. A buzzing sounded alive in my brain. Beyond, I heard the cracking roar of thunder and the anger of beating rain against thin glass. Every drop sounded like heartbreak, but I couldn't think of why.

Only: *Become who you are, Caeles...*

What did that mean?

I looked around. My vision blurred, all tilted shadow, nothing more. My neck felt raw and wet; I touched the back of my head and tried to massage away the pain. Slowly the shadows gave way to shapes and colors, and I began to see.

I was in a black Jeep. The passenger side window was dark and blurred from night. The moisture from the cool rain was mixing with the warmth of the car, making the glass swirl with indefinite confusion.

My first thought was, *Nothing.*

And then, as hot air burst into my lungs, I jumped in my seat; a ghost of something in the window, a haunting reminder of earlier. The memory of my Dad flooded back into my mind like a virus, sickening me to a pale white; a realization of loneliness, drowning me in panic and stillness.

Tyler. Was he - *no, please no* - dead?

Dad. What happened?

I closed my eyes and saw death.

Opened: Life.

I closed and opened and closed but nothing changed;

life and death looked so much alike in this dim light.

My hands flew up to my mouth. The scenery outside was flicking by rapidly, barely there. Above, the moon looked blue in the star-dotted sky; I knew I was far from home.

Dizzy, my head rolled back.

"Don't spew in the car, thanks," a voice to my left said, the tone gritted with disdain.

Without looking I knew. My fingers curled into my palms, nails pushing against skin almost breaking. My heart, beating wildly, threw itself against my ribs. My jaw tightened. Against my racing pulse, my mind screamed at me to jump out of the Jeep; do anything but sit here. Escape. *Run.*

My face burned, and even though I felt like I was catching fire, against it all I was helpless.

Against her I felt helpless.

Closed.

Kate. "Seriously. If you get sick I'll break your face." I felt the Jeep gun forward. "I know twenty ways to kill you without even taking my foot off the gas."

Opened.

Against it all, she was here and so was I.

I could hear the thumping of my heart as it threatened to cripple, torturing me as if it was trying to kill.

Tyler has to be alive. I can't be alone.

It was all a dream.

If I closed my eyes, I could remember.

I could hold on to my friend.

My brother.

"Do you ever feel like you don't belong?" I asked.

He tilted his head. "What do you mean?"

"Like you don't fit in with everyone else?"

Tyler smiled and ran his fingers through his hair when he said, "I just want to feel. Have a kiss that changes me, ya know?"

I asked, "You think you can tell if you love someone from a kiss?"

"You can see into someone's soul through their eyes, Calum, but you can touch their heart through a kiss."

For a moment, silence was the only noise.

I said, "It feels impossible to be who everyone thinks I am when I can't even figure out who I am alone."

"Exactly." Tyler smiled.

A monstrous burst of lightning split the sky a hundred ways, sucking the blackness out of the air, gathering with it the glowing stars and the bright crescent moon. Even the light from the headlights faded and we were lost in the flash. The thunder that immediately followed broke the night with one swift blow, and sent the world back in darkness.

We were gone in the light, and in the dark.

I blinked and felt a tear fall down my face. I reached to wipe it away but stopped. Instead, I let it slide down my blood-covered skin and drop off my chin, dotting red on my jeans.

It was the first time I had cried in so long-

I let it fall to nothing.

I took one breath. I could feel the weight of my voice in my throat, feel the way it burned crawling up. "Why did you take me away? Tyler could be dead! Dead! I could have saved him!"

Her lips curved up. "You could have saved him? Please, Calum, look at yourself; you couldn't do anything. And your father is still alive."

"My father? You think I care about him? After seeing *that*?" My head fell from side to side. "What about Tyler? Is he alive?"

"I don't know." She shrugged. "Probably not."

I didn't believe her. I couldn't. "We have to go back! Turn around right now. I have to know if he's alive."

"We can't," she said, her voice spilling out through a haunting smile that moved like ashes on waves; there, then not. "If we turned around now, all you'd find when you got to Lakewood Hollow would be a town burning. And with your father on the rampage, it's only a matter of time before the entire county is destroyed for good. It was already halfway gone when we left."

I felt my ears go red, my teeth tight together against the unresolved. "How can you just sit there and say that? We need to go back and help Tyler!" My voice cracked and sizzled with sadness. My throat was sore and dry. I felt the sting of fresh tears fall easily, noticed the splatters of red everywhere, on my hands, pants and shirt. "Help all of them."

"It's no use trying to save those people when you already saw them die," Kate said.

A boom of thunder made my hand shake, vibrating along with the outside world. I reached up slowly and pulled down the visor. The skin around my eyes was black, and my face was blistered pink. My hair was more wavy than this morning, and strands of it were tinted red. My eyes looked dead. Hollow.

My face was unrecognizable, too splattered with blood and tears. But after everything, I felt a jolt of happiness fly through me, and as much as I hated that, I didn't push it away; I was too relieved to not see my father looking back.

All my energy left in an instant. "What happened, Kate? Will you please just tell me the truth? I'm so... I just don't understand. Are you the one taking all the people, the ones on the news? Is that why you kidnapped me? Are you working with my Dad?"

"Don't be stupid," she said, her laugh like breaking glass. "You're even more of an idiot than I thought."

I threw up my arms. "Well, what do you expect? Seriously! Do you have any idea how lost I feel right now? And all you can do is laugh and call me an idiot? What does that make you then, Kate?"

Her lips stretched tight. Even in the dark, her violet eyes shone bright.

Looking at her reminded me of the first time I saw her, in class with Tyler.

If ever there was a time I could have wished away my memories it would have been then. I desperately wanted to look up at the sky and find a shooting star, make a wish, and go back to yesterday, back to Tyler, but I knew that was impossible. The sky was too dark wherever we were, the night too forsaken. We were driving too fast to even see the stars clearly.

The jeep hit a bump in the road, causing my heart to jump up and down. I knew I should have been livid, but I was too tired. Even anger couldn't have survived today.

Suddenly, just as thunder crashed, Kate shivered.

"You just don't get it," she whispered. Her voice quivered slightly, making me freeze. "You should. You should know everything, but you don't. They said you would understand everything before we got there, but you don't."

"Who said I would understand? Where are you taking me?"

I waited for her to answer, but no words came.

I turned and looked out the window, taking in the rainy scenery. We were still driving fast, soaring down a single lane road through the mountains with large trees running across both sides. They were some of the tallest I had ever seen, their leaves spotted with light greens, yellows, and reds, all muted and blurred in the dark storm of this autumn night. The horrible beauty rushed by me as if a painter had taken the three colors and ran with the paintbrush over the canvas, like a child racing down a driveway with a stick of bubbles at midnight.

I could barely see the world.

After a few minutes of waiting, I gave up.

Attempting to break the silence, I said, "I don't understand-"

"You shouldn't have to," she whispered, her hushed voice somehow overpowering my own. Her eyes were large, glued to the road. Her voice was so quiet I was sure she wasn't talking to me. "If you don't already know, you shouldn't have to understand. It wasn't supposed to be like this. I have no idea what's going on now. Not anymore. Everything that was supposed to be true... This is all so different than what they told me."

Under her breath, she mumbled words I couldn't make out. Then slowly, as if she was afraid to look directly at me, she leveled her face with mine. Violet eyes pierced my soul and I felt like crying, though I didn't know why until she spoke. "My family is dead."

"What?" I said, not sure what to say. I felt my throat tighten.

She took in a breath, deep and long, as if she were taking in the right amount of courage. She looked at me, really *looked* at me for the first time ever, I think, since that first day we had locked eyes in Mr. Brandt's class.

There were tears in her eyes.

Maybe I was wrong about her.

I felt my heart beat a little faster.

She turned back toward the road, breathing heavily.

"My family," she started again, "is dead. They died five years ago, or at least that's what I was told."

"What do you mean *that's what you were told?*" I asked. Something in her words rang true in my head. Maybe I hadn't lost Tyler. Maybe there was still hope.

"They're not really dead," she said. "At least my sisters aren't. I was told my parents were murdered in cold blood, and that my sisters were too. But now I know the truth. My sisters are alive. I was told I needed to find you in order to find them, that you were enough leverage to get the information I need. I was told that if I didn't find you, no matter what, I would die in your place. You are my only chance to live again. Now though... Now I have no idea what's real and what isn't."

Maybe Mom is safe, I hoped. *Maybe Dad didn't get her.*

He said it was all for me.

~~*This is my fault.*~~ *Did I cause this, too?*

Kate's jaw clenched. "But I still can't let you go. If there's any chance I can have my sisters back." She turned to me, her eyes like knives. "I will never let you go."

My throat burned.

Kate's knuckles turned white. "There is a prophecy called the *Legend of the Dreamer* that tells of a boy who is born time and time again because he is the son of the Devil.

No matter who he is born to in each life, he is still always the reincarnation of his original self, the Dreamer. The Devil's son. You, Calum, are that boy, the Dreamer. You're the one pawn everyone wants. You are not who you think you are. Your true, first father was the Devil himself, and because of your bloodline you are the only one capable of stopping a secret war. The prophecy says that you will be the one to end it all. Even the Orieno, the soul-sucking demons fighting against our side, want to find you so they can use you."

She looked at me but didn't; her eyes moved up and down my body as though she were looking at someone else entirely. She said, "But how can you be what they say? You're so weak. I bet you couldn't even throw a proper punch."

My mind was frozen, my entire body rigid with confusion.

"I don't understand," I said, my voice hard and weak at the same time. "This can't be possible. This can't be real."

"I don't think a hero ever believes in himself until the story is almost over," she said. Kate closed her eyes and opened them again, quickly as if she wasn't believing this either. But when I heard her sigh and saw her fingers grip together until they turned white, I knew it wasn't a joke.

A cold sweat touched my back.

Terrified, I waited.

Kate took in a slow, deep breath as rain pounded down outside. "Just listen, Calum. Listen."

Inexplicably, in the dark void of not knowing, my mind painted a picture of Tyler.

Kate's eyes blinked shut. "Let me explain."

Chapter Ten
Song of a Killer

-Kate-

An old Warrior song haunted my thoughts, one I had learned as a child during those grueling years of training. Sung slow, it sounded almost like praying:

Drums, drums, all around
Giving hell to all the hounds.
Warriors, Warriors, raise your hands,
Beat and fight and hurt for man.
Take those red-eyes down for size.
All they do is spread those lies.
Order is where truth is found,
Our faith we praise the Order now.

I wasn't sure why it kept playing over and over in my head, but the fact that it did was comforting. With my eyes closed, I could see myself as a child running against the wind in my old, familiar gray clothes, playing a game of "Catch the Killer" with the other Warrior children. I pictured them falling down around me as I tackled them, winning always, even against Zackery Solt who, aside from being the only Warrior close to my age, had a heart that beat like mine: For blood and only blood. I saw those children's faces as I lunged at them, hands out and eyes wide. I saw their fear, saw how they were terrified at the sight of me, and I knew that my lack of fear would be my greatest weapon. I won then because they were afraid and I was not.

If I had nothing to lose, no one could touch me.

Like Zack always said: "Being afraid is just as useless as being in love."

My eyes opened to this: Fear was a weakness I couldn't afford to have. Only, the one thing that could destroy me was the one secret I kept locked away; no one but Marcus knew my desire to find my sisters. No one but him would ever know that tiny bit of fear I could never block.

But the rules have changed, I thought. *Now I have to tell one more.*

Now I am one person weaker.

I hated that I had to, but knew I didn't have a choice. If I gave Calum pieces of the truth, he would be more open to trusting me, giving me what I wanted. Marcus had told me that; not enough truth to make him my equal, just enough to keep him quiet.

Out of the corner of my eye, I saw Calum. He was everything I despised: Emotional, innocent, even *pretty*. His eyes were too blue, filled with too much light and dark, and his hair was too messy. His shoulders were wide, tight and compact with sinewy muscle, but they fell forward in ugly misery. Still, I could see his veins bump and ripple across his arms when he moved, when he was angry. Even now, his angled jaw was tight with tension, and I knew somewhere deep inside he was strong.

I saw his smile once, that first day we locked eyes, when he was with his friend Tyler, but never since. It had been kind and easy, his full lips tilted up at the edges. When Calum had smiled it reached to his eyes, lighting up his whole face as though he were completely happy. As though his eyes had captured a supernova exploding in a sparkling sky. Even now the thought of it made me want to smile, made me uncomfortable; that easy smile reminded me too much of my father's.

I wanted to be happy again, like I had been before.

My teeth gritted against memories. I despised Calum with every single thread of hatred I had in my heart because of that smile.

But what if Marcus is wrong, and Calum is really as clueless as he seems? I thought, *Blasphemy! But what if the Order is wrong?*

A moment so quick it was gone before it set in completely: *What if I'm wrong?*

I had always been the eldest, forced to play with the children and learn as they did. But I was never really an equal to them. Never. Their weaknesses did give me practice though, and I relished in the fact that I never lost a game. The Warrior song reminded me of that, and of my place in life.

I was a Warrior, forever and always. In that, I could find happiness.

A hard heart beat under my thick skin. My *leviti* was tattooed on my finger, the Warrior's sign of power. It seemed to beat and burn on my finger, and I knew I truly did believe in the Order. After everything I'd been through I was almost ashamed I had questioned it.

No, I thought, rubbing my *leviti*. It didn't matter if Calum was clueless or as lost as he claimed to be. He was still what the Order had warned: Dangerous and deadly.

I felt a familiar blanket of cold drape over me, as

comforting as the song.

Nothing but truth.

I thought, *I will live and die by the Code.*

I pledge my allegiance to the Order, the one and only truth.
I vow my life to thee, over sky above and ground below.
To kill, to die, or to bleed, my eyes only see one Order.
Soldier by soldier, side by side,
Never shall I break these words, or Death will reap the victor.
United we fight, against all opposed.
This is the truth, as is our Code.

As a Warrior for the Order, I knew there were no rules higher than that of our Code. As I looked again at Calum, bloody and damaged and weak, I knew he was no different than the Warrior kids I once dominated.

As long as he didn't smile, I would be fine.

Fearlessness, again, would be my greatest strength.

The Order was right, as always. It had to be. I couldn't believe otherwise.

Instead, I thought of my mission, and dug deep into the power and control I took from it. I knew this: Being fearless gave you power, gave you control, and nothing was more valuable to a Warrior than that.

Nothing.

Then a memory, falling over me, shattering me: My father's smile as he kissed me goodnight. The way he pushed my hair behind my ears, his hands so warm and rough.

Another: I stood with a boy, Adam. His hands against my sides. I smiled as he did. His hands were warm against my skin, so warm I could feel nothing else, until his lips met mine and that was all I knew instead.

Then, there were smiles. Always smiles.

Now, I felt those smiles in my throat, burning and choking me until, like before, I felt nothing else.

I could see Adam's eyes in my mind, so much like Calum's yet so different, whenever I let darkness fall across my own.

It was nothing new; I thought of old memories daily. Those old smiles stuck in my heart, hurting, and like always, I pushed them deeper until they were nothing.

My throat burned.

My heart was on fire.

Nothing is more important.

They are gone.

Gone.

Nothing.

I opened my mouth to start my story, but words failed me. I had never been good with words, which was probably why I was so good with my hands.

With killing.

I blinked and felt the only words I knew how to speak without fail; the Warrior song repeated in my mind and, as I pulled the stolen Jeep to the side of the deserted highway, those grave words of comfort gave me strength.

The rain beat down hard as we slowed to a stop. I took solace in the fact that there wasn't a single car for miles, though probably only because the storm was getting too strong. Or because the entire state was dead or gone or possessed by the Orieno.

I turned to look at Calum again and felt the sudden urge to punch him hard in the face so his nose broke in pieces. Around him I felt too much of who I used to be. He reminded me of a part of my past I couldn't forget. A part I *needed* to forget.

These thoughts had haunted me since the first day I saw him: He made me feel like the girl I tried to forget, not the Warrior I was.

I ground my teeth together and thought of Marcus' words: *Tell him what you must to get him to the compound, nothing more and nothing less.*

Calum's voice was filled with need, with an angry desire for answers. "Kate? Tell me the truth. Tell me what's going on. You owe me that much."

I recognized his need, that unshakable desire, but he was wrong.

I owed him nothing.

I felt a laugh, sick with bubbles, slide up my throat and out to this: "Truth."

There was so much about the truth that I wanted to change. At night, when I was alone, sometimes the heavy truths of my world hit me so hard I couldn't breathe for hours.

More secrets I kept.

I took a deep breath. I needed to feel Calum out, to see what truth he was after so I could hide the rest. I wondered, maybe, if I wouldn't have to tell him much after all. "What do you want to know first?"

His chest rose and fell. I felt time crawl by in what seemed like hours, days even, while his eyes closed and opened and closed. It was an eternal moment wrapped in something smaller; a moment before a truth.

Calum's eyes opened in a blur of brooding blue. His lips parted as his shoulders lifted and he turned to look out the window. In the glass, or maybe just because of the rain, I saw the wetness of his eyes. His voice was deep and quiet when he said, "Tell me your story."

I felt my heart explode. "What?"

I remembered.

Adam.

Together we were under the apple tree in my backyard, our legs entangled, the wind whistling softly around us. His touches seemed to linger forever on my skin.

"I'm so glad I got to meet you today," Adam said as he bit into a deep red apple. The juice stuck to his lips, and I couldn't help but bring a hand up to touch my own.

I felt as red as the apple in his hand.

I whispered, "Me too."

"Let's hide here forever."

My entire heart screamed: "I will if you will."

He smiled and laced his fingers in mine.

"You know," he breathed, "yesterday was my birthday."

"Tell me about it. How old are you now?"

He grinned. "Mom says I'm thirteen going on thirty."

I laughed. It felt good to laugh with Adam.

"I only just turned twelve last month."

"Twelve is my favorite number." He turned his face to me, still smiling. "You know what I wished for when I blew out my candles?"

I held my breath. "What?"

I felt his thumb rub against my palm. "You."

My heart was beating too fast, but not fast enough.

I felt like running and crying and laughing all at once, but I could only smile.

"Me?" I asked.

We were all breaths and whispers, nothing more.

He nodded. "But now it's your turn. I want to know all about the girl I met today, the girl in the pretty red dress who couldn't stop twirling in the park as the world passed her by. You looked like you were about to fly away. I want to know about that girl. Tell me your story."

Calum turned his head toward me, but all I could see was my lost boy: *Adam, Adam, Adam.* All I could see was his wild brown hair and pale blue eyes. All I saw was him.

I whispered, "What?" and the forgotten softness of my voice made me think of times gone by.

I am not that girl anymore, my mind screamed. *She is dead.*

"Tell me your story." Calum's voice was louder, and with the loss of those sweet whispers the image of Adam was gone. "Tell me why you took me, why you'd rather let me die than let me go. Why *me*? Why you?"

The thought invaded my mind in an instant, and then was gone: *Because you remind me of someone I used to know.*

And then, shocked: *You remind me of me.*

"Tell me your story," he said again, quieter than before.

"Okay," I said. I reminded myself that I could kill Calum with just two fingers. Three, if I wanted to make the pain last.

Still, I'd lived nearly five years in the Order without questions, so this sudden avalanche of them was choking. It felt like I couldn't breathe correctly. I didn't know why, maybe because he reminded me of so much, but I had the urge to trust Calum.

I couldn't.

I didn't know where to begin. I didn't *want* to begin. Somehow, that moment felt like the beginning would end everything. Could I trust myself to begin?

I had to.

"It starts with my family." I forced my voice to relax, made myself calm, but it didn't help; I could feel myself growing weak and pathetic as I remembered what once was. What would never be again. "My family is the reason I'm part of this war, and you're the reason there is one. Our stories kind of intertwine."

His face was tilted to the side. Softly, as if it were a reflex, he pulled his right hand up to his hair and brushed it behind his ear. I could hear him breathing and I tried to mimic mine to match his.

In and out and in.

I'd forgotten what it was like to breathe in time with someone else, almost as if we were one.

"Why are you smiling?" Calum asked.

I turned away. "I'm not!"

"Okay," he agreed, eyebrow raised, and I found myself wishing he would have argued instead.

He was *so* human. Had so many emotions dance across his face. So not me. Yet he wasn't human at all. How he didn't realize it was beyond me. Even a fool could see if they looked in his eyes; it was like he could see your soul and nothing was safe. No secrets could hide. Surely, the Order was right. Calum Wade was a descendant of the Devil.

What was I getting myself into?

I looked straight ahead, eyeing the empty road. In my mind I pictured myself twisting a rope three times around Calum's neck, then hanging him from a tree so his feet wiggled below. I wasn't sure which part of the image I liked better; the part that he was powerless-

"Kate," he urged.

or that he was close to death.

"Five years ago I thought family was forever," I began, and walked into an old dream I could never make true. I choked against it. I felt the girl in the pretty red dress hug me, sad. "I remember Christmas as though it were yesterday: The feelings, the food, the warmth. I remember laughing all the time and playing with my sisters. Being free. Now everything is different; I know those feelings only exist when you're alone. True freedom exists when you have no one but yourself."

Calum's lips puckered, and his eyes went still.

I didn't care that he didn't agree now.

He would, and that was enough.

"Five years ago, when I was twelve, we were having dinner together like always. Mom and Dad always made us eat together." I shook my head. "I think I hated it sometimes. I know I did that night because I wanted to meet someone after."

Calum breathed, "Who?"

"No one," I said, but I remembered a photograph I kept secret under my pillow: Adam with ice cream dripping down his nose, a silly grin on his face. He had one of me, too. I laughed so hard that day I cried. "It doesn't matter anymore."

Two days later, that photograph had burned to ash with the rest of my memories. With my life.

"I used to think my parents were perfect. Mom and Dad both had matching tattoos on their right hands, just big enough to fit under a dime," I continued. "I always thought it was so romantic that they had matching ones, but now I know the truth."

"Truth?" Calum asked. He looked nervous, as though my words were knives held against his flesh, puckering the skin but not drawing blood.

It was a nice thought.

"The tattoo, a circle with interconnecting lines like a net, is the symbol of the Order. My parents were members of the same group I'm in, the one that protects the world from all evil. Only, they betrayed us. They didn't deserve..."

Calum leaned over, too close, and then back as if he didn't really mean to. "What didn't they deserve? Is that the same symbol you have on your finger."

I shook my head. I frowned, thinking of what I believed, and what I didn't. I choked, "No. For what they did, they didn't deserve to live. They were spies."

I thought he might object, or be shocked. But instead his eyes were wide, and I found that they were understanding. It made me wonder.

"I'm sorry," he said. "My parents... I know what it's like to love and hate a person the same."

I nodded.

Inside, I cried.

"Mom was always smiling," I said. "She was always laughing. Dad was like that, too, I suppose. And my sisters, I remember them being so small; Karen and Kelly were only five when it happened. That night, everyone had just sat down in the living room after dinner. Dad was about to read us a story, some grim fairy tale, when all of a sudden we heard a dish shatter in the kitchen. Karen screamed. I screamed."

I felt myself lose control. Things too painful to push away crawled up and in a moment I was gone. "I looked at Dad and saw his eyes wide and alarmed. I remember his voice shaking when he called Mom's name, 'Emaline?' He kept calling but she didn't answer. Kept saying her name until the sounds of it blurred together. His hands dug into the couch as he flung himself up to see if she was hurt, but he stopped. Froze there in the middle of the room as if he was waiting for something.

"Just as he was about to run into the kitchen, we heard Mom shout. I could hear the tension in her voice and she screamed out again, like blood had caught in her throat. I jumped up and was behind Dad. Karen and Kelly were yelling at him from the couch, but they stayed put. Dad pushed me back and told me to take them away, to go upstairs and hide. I didn't know why. I should have stayed with him to help, but I took my sisters and ran.

"From the stairs I heard Mom shriek again and Dad yell in pain. I remember the gun shots, the weird slurping sounds coming from the kitchen, and I remember taking my sisters upstairs to their room, noiselessly, so that whoever was in our house would not hear."

Irritation kindled behind both my eyes. I could feel tears forming, but Warriors did not cry and so I stopped. I let one hand brush through my hair, let it fall over my face.

"Karen, Kelly, and I hid in their closet," I told Calum through strands of hair. "I didn't know what to do. They were shaking. I didn't know what was going on. I didn't understand why my Dad made us run away. My hands were over my sister's mouths to stop them from screaming, and I prayed that they wouldn't make a sound."

The air in the Jeep seemed so thick I couldn't breathe right. Now, unlike before, my breath was different than Calum's. Mine was uneven, shaking with memories. His was still, or not at all.

I remembered this part clearly; I lived it every night,

every morning, every moment in between: "That's when they walked in. There were three of them, two men and a woman with black masks over their faces and dark gloves over their hands. They moved so quietly I was scared they were ghosts. Kelly's hand was on my leg, grabbing it tightly, digging her nails into my skin, but I didn't feel a thing.

"They ripped open the closet doors and threw thin bags over our heads. The woman told me they would kill my sisters if I screamed. I knew by her voice that she meant it. She warned that if I made any noise she would rip out my throat.

"Karen and Kelly were dragged down the stairs, their tiny heads bashing into the steps and I couldn't do anything to help them. The people were too strong. One man kept repeating, 'It's your time. It's your time to go.' I only asked once, but once was not enough to get me an answer. I kicked and pulled at his hair, wishing for my parents the whole time but they didn't answer my cries. No one answered. I clawed at his face, wanting him to bleed, but I was too weak."

"Why would they do that?" Calum asked. "They didn't tell you why they wanted you?"

I heard the unsaid words in his voice: *You didn't tell me either.*

"No," I said. I brushed my hair behind my ear, but let it fall again. "They didn't say why. The man just kept holding me tighter. His hands... I felt like I was choking the whole time even though his hands were nowhere near my throat."

Even now, I couldn't breathe.

Calum's eyes were unmoveable, focused on the rain as it fell against the windshield, but I suspected that, like me, he wasn't really seeing rain at all.

My own hands moved to my throat. "It happened so fast. The other two pushed Karen and Kelly into a car. I was thrown into the back of a truck and hit with something heavy, a rock maybe. Everything went black. When I woke up, I couldn't tell how much time had past. We must have driven for hours. They kept telling me I was going to be better, and that everything would be all right in time. That I was going to become just like them."

I froze.

I breathed.

I knew what I had to do; this was the last I could remember, the last moment I could be so vulnerable.

I looked at Calum.

He was not Adam.

He never would be.

Whereas Adam's eyes had been a pale, sweet blue, Calum's were as blue as death, and looked as though they could suck out your soul.

I became a shell, unbreakable.

I said, "I had no idea where we were. No idea about anything. But I knew one thing; I would never be the same again. I heard whispers, and then the world went black again. When I woke up I was in a cave and a man was standing over me, dressed as black as night. The three that had wrecked my life were gone. This man's skin was covered with glittering red tattoos and a red ruby glinted in the middle of his forehead. I remember thinking Marcus was the most terrifying man I'd ever seen. He told me that he was the leader of a group called the Order, a secret society of enchanters who continue to fight against all that is evil."

For one brief moment, I wondered if I was revealing too much. If I was breaking the Code somehow. But the way Calum was looking at me, as though he was beginning to trust my words, made them fall faster.

"Marcus told me that he had taken action and saved me from my parents, that they were traitors to the cause. Marcus had been looking for my parents for years. Once he had located them, he said he couldn't let them live. The crime they committed was too great. He said my parents had once been great Warriors in the Order, but that they had betrayed the group and gone rogue. They had been spies for the Orieno."

Calum's voice was hushed when he asked, "What did your parents do that was so bad?"

I laughed, loud and dry and short. "Aside from being spies against the one society in the world that can protect us? They killed people. A lot of good people. When they decided to go rogue, they went against the Warrior Code, the law we live by as Warriors, and killed nearly every one of the Warriors the Order had back then. No one knows why. No one is left from that time except Marcus. All the other Elders were killed and they had to create a new Council after."

I shuddered. "Marcus is the only one that remembers exactly what happened that night. Even now we don't talk about it if we can help it. *I don't talk about it.* The Order doesn't even tattoo their own symbol on themselves anymore. It's forbidden. Only the Elders have the Order symbol on them, and the Warriors have something entirely different."

Calum pointed at my finger. "Like yours?"

"Yes." I raised my hand. "This tattoo is my *leviti,* or my death mark. It's branded on all Warrior members so that we can keep track of our rankings, and we do that by showing how many we've killed by inking our death counts in red. It's also kind of a rebel symbol against my parents."

Calum's eyes were wide. I noticed that his hand had moved slowly closer to the door handle.

He was counting my kills.

I smiled, rubbing my *leviti*. "We are going to my home, Lake Iris. The Order has small covens all over the world, but this is where the main coven is located. But what you need to understand, Calum, is that the Order is magic. They are enchanters. They use the energy around them to fight against evil. Each member of the Order has a small amount of power over the Earth's life energy, over the five elements, but together they are a great force. The Elders, though, have each mastered one of the elements completely. Along with Marcus, there are four others. One for each element."

"They have superpowers?" Calum asked, his voice cracking. And then, "Covens? As in witches?"

I shook my head. "No, they're different than witches in the sense that their powers are completely natural. Magic from the elements is *right* and true. Really, everyone could use it if they had the knowledge; they use the natural life energy that is everywhere. Witch's magic is more about blood and sacrifice; it's unnatural."

I gritted my teeth together. My fingers closed and I felt my nails dig into my palms. "The Orieno, however, are made up of groups of followers that are lead by the Orieno Siblings; the two brothers Morphis and Betor, and the sister Phantas. Together they are what the Order call dream demons. They feed off the humanity of people by going into dreams and corrupting human souls. Morphis, we know, is the leader of the group. He's mostly the one running from dream to dream, destroying the world's people one by one. He likes to observe the person's dream for a while, let it play out for a bit. Then, when the victim is completely entranced in their dream, he makes his move. He transforms some part of the dream into the dreamer's worst nightmare, that thing they fear the most. When that happens, there's no stopping him; people are too weak to fight him. That's how the Orieno create their followers, normal people who have been thrown into a sickness, a phantom disease that controls them. They grow pale and lose the ability to think for themselves until they're so far gone, they begin to lust for blood, for anything living they can kill and make their own. Blood begins to be the only thing that keeps them alive. It is what gives humans life, so it is what they take to sustain life. Toward the beginning of the change they can look more human, but as the disease grows stronger they become completely inhuman. They take instructions from the Siblings, feeding when they're told, *on who* they're told. They become the soulless who walk with the three damned Siblings. Once the change is made completely, a person's humanity is lost forever."

Calum was breathing heavy. "Is my Dad...?"

"He is," I said. "But we don't know exactly how. He's too powerful to be the victim of an Orieno attack. We don't know what makes him different than the others; why he moves so quickly and can walk through daylight when the others can't."

The way Calum's face fell, the way his eyes grew wide so the blue was overpowered by white, made me wish things were different.

I almost felt sorry.

Calum's mouth opened and closed, but no words came out. He was pale, white as if the moon were shining only on his face.

I continued, "If the Orieno got hold of you they

would have the power they need to destroy the world. That's why we can't let them get you. Not yet."

You don't care about him.

Calum was silent for a few minutes. Then, "He's not my father. He's nothing."

I kept silent.

I understood that much; how someone can be dead to you without even trying; how your world can shatter in the blink of an eye; how being powerless feels.

It feels like you're dying, I thought. *To me it is living and breathing death.*

Calum shook his head. "But why did they wait all this time to find me? Wouldn't they have wanted me a long time ago?"

"You *would* ask that," I sneered bitterly. "Up until recently the Orieno were too weak to do much of anything. Even if they did try to defeat us, the Order has always been strong. But now, because of my parents, we have little Warrior strength. We've been getting weaker, and the Orieno have been getting stronger. We've both been looking for you, and because of your Dad's highly publicized bloodbaths, we found you at last."

I didn't say: *I've been searching for you since I was twelve. We only found you because I did nothing else but look.*

In a voice that was hollow, cold, he said, "I still don't understand why they need me. Why were you both looking for me?"

"That prophecy I told you about? It tells us about a boy, *you*, but it also shows what we think is the end of the world. The *Legend of the Dreamer* shows us the way our savior, the Dreamer, will rescue us all. The Order believes it to be true. It's said that the Orieno have a prophecy that is similar, though it tells them *how* to end the world with the help of the Destroyer. It's called the *Script of the Hunter*. Glimpses of it have appeared throughout history. From these fragments, the Order has discovered that the Orieno need a child born to the Devil himself to fulfill their legend. If we don't stop them, if we don't stop *you*, then the world as we know it will be over. Hell will be the only thing left, and it's impossible to live in a place so damned."

"But Kate," he said. "I would never do that. How can you *still think* I'm this Dreamer guy? I don't have *any* kind of power at all. I never have!"

"You *are* the Dreamer." I glared at him. "The Order will explain it to you; a binding spell was put on you so your true self wouldn't be seen, even by you, until the binds slowly fade away. Marcus believes it was a witch, the old Woman of Prophecy who did it, but he can't be sure."

"What do you mean? Shouldn't he know? Isn't he in charge?"

I went still. "He is, yes, but he wasn't the Order member in charge of your safety. Before all the former Elder members were killed, except for Marcus, an Elder named Brigid was in charge. She was a great healer, I've been told. She controlled fire and used it to burn away sorrow."

Calum said, "So then Marcus took her place?"

"Marcus was the only one left," I spat. Then continued, "Brigid gave two Warriors the responsibility to protect you and hide you so no one but them knew where you were. Those Warriors knew everything about you. They were the ones that took you to the Woman of Prophecy for the binding spell; it was their idea. For safety reasons, no one else knew where you'd been hidden. The whole thing was one big horrible secret. No one even knew about the spell or *you* until the Order questioned them years ago."

Calum tilted his head toward me. "So, where are they now? Why wouldn't they help me?"

"They're dead," I said in a voice rough as cracked stone. A feeling took hold of me, as though icy water was dripping slowly down my back. "My parents are dead."

"I'm sorry," Calum said after a while.

I shook my head. "It doesn't matter. But if you were taken by the Orieno, you wouldn't have a choice if it came to destroying the world. They are more powerful now than you could ever imagine. *They are living death.* They suck your soul dry until you are *nothing.*"

I shuddered. "Too many people have died. Too many of us and not enough of them. It's my job to kill those who stand against us, those who stop us."

I held up my right hand as though it meant more to me than it did. "I've killed many, more than any other Warrior my age. But it's not enough. It never is. I won't stop until I have this entire *leviti* filled with red."

Calum's voice was quiet. "And then what?"

I was impassive when I said, "And then nothing. I fight until I die." I felt the truth of those words sink in, deep into my heart and stick there. Marcus said I had a death wish, but I could always see the pride hiding beneath his cold eyes. Someone needed to fight, why not me?

Calum touched his left hand to his right. I remembered doing the same thing before I got my *leviti*. I would watch the few older Warriors and wish I was more like them than me.

He paled and whispered, "How do you know who is working for the Orieno and who isn't? How can you tell?"

"Their eyes," I said, feeling a chill run down my back. "To me, it looks like a deep, burning fire. It's terrifying. We call it the Devil's glow because demons have it too."

Calum stopped breathing, though I was sure if I listened closely I would hear his heart pounding fast. I remembered his father's eyes, the blazing fire in them burning like Hell. No doubt Calum was remembering, putting the pieces together in shards of anger, betrayal, and loss.

I remembered doing the same.

Jaw clenched, I whispered, "I am going to find my sisters."

Calum was facing forward and, like me, he wasn't moving. Outside the rain poured down. The air in the car was cool, quiet, and smelled like sweat. Other than the rain, darkness and silence became the only constants.

"What will you do when you find them?" Calum asked, and then added sharply, "kill them, too? Like me?"

"I'm not going to kill you right now," I answered truthfully. "You are safe with me. And when I find my sisters I will do everything I can to protect them."

"Will they join the Order with you?"

Terror seized me; I thought of that question often. It came every night after I relived my parent's deaths, after I saw the blood and the betrayal over and over again.

My hands shook. I was certain, more than anything, and my voice burned raw in my throat when I said, "No. I wouldn't wish this life on anyone."

Calum didn't answer me, but nodded his head.

We sat together, surrounded by nothing but the falling rain. Under my breath I started to hum the slow melody to the Order song, its rhythm comforting and familiar.

Drums, drums, all around
Giving hell to all the hounds.

"Kate?" Calum whispered. His hands were folded in a cross on his chest, his shoulders hunched as he looked out the window.

I didn't answer, but continued to hum.

Warriors, Warriors, raise your hands,
Beat and fight and hurt for man.

"Is my Mom alive?" he asked.

It was the worst possible question.

"I don't know," was all I said. "I don't know."

For some reason I kept wondering if I should sing my song for Calum. Would he see the truth in it? Would he recognize the good my fellow Warriors and I gave to the world?

"Thank you for saving me today," Calum whispered so I almost didn't hear.

Then the song blared louder, extinguishing my thoughts. I felt ashamed I was questioning something I knew was so right.

I pushed all my feelings away and became a wall of stone, impervious to emotion, with only the old Warrior song in my head.

"Kate?"

I felt my throat close around lost smiles.

They are gone now, but not forever.
I need my sisters back.
I will get them back.

There is nothing more important.

Nothing.

-Calum-

I stared straight ahead, not knowing what to do, or what to think. Moments passed between us like long hours instead of minutes, giving the illusion that time was moving slowly.

The pattering of rain. Only it and nothing else.

Silence between us.

I thought: ~~Dad~~ *That man did it for me, that's what he said. All those people dead-*

the writing on the wall-

for me.

~~Dad~~ *He is possessed.*

~~Dad.~~

~~Dad.~~

~~Dad.~~

~~Dad is~~ *I am responsible.*

I said Kate's name once more, remembering how she said the entire town of Lakewood Hollow was gone, burning, but got nothing in response. I knew she was gone again, and now that I knew she was a Warrior it made sense. I didn't hate her anymore, not really. I was feeling something much stronger toward her, something I couldn't exactly name, and because I couldn't name it, I found myself afraid.

Things are so scary when they can't be named.

Maybe it was understanding; she lost her parents, and I might have lost mine. She was part of this war and, apparently, so was I.

Maybe it was something more.

But how could I be someone I knew I wasn't? How could I be this Dreamer?

I couldn't deny what I had seen back at Lakewood. Death. My father *was death*. Never before was I so afraid at what I might become.

Am I guilty? Am I so like him now?

Kate.

My fingers trembled, so did hers.

Together, we were alone.

There was a sadness in her eyes, one I knew she tried to keep hidden, that made me believe she was right about everything. I didn't think even she knew it, but Kate was haunted by just as much sadness as me.

Maybe more.

"Kate?" I asked. "Do all Warriors have violet eyes like yours?"

"No," she whispered. "No one does. I've never met anyone with eyes like mine. It's a genetic thing, I guess."

Then, as a song of silence floated swiftly in the air, I felt myself slip into the darkness of night and knew I would be asleep in minutes.

He did it for me.

I have to find a way to make this right.

"Kate?" I whispered again. "Is this my fault?"

Still, her violet eyes were impassive.

-Kate-

I TOLD MYSELF I DIDN'T CARE.

Calum.

As sleep settled over Calum, I couldn't help but notice that he turned and hugged himself until he was pushed so close to the door I couldn't touch him if I wanted to.

I couldn't care.

Adam.

"What are you doing?" I asked Adam through the darkness. We were in a secret place in the forest, one we'd found several months ago, with only the stars for light.

"I'm glad you snuck out tonight," he whispered. "And I'm sleeping."

I laughed. "Okay, I know that. But why are you sleeping all weird like that? Why are you hugging yourself?"

Even in the dark I could see his grin. "Because you won't."

The night was cold, late September air beating around us, but I felt my cheeks warm and burst into flame.

He laughed, "Come here."

I shook my head but said, "Okay."

I inched closer, nervous.

He moved closer too, and put his arms around me and squeezed. I could feel his nose tickle my neck, feel him breathe in and out and in. He smelled like soap and leaves and burning air.

"What are you doing?" I asked.

His arms pressed against me.

"I'm holding you," he said.

Now, I felt the coldness of the autumn night fall tightly around me. I pressed my arms around myself, safe in the darkness, but it didn't feel the same. The coldness, the bitter loneliness, was as sure as death around me.

I couldn't care.

He was not Adam.

Only my sisters mattered now.

CHAPTER ELEVEN
ANGEL TEARS

-CALUM-

NIGHT BLED INTO MORNING AND BACK AGAIN, though I slept through most of both. I didn't speak for hours, only to accept a few meal bars from Kate because I had to. I wanted to sleep, to hide and forget and disappear, but the moment between dreams and reality was too much to bear. I would hear a voice sounding like a song, so quiet I could barely make out the words. So quiet it was all I thought of. So quiet it screamed, every note shaking with urgency. So afflicted with need I couldn't ignore it.

> *Touched by life and death.*
> *He'll pluck them one by one,*
> *Watching as they fall to the ground.*
> *Be careful, Caeles. You must decide*
> *Which is life and which is death.*
> *Break this prison in a place between.*
> *Wake! You are our only hope.*

More than once I tried to fall back to sleep in hopes the voice would give me answers, but it was only those few lines repeated more quietly each time. After they had faded completely, I dreamt of Tyler, my Mom and Dad; drops of course salt on open wounds.

Still, I continued to wonder about the voice. Who did it belong to, and who was Caeles? Who was counting on me for hope?

I gripped the sides of my seat, digging my nails deep into the padding. A low howl of whispered wind made its way through the windows. I thought of my dream of the woods, of the birds falling like bombs. Of hearts drifting down. Had they been symbols for this war Kate spoke of? She said I was the Dreamer. Were my dreams warnings?

Hide beneath the rising sun.
Follow the light road.

I thought, *Impossible.*

Even my dreams, if they were truly warnings, were hopeless. Now, in this cold autumn, there was no sun, and it was too dark to find the light. The wind never stopped blowing, the rain never stopped falling. Chills crawled over my body, like always, and I thought of Tyler.

Next to me I heard Kate mutter to herself, "Not him. Not him." I'd asked her about the voice, but she didn't answer.

I was too tired to care.

We drove past cities and towns, the smooth road growing like a winding vine. The buildings and polluted air slowly turned into mountains and wispy clouds, spoiled only by the normal gray of the season. The cold shadows of dusk were just beginning to brush the bottoms of trees. Like running through a painting of a ghost story, everything was a blur of muted color. The falling sun hit the trees and their branches made apparitions appear in the gray: Tyler, Dad,

Mom.

"Are we still in Colorado?" I asked Kate, turning away from the ghosts.

She nodded. "Further up in the mountains now. Far away. No one ever goes up here except Order members that live in the town near Lake Iris."

This area was different; I didn't remember Colorado ever looking so terrifying, so deadly. It had changed.

Or I had.

I swallowed a gulp of air but couldn't exhale.

Then suddenly, because the thought had been on my mind for hours, I asked "Do I have powers?"

My chest slammed against the seat belt as Kate tapped the breaks hard.

"Why would you say that?" she asked in a voice that was as much a whisper as a scream.

I rubbed my neck. "Well, you said that the Order members all have powers over the elements. And you said that I'm the Dreamer from some legend. So, I thought maybe there was something else you weren't telling me. Is there?"

She was silent, forever. Until, "We'll find out when we get to Lake Iris."

Kate drove us through the shadows, their ghostly waves flooding over the car in rapid washes of light and dark. Dense fog was billowing off the mountains, crawling onto the road. It was getting difficult to see, but Kate seemed to know exactly where she was going. With the fog came the slow darkness of night, and before I knew it the air was kissed by the blue lips of twilight.

I ran my fingers through my hair. "Kate? Do you know anyone named Caeles?"

"No," she said. "I've never heard that name before."

She raised an eyebrow. "Another voice in your head?"

"No," I lied, frowning. "So what is Lake Iris, exactly?"

Lake Iris, I thought. Whenever Kate mentioned Lake Iris, I felt a rush of panic run through my veins like a fire trying to burn.

Like fire burning too quickly-

faster and faster until it died.

Too fast.

Always too fast.

Kate cracked her neck from side to side, and when she spoke it was as if her voice had cracked too; it was as dark as the night, as deeply filled with mystery as her eyes. "Lake Iris is my home. It's the Order's training complex and coven headquarters; the biggest one in North America." She gritted her teeth. "We're still second to the one in the Atlantic Ocean, but they're pretty reclusive. Lake Iris is home to Warriors, lesser Order members, and the Elder Council for this location. It's where, as Warriors, we train, and where the Elder members can watch over any Orieno attacks in this area."

Kate spoke of her world in fear and respect, an icy undertone always present in her voice. Her world, to me, seemed as luminous in its magic as it was terrifying in its power to unravel what I'd always known. And I wasn't even sure I believed.

She paused, as if she wanted to say more but the words stuck in her throat. It was then that I noticed the way her eyes flashed, sad as if she were always remembering someone she missed.

Her family, I thought, because when I looked in the mirror earlier that's what I saw in myself; that same sadness was in my eyes because of family.

"Stop looking at me like that," she snapped.

"Like what?" I asked.

"Like you know me." She stomped on the brakes and shoved the Jeep in park; it squealed, metal against metal, in protest. "Now get out. We can't let Marcus wait too long. He'll already know we're here."

My eyes searched. "And *where* are we?"

Kate grabbed the steering wheel with both hands and let her head fall between them. Waves of curled brown made her eyes invisible; I didn't know why, but in that moment I missed them. She sighed. "We. Are. At. Lake. Iris. Seriously, I feel like I'm speaking to a child."

"Funny, I feel like I just got kidnapped by a lunatic."

"Funny, I feel like I saved your life."

I turned away, and then back and said, "Funny, it feels like you took it away."

Then, in the ghostly light that the moon cast as it rained in through the Jeep's windows, light and dark filled Kate's eyes: Shades of purple and sadness and cold, cold anger.

As if made of only bone and shadow, hollow and dark as night, she said, "Get out."

I didn't argue.

I didn't say anything.

We had stopped in a field circled by tall trees, their tops hitting the sky like a halo of ominous hands clapping together. In front of us, beyond the field, the mountain reached a peak, its caps snowy and white a mile above just visible over the trees. A brown owl hooted, jumped from a covered place and flew into the moonlight. The glinting silver of the light reflected off its feathers, and in the night I could see its black eyes looking like pieces of a broken blue moon.

For a moment I felt peaceful. Normal, like I once thought I was. Familiar in the black and blue moment.

Then the owl flew to a tiny pond at the edge of the clearing near a thick grove of trees and landed on a jagged rock beside it. The scene was simple and pretty and filled with far too many shades of gray.

"Get out, Calum!" Kate said again as she slammed her door closed. She swore. "You don't want to know what will happen if Marcus thinks we kept him waiting too long."

I wasn't used to seeing Kate look so shaken, nervous. Somehow it made everything worse. Real and not real at the same time. If Kate, the girl that had a tattoo to show the number of people she killed, was afraid of Marcus, what did that mean for me?

My heart wouldn't stop thumping wildly in my chest, and I wondered if a person could die from that: A heart beating so fast it just stops.

I pushed open the door and stepped out into the field. A rush of mountain air hit my face. It hugged me, swirling a cool breeze from my feet to my hair. The thin air made my head light and, just for a second, I forgot who I was and smiled.

I said, "I can't believe I've never come up here before." I looked up at the stars. They were so close that, as I raised my hand above me, it felt like I could almost touch them. The moon was a giant. I brushed a finger over my birthmark and sighed.

Would I ever find answers?

Kate stood next to me. "I meant what I said early, Calum. We're not exactly close to Lakewood Hollow anymore. That place is gone. Dead. Forget everything you left there if you can." She pointed to the end of the clearing just over the pond. "Below us is the town of Ashfall where a lot of the lesser Order members used to live. It's far, a few hours away, but close enough that we used to call it home. The Woman of Prophecy, who keeps the ancient scrolls of legends and psalms lives there, too. Ashfall was founded by Order members so that we would have a safe haven. Well, before the Orieno."

I didn't believe.

"There's no town called Ashfall in Colorado. I've never heard of it."

"You wouldn't have. It's protected by the Elder Council and is warded to be invisible and unchartable. No one knows it exists except members of the Order, or unless a member of the Order reveals its location."

I raised an eyebrow. "Like you just did?"

She frowned. "Yes."

"What other secrets do you have?"

"Everyone has secrets, Calum."

I turned to face her. "You know what I meant. What other secrets do you have about the Order? Is there anything else I should know before we go meet this Marcus guy?"

Kate's eyes flashed. "Show Marcus respect when you speak about him! He's an Elder, Calum!"

I stayed silent and waited.

I thought, *Tyler would have stood up for his dad like that.*

A shiver ran through me and I realized this: I wouldn't stand up for my father or my mother, but one was very different from the other. My mother I wanted to save. My father...

I wish my father had died instead of Annabelle and

Jason and Chad.

    I wish he was never my father.

    My stomach dropped and I clung to a small sliver of hope that Tyler was still alive. When I blinked away tears I thought I saw a flash of bright white in the dark of my mind.

    I was back to being lost, though this time it was different, as if the mountain air and the stars made me stronger. Since Kate had taken me away from Lakewood Hollow, that life seemed to be far away. Gone, like she said, but not forgotten. It felt like I was moving forward, and although the tears for Tyler and my Mom flowed freely, it was beginning to feel like the only way to fix the past was to look to the future.

    Maybe I did believe.

    Maybe, if I wanted to move forward, I didn't have a choice.

    After a while, Kate rolled her eyes, walked over to my side, grabbed my hand, and dragged me over to the side of the mountain past the edge of the clearing. Slowly, heat traced from my hand up my arm, making its way to my chest like a slow-creeping poison; Kate's hand gripped my own as if she thought I'd run away. A faint, warm dizziness was filling my head, but I ignored it, pushing it back to nothing.

    I was good at that.

    "Look," she told me, turning her head up toward the sky stained with stars.

    I looked up, too. I thought of my dreams, of my skin that turned as black as the night above. The sky was bright with a million tiny suns, and a moon that shone like thousands. My hand moved again to my birthmark and for some reason the whole thing, the sky and the stars and the moon, felt familiar. I thought of the voice. If I was supposed to be Caeles, if that voice was right, I wished I knew what came next.

My hand tightened in Kate's until she was crushing my fingers right back, until the warmth became too hot and the closeness became painful. Either she wouldn't let go or I wouldn't. With our tangle of fingers intertwined like they were, I couldn't tell.

"Do you see it?" Kate asked, letting go of my hand.

I turned to her and then back to the sky. "It's beautiful," I said, the words stuck somewhere in my throat. I tried to pretend my hand didn't feel cold away from hers. I tried not to think about my racing heart, or that I wanted to step closer to Kate as if she was more than the girl that stole me. I thought of the stars and the voice and Kate. I whispered, "If only it were real."

Kate stared at me as though she were trying to read my mind, and then said, "Don't you see it? How the stars are so much brighter here?"

"Sure, because we're so high in the mountains like you said. I remember that whole you kidnapping me and driving for days thing pretty well."

"No. That's what people think, that the stars get brighter the higher you are, but the truth is that the stars are always brightest at places where the enchanters meet or have covens. And at Lake Iris the stars shine brightest of all."

I didn't answer. Looking up at the stars made me feel like I was closer to something. Home, maybe. Here, I felt so right that I could almost feel my body vibrating with the need to be something more. When I looked at the stars my eyes saw only them and the rest was gone. I wondered if there was any way I could climb the mountain even higher so I was closer to the world above.

I asked, "Why are the stars so bright wherever the Order is? It's like a whole world up there, with the moon shining like a white sun on everything dark."

"Yeah," she said. "It is." I could hear her breathing in the quiet night, and I turned to look at her so the stars disappeared and it was only her. "Look at the North Star. Do you see that it's the brightest of them all?"

I tore my gaze away from Kate and looked up again to see the star she pointed at, bright and wild. I sounded like a child, so bewildered by the vastness of the sky, when I whispered, "Yes."

"Here, the stars shine like beacons because they feed off the energy the Order emits. Remember how I told you that each member of the Elder council has control over one element? In order to keep their powers focused, they have spells woven by the Woman of Prophecy deep into bloodstones sewn on their bodies. You'll see them. All of the Elders in each coven have them on their foreheads. Because the spells focus their energy so much, the stars feed off the excess life energy that the Elders don't use. Think of it like a cosmic form of photosynthesis; when the Elders use their elemental powers, they only use a fraction of the energy needed to control their element so the leftover energy is dissipated into the air, feeding the stars, making them glow. Marcus told me it's life and death, what they can do. It's give and take. *And* legend has it that because the Orieno are so much like living death, once the last demon is killed the stars will glow their brightest and shine new life on a world once dark."

"Incredible," I whispered.

Beside me, her voice steady as the mountain, dark and dangerous as the night around us, Kate said, "I know. I can't wait for them to die."

My eyes broke from the sky. Kate's fists were white, balled tightly at her sides. In the mountains, where night was a dark void lit by moonlight, Kate's eyes shone like daggers reflecting the burning stars. Once violet, they were now black as night. As death.

My mind screamed, *It's my fault! I am responsible.*

But then, *No. The Orieno and the Bloodletter are the ones who spilt the most blood. I can't wait for them to die, either.*

Kate breathed, "They all deserve death."

I understood.

But death can't be the answer to everything.

We would be no better than them.

I wanted to.

I wanted to believe so badly I could feel the want stick and burn in my chest like fire unwilling to die, felt it kindle in my heart until it dripped down my face in a single tear.

Kate's voice echoed in my mind: *You're the key in this war we're fighting, the one pawn everyone wants.*

I didn't trust myself to speak.

I want to believe I'm something more than this.

I didn't trust myself to do anything.

"Follow me," she barked.

I didn't trust Kate either, but I didn't have a choice.

She led me through an entrance, a small opening in the mountainside, and into shadows darker than night. Here, there were no stars to guide the way. No moon. Nothing but my hand in Kate's and the shivery feeling that I was walking toward something treacherous.

I couldn't see her anymore, and for some reason I felt the desperate need to remember what she looked like. I saw her eyes in my mind and, for now, it was enough.

Slowly, as Kate and I walked through a maze of hollow tunnels, my eyes adjusted to the darkness. The smell of rich earth filled my nostrils; it was the kind of earth you could taste. I could hear water dripping down from rocks above, sliding down the stone tunnel walls as tears had down my face. The slight *drip drip drip* was continuous. After a moment it was all I could hear.

As sounds from the outside world faded, and the tunnel air became so thick it choked, dread seeped into my heart. We had come to an end, a tunnel with no exit. It was either back the way we came, or nothing at all. "Kate, is this a joke? Really. Is this just the place you took me to kill me? Are you working for the Orieno?"

She stayed silent, but her hand gripped mine until I felt the blood slow in my veins. I thought of her *leviti* and knew she wanted to mark me in red.

She let go of my hand. I pushed myself against the stone wall and tried to blend into the shadows. I heard nothing but the thumping of my heart and the rapid, raspy breaths I stole.

I waited for her to attack, kill.

I waited to die.

But even before she moved, I realized it wasn't Kate I was afraid of, not in this moment. Not really. She I understood. She was torn, broken like so many people were. Like me.

I was afraid of death.

I didn't want to die. Not like this, pushed against a wet wall in a dark tunnel. Alone.

I'm something more than this.

I had to be.

This couldn't be it.

I put my hands up to my face, guarding it. I didn't know much about fighting, but I knew this: Those who gave up easily, lost more quickly.

I was afraid of death, and so I couldn't be afraid to live.

I felt my entire body tense. The air was heavy against me, trapping me against the stone. I held my breath, but the wetness found its way into my lungs and stayed there, filling them up until I couldn't take it anymore.

"Kate?" I whispered into the dark. I sounded small.

She sighed. "Put your hands down. Just watch what I do, okay? If you can see anything in the dark, that is; you shouldn't be used to it just yet."

But I almost was. Here, there was no sky to fill the darkness in the tunnel. No breeze came through the maze to push through light. There was nothing but dark shadows, thick as the air, moving like black liquid through the void. But even so, I was beginning to grow used to the dark. I was beginning to see. Not completely, but just enough so I could see Kate as if she were a ghost, outlined in gray, born of night with violet stars shining bright.

"I can kind of see you," I said. "I can see your eyes."

She paused and blinked. I could see the ghost of her shrug its shoulders. "Hmm. The binding spell must be wearing off more quickly than we thought. The wards here should have prevented you from seeing anything." Her voice wasn't as steady as it normally was. She sounded nervous. "Now stop talking and really look. Watch. I can't get us in there if I'm not concentrating."

I said, "In where?"

She was silent, the calm before the storm, quiet and still. Her stillness sent chills up my spine. I knew this:

Before a belligerent storm hits, there is nothing to do but wait; wait for the loud screams of danger; wait for the illuminated brightness of panic; wait for death to come and end it all.

Before the storm there is only waiting-
and silence-
and space between-
a calm horror of unknown-
and silence, silence, *silence.*

I didn't say anything, but watched her hands as she reached them slowly up to touch the wall. She muttered something but her voice was too quiet for me to hear. The second she touched the rocky surface, her *leviti* started to glow a faint pink, like blood mixed with water, before turning as red as a sky at sunrise. The light from it began to envelop her entire body, swirling in a fine pink mist around her. It moved as though alive, dancing on her exposed skin.

Fire felt like it burned in my chest. "*Kate*?"

She said, "Take my hand." Her voice sounded distant. She didn't look at me but focused on the wall, on her hand as it glowed as though she stole it from a fire, all embers and flames and skin. "Be quiet."

I grabbed her hand and she started muttering again, letting words fall out as though they were her only hope to survive; her voice sounded desperate as it began to live in the shadows around me. "*Praecipio vim virtutum luce. Sum fortitudine. Ego sum lux. Hac virtute lucis intus, aperta ianua mando secretum,*" she said. She kept repeating it, her voice growing louder, crashing into the tunnel walls and off until her voice seemed to be more inside my head than out. Chills ravished my spine. She chanted, "*Praecipio vim virtutum luce...*"

I gasped as the wall in front of us began to shake

and vibrate. After a few seconds, the entire tunnel was on the verge of exploding around us. Mist crawled over me, so thick I couldn't breathe. I was only mist, and as it became my skin and my lungs and my veins, I felt it take my heart as well. I knew soon I would be nothing more.

I closed my eyes and, as Kate's voice roared around me, I thought of my nightmare that had become alive in this moment:

The air was thick, wrapping itself around me and pushing into my lungs.

I opened my eyes and, for a moment, thought I saw a flash of purple.

A face in the mist.

I opened my eyes and Kate was all I could see; her violet, luminous eyes stole my breath and my world and I was gone.

I thought, *This is the end.*

Before the storm there is only waiting, but after there is only destruction. Death.

Then without fear or explanation, Kate walked through the stone wall she touched, as if it were made of nothing but colored air, and pulled me through.

Again, blackness erupted around me as though death had made me a friend.

Or an enemy.

~

My ears popped.

First, the sound hit me; water crashing so angrily it screamed. The sound was a hundred waterfalls falling at once. It must have been. It was nothing and everything, so loud it became quiet in an instant, shattering into something so beautiful I thought maybe I was actually dead.

But I breathed deeply-

and I was so, so alive.

I wrinkled my nose against the humidity and the cold breeze that cut through it. I closed my eyes for just a second, and gulped in the raw, clean air. It was sweet and frigid, filling my lungs with so much life they felt as icy as death inside me. This air reminded me of rain, of the way it fell from the tops of the Rocky Mountains down to towns below in sheets and storms.

Of rain so alive it killed.

When I opened my eyes I felt the breath I'd taken live and die on an exhale.

The cave was enormous, lit by a thousand tiny lanterns and filled with hundreds of people as if an entire city had been hidden in this hollow mountain. Jagged stone walls rose up toward a ceiling that wasn't there, trapping the place in an angry cage of gray. Everything, including the floor, seemed to be made of stone. Four fast moving waterfalls, shimmering green and blue and white, ran quickly down the high walls as if pretending to be the four points of a compass. They jumped over misplaced stones and onto the tops of buildings and houses, draping them in curtains of blue-green water, frothing white where they hit gray, and flowed gently into a rapid river that circled the edge of the cave. The river must have drained out somewhere, but there was no end in sight. There was only water and stone, the two mixing together, one.

Amidst the water and stone were people, all dressed in the same black pants but different colored shirts: Blue, red, green, yellow, white, and gray. Each person had determination in their eyes, the same burning purpose I saw in Kate. They moved with grace, and the ones in gray ran like birds against the river. None of them seemed to have realized we had stepped out of the mist and through the stone as if it were nothing.

As if everything was normal.

Tiny flecks of what looked like mirrored snowflakes floated through the air like fragmented thoughts from a thousand angels. Each fleck shone a rainbow of whites, not colors, reflecting everything and nothing at all; it was as if they were made of pure light, white as the center of the sun.

And then belief hit me: *Lake Iris*.

It had to be.

The lake stretched wide, resting in the very center of the cave. It was a vast black thing, still as death and as placid as if ice had formed on top. The lake, so still and dark with the swirling white flakes reflecting off its surface, became the night and the stars.

"We have to hurry." Kate's voice brought me back to reality. "Let's go. Move. Now!" She pulled me forward and, without meaning to, I found myself falling into her, touching her, holding her, and it was like the first time all over again:

My heart was all I could feel until:

I can't breathe.

Too much, too fast.

Our eyes met.

I can't breathe.

One moment lingered in time.

Hope.

Blue against eyes so black they looked violet.

Is this the beginning?

Her eyes narrowed-

Or the end.

and found mine and would not look away.

I can't breathe.

"Sorry," I mumbled. I pushed away and blinked and the moment was just a lost memory I wanted to remember but didn't know why.

Kate backed up slowly, her eyes wide, turned-and ran.

I was left behind, broken and alone.

I wondered if that's how it always would be.

Desperate, needing, wanting: I ran as fast as I could to catch up to Kate. My legs moved under me as if I was a magnet and so was she.

I screamed, "Kate!" but it was nothing more than a lost breath; as I ran my voice flew behind me. "Wait!"

She stopped.

Then, opposite to opposite, we stood in front of each other, unable to move closer.

I asked, "What were those words you said back there?"

"Just words," she said. "But words have power when they have purpose. Basically, it was a passcode to get through the wards that protect this place."

"What does it mean?"

"*Praecipio vim virtutum luce. Sum fortitudine. Ego sum lux. Hac virtute lucis intus, aperta ianua mando secretum,*" she repeated. "I was told it means 'I command the power of virtue, of light. I am strength. I am light. With this power of light inside me, I command this secret door to open.'"

"Can anyone say the words?"

"Sure," a voice like thunder said behind me. "But not everyone can use their magic."

A boy stepped beside me, and I felt my breath

catch. With his thick arms crossed over his gray shirt, and eyes popping green against his dark skin, he made me think of Tyler.

"What do you want, Zack?" Kate asked, leaning back on one foot.

He smiled and rolled on the heels of his feet. "Nothing. Just wanted to see who you had with you and why you're sharing our secrets with him. Who is he?"

"He's no one."

Zack raised an eyebrow. "Is this him?"

"Go away, Zack."

"What if I don't want to?"

Kate stepped closer to him. "Then I'll make you leave. You don't think I could?"

Zack just grinned and ran a hand over his dark, short hair. "Oh, I know you could. I'm not stupid."

I could see Kate almost smile. "No, you're not. An idiot, maybe, but not stupid."

"You gonna show him around?" Zack asked, looking me up and down. The veins in his neck burst with every movement.

"No," she said. "I have orders."

Zack's eyes went wide, and his dusky skin blotched with pale light. "Oh, sorry. Go. Didn't mean to keep you."

Kate nodded, her eyes almost sad. "Talk to you later."

Zack turned to leave, and Kate grabbed my arm to pull.

"Wait!" I called to Zack. "Hold on."

Slowly, he turned around to face me. His eyes were bright, shining with a quiet sadness that reflected the light in the cave. "What?"

"Who do you think I am?" I asked, and held my

breath.

Zack's eyes turned to Kate, and then slowly back to me.

"I think," he said, "that you're someone who has no idea what's about to happen to him, and that makes you afraid of what's to come."

My voice caught in my throat. "Do you know what's going to happen?"

His smile was sad. "That's the problem, isn't it? No one does."

Without another word, he turned and ran.

"A friend of yours?" I asked Kate.

"I have no friends," Kate said. "He's just someone I used to fight."

"Is he the one you wanted to meet after dinner that night?"

Her eyes blazed. She spat, "No, Calum! Zack's not like that at all."

Again, without warning, she turned and ran. This time though, she stopped before I had the chance to scream.

I bent over and put a hand on the back of my neck before I stood straight and brought it down to my heart. My chest was too full, and not enough so. My heart skipped beats, my lungs were in my throat, and my pulse raced.

With a stitch in my chest, I breathed, "Why-
Do I feel like you-
did
something to make me think about-
you
always?
Like I need you.
Like I should-

run?"

away, I thought. *But no. I don't need anyone.*
Do I?

"I ran because we have to meet Marcus," she said unwavering. "In case you forgot, *you* wanted to figure out what was going on with you, remember?"

She was lying.

She had hidden so many things from me, given me so little that it felt like too much, and so I knew her eyes. I knew when they hid secrets, and when, like now, they lied.

Her eyes spoke the truth even when her voice stayed silent: *I will never tell you the truth about why I ran. It is a secret worse than everything I've kept before, and so I will not tell you. Ever.*

I wondered if this was about the family she missed, or if maybe there was someone more.

The lies, so many hidden lies, began to grind against my mind, began to eat at my heart until all I could think was:

Lies.

Kate.

Lies.

Dad.

~~*Dad.*~~

Lies.

Kate.

Why did I run after you?

Kate.

Why do I care?

I blinked and tried to believe, "I don't care."

I won't.

I can't.

"What?" Kate's eyes threw daggers at me and her

fists curled into hammers, shaking. "You're telling me that you don't care? You were the one that nearly cried like a baby in the Jeep before I told you anything! You're the one that begged me to tell you what you are and now-"

"You still haven't told me what I am! I'm some bastard offspring of the Devil, some guy who has no choice but to destroy the world? You've told me that but not *what* I am. Thanks, Kate, but forgive me if I'm not jumping up and down right now."

"I don't *know* what you are!"

"You said you knew!"

"No I didn't!" She shook her head. "I only know that the Order thinks you're the one from the prophecy. *They* want you. I said Marcus knows what you are. He has answers. Which is why we need to hurry."

I glared. "Fine. Lead the way."

But she didn't move.

Instead she said, "You need to care, Calum."

"Why? It's not like I have anything to care about."

Kate's eyes slanted down, the purple in them fading to familiar black shadows beneath her long lashes. Her voice ran at me, hard and fast and, when it found me, was as though acid had merged with breath. "*You don't know that!* You don't know where your Mom is or that Tyler guy you keep talking about, and you sure as hell don't know what the future will bring, so *don't* say you have nothing. Don't you *dare* lose sight of what you could have if you did care!"

Cold.

I do care, I thought, the cold realization of it unleashing itself in my blood until it was all I could feel, all I could think.

What Kate didn't realize was that I *did* care.

192

About Mom and Tyler.

Me.

Her.

I cared *too* much.

I sighed. "I care. Okay? I do."

I just didn't know why, or when it had started. When Kate had become someone more. Maybe because she was broken and I understood that. I saw it in her eyes; the way she lived and breathed for her sisters; the way she moved toward them without knowing where to go; the way she needed them more than even she could know. Maybe it wasn't that I understood it, but that I wanted it. I lived to find it just like she did: A place to belong, family.

I remembered again that first time I saw her. Her dark brown curls fell in loose waves past a face riddled with anger, though now it was luminous in the light from the lake beside us. I saw those freckles that looked liked stars dancing on her dark, golden face, just above where her lips pursed like two slashes of blood. She stood tall, her shoulders high and back, the veins in her neck popping and, with flakes of silver falling in her hair and on her skin so she seemed to glow with light, she looked like an angel of death.

I wanted to smile-

to laugh-

to touch-

to kiss.

No, I thought. *That wouldn't be good. And if it is, it will just be good and gone like always. Like Tyler. Nothing stays good for long.*

I can't let it be good for long.

She doesn't care about me anyway.

She took me from my life.

I wanted to run.

I remembered Kate saying, *"Funny, I feel like I saved your life."*

I wanted to run from her, but I could feel in my heart that I was something more than the person I had been in Lakewood Hollow.

Sometimes you can only go forward.

Sometimes it's impossible to look back.

Maybe she did save me.

Words fell from my mouth before I could stop them. "Is that the only reason you kidnapped me? Your family?"

She gasped. "What?" Her mouth opened and closed, and then she said, she *shouted*, *"Yes!* What other reason would I have?"

"I don't know," I said. I took one step back. "Do you... Do you..."

"Do I what, Calum?" she snapped, but her voice was softer than before. She tilted her head to the side. She ran a hand through her hair and, for a moment, her *leviti* was gone. Her eyes searched me up and down. They were taut with irritation, but beneath those shadows I saw the girl that missed her family. The girl that told me a story. Beneath it all she was just Kate. A girl.

For some reason, that made it worse.

Do you care? I wanted to say. *Why do you look at me like that?*

I looked down and felt the unsaid words stick in my throat. "Do you know what all this is?" I looked up and pointed to the falling specks of silver. "Looks like diamonds floating in the air. Like glass rain."

I turned, my eyes locked with hers, and I had to look away. I had to, but I couldn't, and one hundred moments happened in one beat of my heart. One look between us and my heart didn't know what to do: Beat, boom, stop, stop, beat, stop, stop, beat.

Beat.

She smiled. "Glass rain. I've never heard that before."

Boom.

Kate's chest moved up and down in jagged breaths. I could feel my own lungs struggling for air.

I whispered, "What is it then?"

"They say every fallen Warrior leaves a trace of his or her power when they die," she breathed. She was so quiet, her voice nothing more than air, and I wondered if it would blow away before I heard it.

I stepped closer, just one foot forward.

She blinked but didn't step back. "Marcus told it to me like this: These are the tears of those fallen Warriors that have become angels, the Heaven's Guard, who proved themselves in the name of the Order. These are the tears of the group of Warriors that still protect the Order from where they rest in the sky. When a Warrior sacrifices himself in the name of the Order, they find a place in the afterlife always helping a Warrior or Order member in need." Her voice grew quiet, fading to only a shiver in the air before dying away completely.

"Do you believe that?" I asked.

"I always thought I did. I want to. I believe the Order is truth so I've never questioned Marcus about the story, and it's nice to believe in a happy ending, you know? I like the idea of Heaven's Guard, a group of powerful angel Warriors that fight eternally to save the world. I'm a Warrior. It's what I should believe in. Even if it doesn't exist, it's nice to hope it might." She looked at me. "Do you believe in happy endings?"

"I don't know." My head felt heavy. I cracked my knuckles, then my neck. "I really don't know. I mean, my Dad is the Bloodletter. My Mom is basically an alcoholic, and my best friend could be dead. I have no one in the world to make me believe in happy endings, but I want to. *I want to.*"

Her eyes agreed with me.

I moved closer to her until we were almost touching. The two of us stood still, our shoulders nearly together and heads lifted up, while the rain of angel tears kissed our faces. I opened my mouth, pretended I was a child wanting to catch snowflakes, and stuck my tongue out. I felt a tingle where a tear landed. Warmth spread from my head to my toes.

I felt like flying.

And then, "We need to go. Now!" Kate backed away from me, and then turned to run. Her eyes were wide, darting left and right as if she were scared of someone I couldn't see. She snapped, "Move, Calum! Why are you so slow? Idiot. Follow me. Let's go!"

She ran, but all I wanted to do was stay-

in that moment-

in time standing still-

and just for a second, keep something good.

But time wasn't stopping, and so I ran as fast as I could to catch up to Kate, and as soon as I was close enough to feel the brush of her long hair blowing back against my face, I slowed enough to pretend I was standing still.

I couldn't fool myself, though.

My heart, beating faster than I ran, gave me away.

All around us the men and woman gave us curious looks as we passed, though I had a feeling their eyes only saw me. The stranger. The one that didn't belong. The ones in gray shirts looked especially angry, their eyes slanted down, lips curled in my direction. I could feel sweat dripping down my face already, while everyone else seemed to move so gracefully swift like Kate.

I saw a woman in red, her hair like embers burning, touch her hand to a cold lantern and light the flame with a snap of her fingers.

Closer now, I could see that their skin seemed iridescent, the same glow I had noticed in Kate that first day, almost lit from the inside out.

I wanted to ask about it, but I couldn't find my breath.

Part of me felt I might be dreaming.

The other part of me knew I wasn't.

Kate and I ran further into the cave, straddling the edge of the great lake. I noticed, as we sidestepped the runners in gray, that there weren't many children around. The only ones I could see were circled near the lake. They were dressed in the same gray shirts as the runners. Three of the children were playing, two of them twirling the ends of a rope while another bounced up and down in the twine vortex, singing a song to the beat: "Drums, drums all around..."

I stumbled, tripping on the point of a lone rock that was peaking out of the otherwise smooth ground.

Tyler and I had played jump rope with Kendra in Birdsong Park many times before. Every day, actually, for an entire summer when Tyler was Kendra's babysitter while Mrs. Little finished classes for her Master's degree. Tyler and I had made up different versions of songs for Kendra to jump to, but we'd never sung one so haunting.

The eerie song sent shivers down my spine. One of

the children, an older boy about twelve or so, seemed to be bossing the others around as if they were playing house and he was the father. He was shouting and screaming at the others. I saw him point to his eyes and then at theirs, shaking his head back and forth and back again as if the world depended on it.

Run, I told myself. I focused on the curled brown hair in front of me, flying back like a hundred sparrows flocking together. *Just keep running forward and don't look back.*

That thought was brilliant in my mind:

Just keep running forward.

Don't look back.

Don't ever look back.

But as the memories of Tyler and Kendra, Mom and Dad, chased behind me like shadows, I knew not looking back would be impossible. Even now I could feel those memories closing in, and soon they would find me, break me, and I would be helpless to ignore them.

How did I last so long by ignoring so much?

Kate pushed me into a building near the back of the cave, built underneath the largest waterfall. The water gushed down over the top of the building making the stone smooth and shiny. Inside, the building was dark and the air was damp, tasting dank and wicked as if death was visiting.

The room felt wrong.

"Kate, what *is* this place?" I asked.

"Shh," she hissed, throwing her hand up to silence me. "Be quiet!"

"Kate," I said, "you can't leave me in the dark."

"Shut up! You'll get us-"

Boom.

At first, I thought it was my heart breaking.

Boom.

Steps. Footsteps sounded in the distance, growing ever closer, as if gravity were stomping down in metal boots.

Boom!

The door on the opposite side of the room opened with a bang, splintering on the floor in a thousand pieces. It became nothing in the blink of an eye, destroyed in a *boom.* And, as the broken bits of door fell to the floor, the air in the room seemed to flow towards the shadow of a man in the dark void of shadow and dust.

"Katherine," the man said in a deep, coarse rumble of a voice that made my blood slow. Made it burn. "You have returned. And with company. Good."

"Yes, sir," was all Kate said, her head and shoulders slouched forward. She was as quiet as the dead. Her body set like stone.

As the man moved closer to us, gliding into focus, I saw his ancient face was wrinkled and his gray hair was long, coming down almost to his waist. On his forehead, the stone spell Kate mentioned earlier reflected what muted light was in the room. It sparkled like a garnet diamond without needing any movement to shine. Surrounding the blood-red jewel were intricate twines of red tattoos, spiraling tribal swirls that circled his black eyes like a mask. And, although they were slanted in a deep smile, his eyes did not feel warm or kind but black and cold and dark.

"You are Calum Wade," he said without question as he studied me. A low hiss sounded from his mouth. "The son of the Devil."

I was frozen.

I am not my father. I am not.

He continued, "You are a mystery, Calum. A

dangerous mystery."

My mouth shook with words I knew I should have said: *I am no one but myself.*

Questions I should have asked: *What am I, really? Who are you? What do you want with me?*

I opened and closed my mouth, but nothing came.

I was nothing but silent.

The man smiled with his lips closed and, though the smile didn't reach his eyes, he looked like he was enjoying my misery. "My name is Marcus, though you may not address me at all. I am the leader of this coven."

He did not blink. He moved closer, lowering his face so that it was in line with mine, and narrowed his eyes.

"We will have to hold a trial for you," he said slowly, his breath like fire. His teeth were so pointed they looked like fangs. "I am unsure as to whether you are truly the Dreamer, the one who will save us all, or if you are the Destroyer who will side with the Orieno. Or, simply, if you should die and be gone with. As of right now, you know too much to live freely regardless."

Cold sweat ran down my back. *Die?*

Then, as if what he had said was as common as hello, he jumped up and walked back toward the shattered door.

"Katherine," he said, turning to leave the room. "The trial for him will begin in one hour. No more and no less. You were late bringing the boy here, and I have forgiven you, but do not be late for this. You know what will happen if you are."

A trial? I thought. What had I done wrong?

In my head I felt like screaming.

-Kate-

I WAS SUPPOSED TO KILL CALUM.

I remembered that night, four years ago, as though the cold winter darkness had seeped into that cut in my palm, leaving vivid memories in my veins as the blood spilled out.

That was the one word that always came back when I remembered my oath: Blood. That night there was nothing but blood and this:

"You are significant to this prophecy, Katherine," Marcus told me. He smiled as though I was important, and in that moment I felt like I was. *"You know very well that your parents were traitors to the Order and that it is your job to avenge your family legacy without them. "*

I nodded. "But my sisters?"

Marcus waved his hand in the air. "I've already said that I would help you find them, but you must do something for me first. You see, in order for me to find your lost family, I need you to take a concern from my mind. I need you to make a blood oath that you will kill a demon."

"Blood oath?" I cringed. Those two words made me nervous. I had only known Marcus for a year but I trusted him. The sight of blood still made me dizzy, and Marcus was always saying he had been the same way when he was young, so I knew even then the feeling would pass. "Like the blood ceremony the Order will do when the first enchanter returns to help us?"

"This is a little different than that one. Much safer, I promise. This time, I need you to make a blood oath that you will one day kill the demon that is prophecized to destroy the Order," Marcus said.

I felt my heart run away. Sweat began to drip down my back as I said, "But why me? I- I don't know if I can kill someone yet. My training isn't completely done."

Marcus leaned close. "Your training will be completed in just a week." His breath smelled like burning leaves. His eyes grew wide with sympathy, and he smiled. "You are everything. I need someone who has a pure heart, so I picked you." He sighed. "And after what your parents did to the Order, killing all those innocent people, I thought you would want to help us prevent a massacre like that from happening again. Wouldn't you like that, young Katherine? I thought you wanted to avenge your family name. Don't you want to save your sisters?"

I looked into Marcus' eyes and saw what I had always seen: Truth. This was the man who had rescued me from my parents after I found out they were murderers. This was the man who had given me a home.

I owed him my life.

I stood tall. "Yes. I'll do it. I'll help. I'll make the oath. I want to save my sisters."

"Good," Marcus said. He reached behind him and, from nowhere, revealed a golden chalice covered in ornate red rubies the color of blood.

"What do I have to do?" I asked. "What is a blood oath, anyway?"

Marcus pulled a silver knife from a hidden pocket in his robes. "It's simple, really. You only need to cut your hand a tiny bit, and then drip your blood into this chalice. I'll do the rest."

I felt my face pale. "I need to cut myself?"

Marcus only smiled. "Don't worry. I will be here the entire time. I won't let anything bad happen to you. You can trust me to finish the ceremony if you feel like you can't. You do trust me, don't you?"

I nodded. "Yes. Okay."

He handed me the knife. "Cut your palm deeply."

My head shot up. "Deeply? I thought you said just a tiny bit?"

Marcus shrugged his shoulders. "I just want to make sure you cut deep enough so that the blood will drip into the chalice. You don't have to cut deep, I suppose, but don't be afraid."

The knife was shaking in my hand. "I can't-"

"You must," Marcus said, his voice hard. "I can't do it for you. The knife must be held by you for this to work. Remember your sisters."

I breathed in and out. "Okay."

I felt the cold blade touch the smooth skin of my palm. A tingle of pain shot up my arm and made my face twist in agony, but I dragged the knife across my palm anyway. I stayed quiet.

Then, as fast as lightning, Marcus reached over and pushed down on the knife, hard. Fire burst through me as the knife cut deep.

Red.

All I could see was red.

A question tore out my throat. "Why?"

"You've known me for nearly a year, Katherine. You can trust me," he said. "We don't have much time, and we need more blood than what you were giving. It will be faster this way. Easier for you."

Red drifted to black as the edges of my vision began

to fade away. Still, I felt the warm trickle of blood down my hand, heard the drip drip drip of it fall into the chalice.

I tried to stay awake.

"How will I know the demon when I see him?" I asked, feeling the energy drain from me as my blood poured out.

Marcus grinned and licked his lips. His eyes were locked on my blood, but he said, "You will know the true demon to kill when the time is right, but for now you must remember to find the Destroyer. You will recognize him by his eyes. He is the son of the Devil, and so his eyes are like his father's, like the depths of Hell; they will be as blue as though they were filled with cold, dead bodies, as filled with darkness as they are filled with a deceiving light. They are eyes that trick their victims into savage evil."

I could feel the world slipping away. Dizzy, I whispered, "Blue eyes..."

Marcus' tongue shot out and in, and his eyes floated back in his head. He was breathing heavily. "With this blood oath, you will be the only one with the power to stop the demon's heart. You will know him, Katherine. You will know in your heart when it is time. You will have to be the one to kill him."

He took my bleeding hand in his and covered my cut with a red piece of cloth. Then he took the knife I had used on myself and sliced his own palm open. I watched, feeling myself sway left and right, as my blood mixed in the gold chalice with his.

It seemed like forever until he was done bleeding himself, until he began to chant in a language I didn't understand. I wondered if I had passed out, because suddenly Marcus' chin was a deep blood red, and the chalice was touching his lips.

He was drinking our blood.

I wanted to cry, but I didn't have the energy to do anything except open and close my mouth.

Suddenly, Marcus threw his head back and words ran from his mouth. He began to chant faster and faster, and it was as though the words had become alive in the space around us. Lines of red dripped from Marcus' mouth and down his chin.

"Drink!" he said to me. The blood chalice was tilted to my mouth and, before I could stop it, I felt the warm, metallic taste flowing down my throat.

"It is done!" Marcus shouted. "Now you are bound by the blood in your veins to kill him. If you fail, you will feel the wrath of blood do to you what you could not do to the demon."

I felt the world tilt and, as I tried to reach a hand to my face to wipe the blood from my chin, I gave myself over to the darkness that had been threatening for so long.

~

I almost told Calum.

When he asked me about my family, about why I needed him so badly, I almost told him that truth.

But then-

Calum's hand in mine.

His voice. *Tell me your story.*

-I didn't know if I could, so I lied.

Calum was stronger than he looked. I could hear it in his voice and see it in his bright eyes, in the way he questioned everything and then took the time to think. To wonder about the possibilities. I could see the way he *wanted* things: Family, friends, love. I could see the way he looked at me like he knew me. Like he cared.

Like he wasn't the Destroyer I knew him to be.

He made me want to scream.

Made me want to run.

His hands.

His voice.

His eyes.

I trusted that Marcus thought Calum was the Destroyer, but what if he was the Dreamer instead? What if my lies to Calum were truths I didn't know just yet?

With Calum, I was beginning to not trust myself and I hated that. Times like this I couldn't remember who I was now, only who I was before.

Most of all there was this: *He is not Adam.*

Calum was his father's son.

I *had* to kill him.

Chapter Twelve
Forever Damned

-Calum-

I was flying.

Radiant blue sky surrounded me with no sign of stopping. Only white and fluffy clouds, as if snow had been whipped and formed, spotted the sky like beautiful, irregular diseases, and as I rushed through them I could feel beads of dew wet my hair and skin. This entire world, this sky, seemed magical. Every breath I took tasted like freedom. Like life.

Then a voice surrounded me, the same one I'd heard before. "Caeles. Embrace this life."

"Who are you?" I said, feeling lighter than even the air.

"I am what you were before you forgot. I am so many things, but you may know me now as your brother, the Giant."

"Brother? I don't know what you mean. I have no brothers." I felt my voice grow harsh, and I knew my time must be limited.

The voice sighed. "Look to the stars for guidance. Become the one you are meant to be. Don't forget that this life is not the only one you will die in; there were others before and there will be others after.

"Can you not feel it when you look at us? Can you not sense your power when you look to the sky? Give in and become who you were always meant to be. Only then will you win the war and learn the truth. It is the only way to cure the hellish curse that you were born with...

"There is no time left. To set us free and save the ones you love, you must find what you lost. See the truth and free us..."

And then I felt myself drop. The breath I wanted to take stolen from me by the surprise. Need flooded through me. I wanted to breathe again. I wanted to taste life. And, even though the next second granted my desire, I knew I'd never get that stolen breath back. All because of that drop, that moment.

It was only a few feet, but I had dropped.

In midair.

How?

And then suddenly I felt hot hands grab me, hold my arms and legs with insatiable fury. Down they pulled, always down.

Down.

In a second I was about to hit the ground.

Down.

Down.

In two, I was beneath it.

Down.

Down.

Down.

In three, the depths of Hell ate me alive, and fire licked at me like the hands of people trying to escape.

~

I woke riddled with agony so vividly real it hurt. Lying against the same rock I'd tripped over near Lake Iris, I opened my eyes, blinked back sweat that was a mask over them, and saw Kate frowning within a tilted world hazed with blue.

"What?" I asked, wiping drool from my lips as the world righted itself. Pins and needles poked at my skin, feeling like tiny fingers prodding. Pulling.

"You were screaming." She raised an eyebrow. "You were screaming about fire."

"It was nothing," I said quickly. "Nothing."

She laughed: Daggers and disbelief. "Right. Still can't believe you are your father's son?"

I didn't answer, but thought of Hell and remembered:

Be careful, Caeles. You must decide
Which is life, and which is death.
Break this prison in a place between.

"You fainted right after Marcus left," Kate said. She got to her feet, stretched, and ran the hand that branded her *leviti* through her hair. "Are you... Were you... Marcus said you won't be able to use any of your demon powers until they remove the binding spell at the trial, so don't even try."

"Shut up," I said. I whispered, "Stop lying."

Her eyes went wide. "What?"

My skin was on fire, burning as though my dream had been real. And then old wounds from old dreams began to blare in my mind, the memories of pain alive in chills on my skin.

My voice tore my throat in a hundred ways, flying up and out without stopping. "Shut up! I'm not who you think I am! I will *never* be my father's son, or the Destroyer, no matter who tells you otherwise. So. Just. Shut. Up!"

My mind screamed, *I have a different destiny!*

I have to.

I remembered thinking, *I am not me*, and words I had once written came back:

> I am ~~nothing without truth~~ someone
> more than this.
> I am someone.
> ~~Am I even alive?~~ Who am I?

Then, the words underneath:

> ...nothing without truth...
> Am I even alive?

I sighed. "I'm sorry, Kate. I really am. But I'm not who you think I am, who everyone seems to think I am, and it's driving me crazy. And it's not just that. It's the fact that I miss everyone: Tyler, my Mom. All this stuff you're telling me is making me miss my old life and I don't even know if it was a real life to begin with. How could it have been if I wasn't who I thought I was? The past seventeen years are just one big lie to me!" I sighed. "And now I know the truth and it's *nothing* like I thought it would be. The thing that is really killing me is that I believe you. Or I want to believe you. And I *do* care! I want to be someone more than who I am right now, but I don't want to be the Destroyer. I don't want to be the Dreamer. I don't even want to be who I was a few days ago. I don't know *who* to be."

I tried to find her eyes, but she seemed to be looking anywhere but at me, as if my eyes were the one place she wanted more than anything to avoid.

"But you know what?" I continued. "I feel more like *me* now than I ever did before. More alive. And that, maybe more than anything, makes me wish I didn't care. Makes me wish I didn't believe. Because being me *now* is terrifying."

Be careful, Caeles. You must decide...

But it wasn't that easy.

Truth doesn't set you free, it shifts your world into something else entirely until you're back to this: *Who am I now that I know who I should be?*

But I didn't think hers was the whole truth.

I asked, "Do you believe in past lives?"

Finally, I found her and she said, "The first time I walked into this cave and saw Lake Iris, saw the angel tears falling from nowhere, I knew I needed to leave my old life behind if I ever wanted to have a new one. I believed in what was before me, believed in what Marcus told me about the Order because it was a way for me to avenge my family's name. To save my sisters. And now that I've been in the Order for all these years, I really do believe in it. So, yes, Calum, I believe that we all eventually have a choice to make about who we want to be, and when we make it, our life becomes a series of *befores* and *afters*. I made the choice to join the Order and fight for what is good. My past life is something I can never go back to."

"That's not what I meant," I said, my voice unraveling in a quiet, frantic storm. "I keep having these weird dreams and I'm beginning to wonder if I used to be someone else. Had a past life that I don't know about. There's this voice that keeps telling me to look to the stars, to what I once was in the past. It keeps calling me Caeles, keeps saying I have this curse, and I think maybe that's who I was in some past life."

"Well, your curse could just be about the prophecy, or the binding spell the Order put on you. But you really think you were someone else?" She paused. "Like, *when* do you think you were this other person?"

I shrugged. "I don't know, but I think the voice does. I feel like it knows me, or knows who I was. This voice keeps telling me to give in and become who I'm supposed to be. I don't know what it means, but it's not going away, and the more I think about it, everything the voice has told me feels like warnings."

"For what?"

I breathed through my nose. "I don't know. I thought it was just me going crazy at first, but then the Bloodletter happened and here you are calling me the Dreamer and the Destroyer, and I wonder if the voice has something to do with that. Like maybe it's someone trying to help."

Kate's eyes glazed over with anger. "You think it's the Devil trying to send you messages?"

"No, Kate," I said, matching her tone. "I don't think it's anyone bad. I think it's actually someone trying to help me become good. Help me break away from the bad."

"Destroy the Devil inside?"

I was quiet. Then, "Yes."

"You know, Calum," Kate said as we both got to our feet. I stepped beside her as we walked. "You can't change your past, but you can control your future. I still don't know how good it is that you're hearing voices, but maybe you should talk to Marcus about it." She paused. "He's been something of a dream weaver since I can remember. He's how I found out my sisters are still alive. Next time you're in a dream, just give in. My guess is that you've been holding back a lot. You can't fight something unless you're willing to look it in the eye."

I thought of Hell. Of falling down, down, down. "But what if I don't have a choice? What if I'm damned from the beginning and don't have any choice in who I want to be?"

"There's always a choice," Kate said but didn't meet my eyes. Her nails dug into my arm as she pulled me along. "But sometimes you have to fight for what you want, *who* you want. Don't for one second believe life gets better when you just sit there. You'll always wonder what could have been."

And then, her voice so quiet it was almost lost in the maze of angel tears falling down, "Who could have been."

-KATE-

HE COULD HAVE BEEN.

I had imagined what ~~would~~

~~should~~

could have been so many times, the pictured memories felt real.

I *wanted* them to be real.

But they weren't and it killed me.

Every single time it killed me, because all I wanted was this:

Adam whispered, "Hi."

I smiled. "Hi."

Our hands seemed stuck together, one. I wouldn't have been able to tell which were his fingers and which were mine, except for the fact that his hands covered mine completely.

He lay on top of me, the tall grass closing us in a different world, a secret world only ours, and this close, his body crushing me, I felt complete. He covered me until I disappeared beneath. I should have felt like nothing as I faded away under the weight of him, but instead, as I looked into his soft blue eyes, I felt as though I could do anything.

"What are you thinking?" he asked, brushing my hair behind my ear.

"What makes you think I'm thinking anything?"

He laughed, loud and sharp. "You're always thinking something! But right now I can see it in your eyes.

Those wild, fearless purple eyes. Tell me. Since tomorrow's my fourteenth birthday, it can be your present to me."

I just grinned and shook my head.

He laughed and growled and buried his head in my neck and-

I felt my heart shatter and storm through my veins until it was all I could feel and everything I was - until I shivered so hard my breath stopped and he-

kissed me there. "Tell me! Tell me! Tell me!"

"Okay!" I laughed, almost crying. "I'll tell you!"

He moved his head so it was all I could see. The smile that played on his face was luminous and made him look younger than he really was. He moved his eyebrows up and down, and his nose fell so it touched mine.

I felt Adam's sweet, warm breath still chilled with the sting of ice cream explode around me, felt his eyelashes bat against my cheek as he whispered in a voice so low it made my chest hurt, "Tell me."

I said, "I'm thinking I love you."

I felt him breathe, felt his chest expand and crush me hard. Felt him sink deeper against me.

Felt him whisper to my lips, "I love you, too."

~

Adam could have been.

All I wanted was that life, what could have been after almost a year of opening my heart. I wondered if I could have been that girl who loved, or if I was always meant to be this girl that couldn't.

Calum broke away from me as we stepped under a curtain of water falling off the rocks above. "What is this place?"

I ignored him and brushed beads of water from my shirt and hair.

Calum's shoulders fell forward and he let out a breath as though it were his last. Drops of water dripped down his face like tears. He said, "I'm tired of you holding things back when I know you have things to say. So, what is this place? Kate?" Then sighing, "Just tell me."

Adam.

"Tell me."
I love you.

I said, "When I first came to the Order, just before I turned thirteen, I would wake up in the middle of the night from nightmares so bad I thought they were real even after they ended. Everything was all blood and darkness and fire... So one night after a nightmare, I just ran. It was the first time I left my room alone, but I ran until I couldn't breathe or care, and I found myself here." I turned to Calum. "Since then, whenever I have a nightmare I come here to think about those things that used to be. To be alone. No one but Marcus really knows my story, and I've never seen anyone inside this place except me."

"It's beautiful," he said.

I stood in the middle of the cavern as he circled, both of us taking in the quiet of the place where things came back.

The rocks here crossed and twisted, crawling up in jagged angles so the ceiling was black and pointed and dripping with dew. We would have been in darkness if not for the light seeping in through the curtain of water falling from the edges where the ceiling curved down, circling us in shades of light reflecting the angel tears outside: Blues, purples, reds, greens. And, though the inside of the cave was nothing but rock, in the walls of water I could see the shadowed, wavy shapes of water and earth enchanters shaping waves and flowers. See distorted blushes of pink and bursts of yellow seep through the falls.

The way the light faded and the sounds quieted inside this place, I felt as though I was in a different world entirely.

"Who are those people outside?" Calum asked, sitting on the floor beside me hugging his knees to his chest. His wet hair twisted like the rocks and, when he rested his head on his knees, fell just over his eyes so they were hidden by shadow.

Just like that the brilliant blue was gone-
light killed by shadow.
Soon, I thought, *I will kill, too.*
Soon the blue will be gone forever.

"Everyone is accountable for something," I said, ignoring the way my breath was catching in my throat as though a spider was weaving a web of lies inside. "Here we have different rules we follow and different responsibilities to uphold. You remember how I said all the Elder Council members control a certain element?"

"*No,*" Calum snorted. "*No,* I completely forgot about the group of superheroes about to decide whether I live or die. Must have slipped my mind."

"You *are* a little on the slow side sometimes."

A smile touched the edges of his mouth, but didn't stay. "Yes, I remember."

"Well, each Elder is in charge of a faction of Order members that control their same element. Because the Elders and the Warriors are the only ones that fight the Orieno directly, the other Order members use their abilities to help the natural balance of life where they live."

"Uh, remember that time I was slow?"

I rolled my eyes. "There are five natural elements: Fire, light, earth, water, and spirit. Each Order faction is represented by the color of their element: Red, yellow, green, blue, and white. The Warriors are in gray uniforms. That's why we saw the members in different colored shirts when we first came in. I *should* have changed already, but I have to babysit someone before his trial. Anyway, those factions do things to help their specific element in the world around us. Those in the earth faction, for example, travel around the nearby cities to help grow trees and plants. The light faction helps control the sun and the moon and their respective rotations. And," I pointed beyond the waterfall, "you can see that the water faction helps out with the falls and the lake and all the water in between."

"That makes the Order seem like a charity organization. Like there's actually some good in this place."

"I keep telling you, Calum," I said, "the Order *is* good. We do good things for people. We haven't been able to do much recently because the Orieno attacks brought our numbers down, but we're trying to fix the bad things that have happened in the past decade. Without us the oceans would rise and flood the world, global warming would become catastrophic, and the spirit of the human race would turn dark and evil. It'd be an apocalypse. So we try. I don't know why you think we're so bad."

"Really? You seriously don't?"

"We're not all bad. Not even the Elders. I mean Gae, the Elder that controls the earth faction, used to play games with me all the time when I was younger, especially when I first came to the Order to help me train. She was one of the first people besides Marcus who gave me hope. She used to enchant thousands of tiny flowers to make a path for me to follow to Ashfall and back. She would time me to see how fast I could run from here to there and back again, to see if I could beat her enchantments as they disappeared before me. Gae helped me so much with my training. I promise, Calum, the Order is good."

"Sometimes one bad thing ruins it all."

"The Elders might not decide you have to die."

"And then what?"

"What do you mean?" I asked.

"Even if I don't die today," Calum said, "what about this curse? What about the Bloodletter? What about my friends?"

"They might be safe," I lied.

"You know that's a lie. I can see it in your eyes."

I turned away. "You don't know what you're talking about, Calum."

"I'm beginning to think you don't either, Kate."

"I know where I stand," I said. "I know what I want."

He breathed, "Do you?"

I said, "Yes."

Still, the spider spun lie after lie between us:

You and *I* are more than this.
I know what you *are.*
I **believe** everything will be okay.
It is *safe* here.
Everything will be better *in* time.
I don't want to be *with* you or against you.
I am **happy** alone.
I am *me.*
I am not afraid of **endings**.

"I don't know what to think anymore," he said. "I feel like I should listen to this voice in my head, give in. I want to be someone more than this, but I don't know what's right or wrong. I don't think I ever have."

"Sometimes you don't have a choice between what's right or wrong," I said. "Sometimes that choice is made for you, and if it's not, you do what is best for the most people. Protect those weaker than you. I don't know, Calum, maybe you need to listen to what the Elder Council, especially Gae, has to say before you decide what you should do. It might help to hear another person's thoughts after they've heard yours."

He frowned. "I thought you said I should fight for what I want and not just sit around waiting?"

"You can't win if you don't know what you're fighting for," I said. "If I were you, I'd figure that out fast. Listen to the Council and maybe in an hour you'll know what's right and wrong."

"What if I don't want to win? What if I just want to survive?"

I almost laughed. "This is a different kind of fight, Calum. In this world you do everything you can to win, because if you lose, you die."

"You're fighting for your sisters?" he asked.

I said, "Until I find them and know they're safe."

"They're the only ones you want? Is there anyone else you're fighting for?"

A water worker ran her hand over the waterfall in front of us, causing a ripple to run the circle in lines of shadow and light. Then, stronger than before, the water poured down in waves of blue so dark it looked green.

"Kate?" Calum turned to look at me and, when I

found his eyes again, he asked, "What are you thinking?"

Adam.

"Shut up, Calum. We need to go. Follow me. You don't want to know what will happen if you're late to your trial."

I turned and ran and didn't look back.

-CALUM-

THE HOUR WAS DEAD-
gone as if it never had been-
and I wondered if I would soon follow.

Beyond the largest waterfall, the world bent and broke in two; nothing but the pounding sound of the falls behind us, and a double door before. Nothing else but me and Kate, two souls facing a door with two sides.

We stood side by side, the space between us feeling heavy as though it were not as vast as it should have been. As though we were more than this. This close, I could almost feel her breathing, almost feel the angry rift between us break.

Almost.

I stepped closer.

Kate, her voice steady and low, said, "It's been said that everyone sees something different when they look upon the Doors of Judgment. Different, but always the same. Always the one thing that defines them the most. The Doors show us the one thing that tips the scales and defines who we were, are, and will be."

I felt further away.

Carved in the stone of the cave wall, the Doors were the only smooth things in a world of jagged madness. There were no lines to distinguish them from the cave, except for swirls and patterns of intricately carved designs that faded like rays of light into the stone; a shape just barely there.

"They say magic runs deep and wild in the lines carved in the Doors," Kate said. "They were carved by the first enchanter, Myrddin Lailoken. He was a seer, a prophet, and the one who saw the *Legend of the Dreamer*. It is said that Myrddin traveled to this mountain from Britain around 500 AD in search of his lost sister, Gwendydd, but instead of finding her he found an evil witch who trapped him in the forest for decades. He went mad, lost his mind completely, and eventually fell in love with the witch."

"You're telling me he loved this witch even though she basically kidnapped him against his will? That's crazy," I said. "But I guess it doesn't matter who you love, just that you do."

Kate only shook her head back and forth before she continued, "On the day they were supposed to be married, Myrddin went to the highest peak of this mountain to ask for a blessing from the gods he believed in. Instead, a single bolt of lightning blasted down from the sky and struck him with a vision, the *Legend of the Dreamer*. Instantly, he evolved into something more. The lightning marked him as a prophetic enchanter and gave him control over all five elements."

"Is that how the Order was started?"

"That's what we believe. After seeing the prophecy, Myrddin killed the witch and traveled back to Britain where he gave four of his closest companions a different power over an element, keeping spirit for himself. Together, in hopes of warding off evil and keeping the prophecy protected, they formed the Order. Each of them then traveled to a different part of the world to recruit members and give them a part of the power Myrddin bestowed upon them. Over time the Order grew to have thousands of members worldwide."

"So, how do the Doors of Judgment come into

play?"

"After creating the Order, Myrddin spent years trying to find his sister. She was his twin and the only person alive that shared his blood. He searched the world but never found Gwendydd. So he came back to this forest where it all began. He went back to the peak where he first was shown the prophecy and waited for lightning to strike with an answer once more. It's said that Myrddin waited for ten years, until he was nothing more than a ghost of his spirit. After waiting for so long, he knew his time was coming to an end, so he crawled to this cave to die. With his last bit of power, he used his spirit energy to carve these doors so that all who stood before them would see the truth within themselves; they would be judged by the spirit of the enchanter who started it all. When the doors were finished, Myrddin went to Lake Iris, swam to the center, and let the last of his spirit dissipate into the water as he died. Even today, some Warriors believe that the lake has healing powers, and it's how we get initiated as Warriors. We are blessed with the water of Myrddin as part of the final test before we receive our *levitis* and become full Warriors."

"Did he ever find his sister?" I asked.

Kate shook her head. "No. He didn't." She blinked and swallowed. "He died before he found his sister."

I said, "I'm sorry."

"For what?" she snapped.

I turned away. "Nothing."

Focusing on the Doors, I let my eyes wander until they were all I could see. Until they were everything, the only light in the darkness. The carved lines twisted and turned as if alive, weaving around an inlaid circle broken in four. Light seemed to be ebbing in and out of the carving, as though the angel tears had gotten trapped inside.

"It's a dream catcher," I realized.

"Kind of," Kate agreed. "It's the symbol of the Order that, according to our history, was based on Myrddin's idea that dreams were the gods showing us our fate. He believed we all had the ability to be prophets if we focused enough on what our dreams were saying." She turned to me. "What do you see?"

I closed my eyes before anything took hold.

No. I won't look.

"I don't see anything."

"Open your eyes and try," she snarled. "You have to otherwise we can't go in, and that really wouldn't be the best move for you, Calum."

No.

I fought it.

No.

I didn't want to see my fate, didn't want to see my death.

No.

Didn't want to see how I would become my father.

And then, Kate's voice was so close I felt like she was whispering in my ear when she said, "Open your eyes, Calum. See where you stand and what you should fight for. See who you really are."

Like a million tiny wolves, chills bit into my spine and fought to stay there, grinding up my back until teeth sank into my skull. I felt the Doors pulling at me from all sides, willing me to open my eyes, wanting me to see. Even in the darkness of my mind I could see its light like a beacon calling me forward.

She breathed, "Take a chance, otherwise you'll never know the truth."

I opened my eyes and, as the sound of Kate's voice washed over me, was lost to a dream. Magic consumed me, and I was lost to this:

The depths of Hell ate me alive, and fire licked at me like the hands of people trying to escape...

And then there was a twist in my mind-
sharp and loud and I was
                                falling so fast too fast
                                                    falling

    down
    down
    down
    too much too soon my voice screaming I yelled I hurt so bad I hurt I cried tears and pain pain pain
                                                    falling fast

    down
    down
    down
    until
    nothing and quiet and calm and nothing
    until the fire faded to nothing, and all I saw was darkness. Then, as it faded from black to blue to white light, I felt a burning in my heart that told me I was alive.

Above me nothing moved, nothing pulsed with life. The night sky was an inky blue-black, poked through with tiny stars. It was a different world, the sky, as though time was standing still and I was the only thing moving.

Where am I?

I fell to my knees. Clasping my hands together, I squeezed them while every fiber of my being ached for

226

something more than this.

I thought, I want to know who I really am.

Please.

Show me who I am.

I unbound my hands and put both over my birthmark.

I wished, Show me who I'm not.

My head tilted up. Above the stars were blinking down as if telling me to wait, the wishing star would be coming soon.

And then the world exploded.

It started with the wishing star, a faint dot of white light flying through the sky toward me; a small movement in the dark abyss of night. Every second the falling star gained speed, every moment it flew closer and closer until it lit up the world and, as I closed my eyes, crashed into me in a collision of bright, blinding light that stopped my heart.

No breath.

No air.

No life.

All was dead and gone from light, until-

I breathed.

I was alive.

I opened my eyes and began to see.

I stood outside of time, in the dark field near the cave leading to Lake Iris.

I was me-

but I didn't feel like myself.

There was a difference; I felt it flow through my veins and beat in my heart. My body was lighter, as though lightning had cut and burned my skin away and replaced it with a hundred tiny clouds. My mind though, was as heavy as a storm; I could feel it crack in a tempest of emotions as tears rained down my face.

Anger.

Sadness.

I tried with verve to look at myself, twisting this way and that to see what was different, but all I could see was white, warm light saturating me from every direction until it was all I was.

Fear.

Happiness.

I was light and, just as the tears dried and became nothing more than saline lines down my face, I felt as though I could fly.

Love.

And then the voice from my dreams: "Free us, Caeles. Give in and become who you were always meant to be. This was it. This was your moment. **Remember!** *Look around you. Free us."*

The light burst to a swell around me once more and then closed against me so it was a shell, armor. I blinked and saw the same sky but a different field stretched out before, riddled with tiny hills and trees and so much blood.

As the field became alive in shades of dripping blood, a scene shifted in smoke and shadow and exploded around me: A Hunter's moon shone down on soldiers dressed in gray and red, shining an eerie glow on their battle armor. I felt the pull of the full moon, like always. Felt the familiar fire deep inside me raging, wanting to burn, and I gripped my hands against the heat. Rain fell from the sky in crimson sheets, each drop a needle against my skin. Water like blood.

The battle erupted in chaos.

There was no order.

There was nowhere safe.

"You know what this is, don't you? You've always known what this is," the voice said over the battle cries, over death and pain and agony.

And I realized I did.

For some reason I knew everything.

The Orieno were in red, the Order in gray: Monster against Warrior.

This was a battle fought a thousand times before-

a thousand times after-

forever, until someone stopped it.

Monster against monster.

"You must end this war," the voice said. "We can help, but it starts and ends with you. It always has and always will."

"What do I need to do?" I asked. My voice warbled as though I was underwater, and I could almost feel it bounce off the orb of light around me.

"Look, for now. See this war for what it really is. See what you must become and what you can do, even now. See who we are."

I looked-

and saw death.

Everyone was covered in blood so dark it was black with the same kind of death. Stab after stab brought down another victim in red or gray, until the field was a graveyard of bodies and there was no room to walk without stepping on the dead and fallen.

"War," the voice whispered, "is very rarely the answer to anything, and never so when the ultimate goal is power. It corrupts like poison in the veins of humanity. War strangles and destroys the good in people until all that's left is what you see before you."

War.

Blood.

Death.

Amidst the chaos, I looked up at the night sky, and wished with all my heart that this war would end.

I wish...

I wish...

I closed my eyes and wished I could finally start living. I wished for my Mom and Dad, and for Kate and her sisters. For safety. For Tyler. I wished for the countless people abducted by the Orieno to be saved. For peace. For truth. For answers.

I wish for life.

When I opened my eyes blinding light was flooding the field in waves of silver glory, burning as if the moon had exploded. As the stars fell faster, faces marked by infuriated lines, eyes touched by anger, and dark hands holding glowing swords emerged from the light, and I could see that these weren't stars at all, but people as black and foreboding as the night sky above.

In moments they were intertwined with the soldiers, blades of light slicing through good and bad and turning all to dust.

"There is life in death," the voice said. "We take their souls just before they die, so both good and evil can have a second chance in the hereafter."

Silently, one of the stars landed in front of me, a smile on his face, and stepped close to me so he was surrounded by light.

"Calum," he said looking me straight in the eyes. "Thank you for calling us."

"Calling you? What? I didn't do anything."

He laughed, the melody like a chorus of chimes in wind. "Oh, but you did. Before and now, you did. When you made a wish, we answered. We are the stars people wish upon. We are the light in the darkness. We are hope. I am Orion, leader of Heaven's Guard."

Kate's words dawned in my mind. "The angel Warriors that fight to save the world?"

"I suppose you might call us that, though we are most certainly not angels." He turned to the battle. "Look around you. We are not angels because we are not completely good, though we're not exactly evil either. We are not passive and we fight when we must. We are protectors. In different times, however, we have been known as the Angels of Mons, appearing to Warriors in need throughout Britain as well as in other parts of the world. The Watchers. I myself have been known as the Angel Moroni to several Elder members, though we are anything but angels and those that classify us as such are greatly misled in their beliefs."

He waved a hand through the air. "The stars you see above are protectors to individuals all over the world. They, indeed, are Warriors still fighting. However, the larger stars, the clusters you call constellations, like me, are guards to the more powerful souls that have a greater purpose. Everyone has a claim to make in the circle of fate."

For a moment I got so lost in looking at Orion that I forgot it was my turn to speak. Orion had hair that cropped close to the sides of his head, with long bangs that spread in a slash down his brow. His hair was so white that it shone like opals, reflecting light as if tiny rainbows were in each strand. He had no wings, but swirls of what looked like ever-moving clouds circled around his body, translucent enough to look like fine mist. Tints of pale blue and white danced through them like veins, enhancing the sheer power they seemed to hold. The clouds moved with each breath he took, and it was easy to picture them slicing through the air like knives, lifting Orion up with ease and grace. His skin, like the others, was as dark as midnight, as if it was made of night. It seemed to be as fluid as a moving sky and, for a second, I thought I saw a shooting star fly across his left arm.

"Calum?" he said politely.

I looked into his eyes, golden like the sun with a halo of light around each pupil. If my eyes were mirrors of the moon, his were reflections of the sun. "Sorry. I just... I'm not even sure where I am, or what I am. You say I wished for you, but I don't think I did. I wished for answers."

"You wished for life," he said. "And so we came to give you yours, like we do every time you ask."

"I don't know what you're talking about."

"We only know what we must. Never the complete truth, and never until we're ready."

"What?" I asked, my head spinning. "What do you mean?"

Orion smiled. "I'll say this much, because it's all you need to know in your current life: There are many theories as to how or why the world is what it is, but none of them are completely true. That doesn't mean, however, that there is or isn't an ultimate truth. In fact, there are many. Each person brings something different to the world, a different energy that no one else can bring because we are all secular beings, but circular in our own ways together."

"What?"

"I never get tired of explaining this to you," Orion laughed. "Forget what you know. Instead of thinking of life and death, or Heaven and Hell, think of everything as one large circle of fate. The past, present, and future are linked together not by time but by our minds. By the people that shape that period within time. The past influences the present, which changes the future. And, if we were to count those people that have not yet been born, our futures would influence their own pasts, presents, and futures. It's an entire circle of death and life, and everyone helps shape it. One being cannot shape humanity, but they can make all the difference in the world."

"I don't..." I started, but then found myself thinking of the Doors of Judgment. "Kind of like a dream catcher? Like the symbol of the Order? That idea of fate?"

He nodded. "Exactly. Who do you think they got it from?"

"I thought the Order was started by that enchanter, Myrddin."

Orion smiled again. "And who do you think gave Myrddin the power to create the Order and control the elements? Who do you think showed Myrddin the prophecy that powers this war?"

"The lightning! It was you guys wasn't it? Heaven's Guard?"

"No," Orion whispered. "It was you."

"Me?" I gasped.

"You. Don't you feel the elements calling to you? Do you not remember the way fire burns for you every true full moon, how lightning strikes close, or even how the moon's light beckons your eyes to the sky? Even without your full powers you can feel it, I know."

I remembered. "You mean when my house caught fire when I was little, that was because of who I am? I did that?"

Orion nodded. "Because the moon was full that

night, your true self was closer than ever and you were able to harness a small part of yourself without even knowing. It doesn't happen every time but only when the moon is truly full, and only when a powerful emotion is linked to that moment. That's why you've only felt that way a handful of times, and why you've found other reasons to blame for those extraordinary events.

"Everything in your life has happened because of who you are. You are the one that saw the original prophecy, the Legend of the Dreamer, and you are the one that gave Myrddin his powers so he would help protect your future. Before you died the first time so long ago, you struck Myrddin down and showed him the truth; because of your bloodline and your curse, you knew you would soon forget it. You created the Order to fight in your honor and protect the world from darkness, the Devil, when you were lost to it. But times have changed. The world is darker now than ever before, and the Order is failing. We need to stop this war, and that starts with you." He stepped closer to me. "It always has been about you, Calum. About who you are. The Order is right about one thing: You are the Dreamer, the one who walks through time, through dreams. But you are so much more than just that."

I whispered, "The Devil. I have evil in me. I can feel it."

He put his hand on my shoulder. "We all have a little evil inside us. To doubt that would be to lie. The question is not that we do, but how much of it we have. And you, Calum, have much more good than evil. It's difficult for you to see that now because of the binding spell moving through your veins, but that was for your protection. Even so, with it you can still feel some of the power you do have. You felt it mostly when you were younger, when your mind was less stable and your thoughts much more free. The witch who placed that spell on you was right in doing so, and unfortunately only she can remove it. The Order, however, is wrong about almost everything else. You are not the Destroyer. You are someone else entirely." He shook his head and grinned. "I missed this. Missed you. Our arguments. Our paths connecting like they always will. Are you ready to know what you truly are?"

I gulped.

I nodded.

Orion said, "Look at your arm, Calum. Look at your birthmark."

My heart fluttered as if falling. "How do you know about that?"

He just smiled. "You've asked that question a thousand times. Each time I answer the same: I have one of my own."

Orion pointed to a spot on his lower, right arm. There, shining amid the black of his skin, were several tiny dots glaring bright. Together, they formed the vision of a hunter ready for battle.

"Orion?" I asked, pulling my hand back in. I had almost touched him. "As in the Hunter?"

He nodded. "As I said, I am a constellation. As are you."

Cruel and wonderful bliss filled me.

I thought, Does this mean I'm not my father's son?

I reached to touch my own mark, but it meant nothing to me. There was no constellation that matched it. Not one I knew of.

"You won't find the answer there," Orion said, still smiling.

I could still hear the battle around us, but it was

softer now. More had died.

"Tell me. I need to know. I need the entire truth."

"Why?"

I was taken aback. "Why? Because someone has to stop this! We just can't sit here and let the entire world suffer, can we?"

"No," he said and sighed. "This has gone on long enough. People are dying when they were never meant to. Too much evil exists now. You are right to stop it. But you won't find your birthmark in the sky, Calum, because it was lost long ago. For so long, you were the one that shone the brightest among us all. You are and forever will be the Caeles, the most powerful of all Heaven's Guard. Our true leader, the North Star."

His eyes didn't lie.

I tried to find words-

but nothing came except: "How?"

Orion's eyes grew heavy. The mist around him slowed as he said, "Your story starts like most do, with love. As you know, your true father was Lucifer, the Devil. You will always be the son of the Devil, no matter when or how or to whom you are born. Your soul will always be the first one you were born with. But there is always hope for you. There is a reason you are alive today. Your mother was the angel Gabriella."

I blinked. I will always be this, but there is hope...

"She was the most powerful angel of her time," Orion said. *"And it is because of her you were able to live. But because of your father, you were cursed to die."*

I choked, "I'm going to die?"

Orion's eyes closed for an instant, and when they opened he said, "Let me explain. After you were born you were supposed to die. Children of angels and demons are

236

never meant to live. However, because they are born with the blood of angels in them, they cannot be killed outright. Instead, they are all exiled to live in limbo in the sky as stars. You, Caeles, are different because you are the only one born to the Devil himself. You are his only son. Because of this he has claim over you, and tried to find you when you were banished to the sky shortly after you were born. However, your mother knew this and asked a member of the Guard to look after you and make you his equal. Me."

"You raised me?"

"I think of you as a son, Caeles. And for a short time we were happy together. But even Gabriella could not have seen what would happen. You were her only son, too, but she didn't live long enough to foresee this trouble. She thought you would be safe with me, safe in the sky away from the fires of Hell, but she was wrong. Lucifer's claim over you was so strong that he was able to curse you. Because you went against him and became a member of the Guard, fighting the very evil he loves so much, he cursed you to die over and over again, and live as a human on earth, each time forgetting your prior lives. He knew the curse would cause you to be lost to the sky for even a brief amount of time. I believe he hoped it would eventually become a permanent loss for the Guard because every time you die your cluster of stars dies too, fading to nothing more than a mark on your arm. Without you, the sky is not as bright. Only the brightest star, the North, is left where twenty-five should be."

Orion's chest rose and fell. The blackness of it shimmering like rain against a night sky. "There is more, I'm sorry. I am truly sorry, Caeles. You must understand that you are currently safe from Lucifer. He cannot touch you now. There is too much love in your veins, too much *angelic blood from your mother. It is the only thing protecting you. However, the last part of Lucifer's curse is this: When you find true love, you will need your mother's protection no more. It's said that an act of true love will break your curse, but be the curse itself. Love is your curse, and it is your salvation. It will free us, and trap you. When that happens, the Devil will find you and be granted the power to kill you once and for all time."*

I shook my head. "No. Then I won't fall in love."

"Caeles," Orion whispered. "I'll say this: Flesh is mortal, but a soul is forever. That's one thing so many of us fail to remember. You may have been born and killed countless times before, Calum, but you are not the only one who has lived as long. Did you ever think maybe you've been searching for someone? Maybe you are not in this alone, and maybe love is the answer to your questions?"

"But I don't understand. Just tell me what I need to know!"

But Orion didn't answer. He just waved his arms from side to side, indicating the battle. "Look around you. The Order is dying, and in moments they will be gone. So will the demons. All that will be left is the destruction and the memory from those few survivors that will create the next war."

"Will this war ever end?"

"There is a chance. You, Calum, are our last hope. You are the one we call on when times are too dark to see any light. You must become the Caeles once again. There is no denying who you are; it's written in the stars."

I tried to speak but couldn't. Finally, "How?"

"Remember. Look to the stars and remember. The answer will come to you. You have called to us in your dreams, but not in your reality. You are missing the key."

He began to blur.

"You have a choice. The Caeles can be good or evil, that's the part that is clouded. Because of your father, many think that you are destined to be evil, but you have a choice. Look to your star for guidance," he said, his voice fading as the dream did. "When you are ready you will remember. When you become the Caeles, the rest of us will rise again. Find the missing key. It is closer than you think. Soon, you will feel the true power of Heaven's Guard. Remember you are never really alone."

"But I can't be who you say. I can't win this war. I'm not strong and I don't feel brave."

"You are the Caeles." Orion smiled. "And being brave doesn't always mean you need to fight to win your battles; there are different kinds of strengths. Sometimes bravery comes from letting your heart make choices your mind cannot."

Chapter Thirteen
Of Life And Death

-Calum-

It was Kate.

My face burned with pain. I felt a hand on my shoulder, shaking me violently, and knew it had to be her; no one else would hit me in the face to wake me up.

I wondered if it would always be her.

Always blue against violet.

I was so tired I couldn't find the strength to be mad. Instead, I felt myself slide further into her grip. My head fell to the side and she stopped shaking me.

I blinked the stars away.

"Calum?" Her voice was quiet. "Are you awake?"

Dizzy, I tried to talk but my mouth was too dry.

Her hand still on my shoulder, I felt her grip tighten before she jerked it away. "What did you see?"

Like before, one moment seemed to linger forever. My heart beat too fast as our eyes met, and my gaze ran down her skin, touching each familiar dimple, every memory of a grin. Every moment of defiance etched in a map of golden lines.

She touched her face. "What? What's wrong?"

I expected her eyes to narrow into hatred, but

instead there was only longing, curiosity.

"Kate." My voice broke up my throat in dry, raspy breaths. I reached a hand up to touch her face. I whispered, "I'm sorry I didn't trust you sooner, but now I know. I *know*."

"Shut up, Calum," she said, rolling her eyes. "You hit your head pretty hard when you passed out. How do you feel?"

"Empty," I said. "I'm not... My dream..."

"What was your vision of?"

"I saw Orion, leader of Heaven's Guard. He spoke to me and told me the truth." I only hesitated for a second. "I remember, Kate. I really do, and I'm not who you think I am."

Her eyes slanted down and she asked, "What do you mean? What exactly did you see?"

"I know who I am. I am the Dreamer. I am reincarnated after every life I live and die. But the Order is so wrong about everything else." I took a deep breath and felt my pulse quicken. "You don't know about the curse."

"The binding spell, you mean?"

"No, Kate. It's much worse than that."

I saw fear in the violet of her eyes.

I said, "The Devil can't touch me as long as my mother's blood runs through my veins. That is my protection and, when I fall in love, it becomes my curse."

"What happens then?"

"When I fall in love the Devil will be able to find me, which means I'm that much closer to death. There will be nowhere left to hide. For anyone."

"So don't fall in love. Easy."

I remember you, I thought. *Your eyes. I think I remember your eyes.*

I shook my head and gulped down fear, feeling the raw, gritty nature of it slide down my throat and sit in my stomach like tar. "In order to unlock the power of Heaven's Guard and save the world from the Orieno, Orion said I need to fall in love, and when I do that will be the key to free them. *Love is my curse and my salvation.* I'm not a demon, Kate. I know you think I am but I'm not. Orion called me the North Star, the Caeles, the lost member of the Guard."

Kate's eyes were oceans of horror, pain. Her voice sounded like knives lined her throat. "The North... I've heard stories about this but I never knew the name of the lost one. But... *You?* Are you saying you're the one that started everything?"

In my mind, I heard Orion's voice as a memory of truth:

You are and forever will be the Caeles...
... there is always hope.

Before I knew what I was doing I grabbed her hands in mine. I felt her pull away but I held on tightly. "Yes. I am the Caeles. I'm the one that showed Myrddin the prophecy I foresaw. I gave him the power to create the Order." I ran a thumb against her closed fist. "I know it sounds insane but this is true. I can feel it this time. I've seen it. I've never been so sure of anything in my life."

I'm sure of this, too: Love is my curse.

I looked in her eyes, and was taken aback.

I forgot where I was. Who I was.

Love might kill me.

Kate's eyes filled with drops of purple rain that refused to fall.

"What's wrong?" I asked, easing my grip on her hand so that it rested in mine. I expected her to pull it away, but her hand stayed. "I know this changes everything, but I think I need you to help me. I don't remember everything, and I need an ally in the Order to help me find some key so I can free the Guard and stop this war. I need you."

"Calum," her voice broke. The tears in her eyes faded to nothing as they grew serious, her face like stone. "I'll help you if you do me one favor."

I closed my eyes.

"Help me save my sisters."

My eyes fluttered open with my heart, and I held her hands tighter. "I promise. But you need to do me a favor then, too."

"What?"

"*Trust* me, Kate. Stop pulling away from me. I know... I mean that I remember... I just want you to try and trust me."

There was a moment when I thought the world might unravel, and then, "Okay. I'll try."

I nodded. "Now, do you have any idea where this key might be?"

She looked confused. "Key? I've never heard of a key. Nothing is mentioned in the story I heard. Are you sure that's what he said?"

I nodded. "Yes! I have to find it to unlock the power of Heaven's Guard. I can't remember anything about what it's supposed to look like. Let's go. We have to get out of here and find it before it's too late."

I didn't say: *Before I fall in love.*

I made to stand but she pulled me back down. "Calum! We need to go to your trial. We have to! You'll die if we don't go, and they'll end up killing me too."

And then the realization hit me: I would die no matter what. Orion had said it. I had felt it. It was up to fate to show me the way. Nothing was up to me.

I had no power against love.

Lucifer had known that when he cast the curse.

It took me a while to remember, but knew I would always die in the name of love -

for even the hope of something like it.

Always.

"Okay. Let's go," I said.

Kate's voice broke. "Don't say anything until I introduce us both, and don't move until Marcus invites us to. Just follow my lead."

I said, "I trust you."

"You shouldn't," she breathed.

As much as my heart was telling me no, as much as I wanted to run and never look back, I took Kate's hand and we stood. Together, Kate and I opened the Doors of Judgment and stepped toward our future.

-Kate-

I was broken.

Slow-beating pangs of emotion filled my chest, my eyes, and my heart: Hurt. Pain. Hope. Fear.

Who am I anymore?

I felt fear most of all.

Fear that I felt more than I should.

That my sisters would not be saved.

That Calum was right: I was losing control.

When all I wanted to do was feel nothing, I was beginning to feel things I hadn't since before the Order. It all had changed the instant Calum had told me his truth.

The instant he held my hand.

I would die for my sisters, but were they the only people who mattered?

Now, I was broken; a shattered version of the Warrior I had been. Calum said that love was his salvation and his curse, that it was inevitable, and I wondered if I would be lost to love as well.

Would love be the death of us all?

I thought of Adam and my heart broke-

Calum and my heart shattered.

Both made me feel like the girl I had been so many years before.

Calum said I should trust him, but I had tried that with Adam. I had trusted before and found myself in a place so lost that truths became broken in an instant.

But Adam was gone.

Still, he had made my heart feel light as air, while

Calum made it beat with raging fire. Adam was safe. Calum was dangerous. And while I hadn't known Calum for that long, he made me remember a time when I was alive with feelings.

In that, Calum reminded me of Adam.

Of me, before.

When Calum told me who he truly was, I realized the only reason I had hated him was because of who I thought he had been. Who I was told he was.

I didn't know what to do.

But I would try to trust Calum.

For my sisters I would try anything.

I thought of the Warrior Code and realized it meant little to me now. I still believed its message, still had faith in the fight against evil, but the words were too binding to live by anymore.

I will be exiled, I thought. *Just like my parents.*

If the Order finds out, they will kill me.

Calum squeezed my hand.

I had thought he would be like his father, but all along it had been me. I was the one who was damned to become the one thing I had been running from all along: A traitor.

I thought of the people I would have to kill, of Calum, and realized I wasn't as different from my parents as I had thought. If I had to kill a hundred people to save my sisters, I would slay them all in a heartbeat.

An odd thought flared in my mind: *Maybe my parents weren't as guilty as I think. Maybe they had reasons for killing that many people. They did bind Calum's power, after all, and hide him without telling anyone. Why would they keep him safe like that? Could they have known what he is?*

I didn't know anything about what my parents had wanted back then, but I knew what I wanted now.

Now, I wanted something more than this life. I wanted my sisters, and I finally had a way to get them back.

For now, it would be Calum and me against the world.

~

Beyond the Doors of Judgment was cold darkness, and the icy air of reality made me realize one thing: No matter what, I was a Warrior to the bone. My blood was hot with angry strength. My soul filled with courage.

I would not be weak in front of the Elders.

I threw Calum's hand off mine. I couldn't let myself be close to him, not now. The Order thought strength and courage could not be found in love.

Love?

I choked on air.

Stone.

I would try to trust Calum, but I could not lose myself yet. Not in the middle of his trial. We had to get out of here alive in order to save my sisters.

I was stone beneath my skin.

Instead of the wild confusion in my heart, I focused on this: Calum was the Caeles, the lost member of Heaven's Guard said to be the most powerful of them all. He was the one that had started everything, and with him it would all end.

Did the Order know about this?

Did anyone?

They couldn't, I knew, and it would be my secret

for now. If anyone, even Marcus, found out who Calum was, it wouldn't be up to me to kill him anymore. Marcus had told me this every day since I was a girl: If the first enchanter ever returned to this time, he would be sacrificed in a blood ceremony, bled dry in the lake, his body ground to dust and sprinkled in the blood water for all to drink and bathe in. They would gain magic of the ages from his body in hopes that it would help them defeat the Orieno once and for all. Marcus told me that it would happen no matter what because the first enchanter would be born again in every time, and would never truly die. And even though Calum was not who they wanted, not Myrddin, he would be close enough.

One immortal life sacrificed for a thousand more.

But he couldn't die yet. Even in terms of my own blood oath, Calum would have had more time to live, and I needed him alive *now*.

Calum wasn't the Destroyer, of that I was sure, but a storm was surely coming, brewing in the sky above. I knew that soon nothing, not even the Order, could stop Hell from breaking open and raining fire on us all.

I looked down at my *leviti*. Would Calum end as a blood-red mark on my finger? Would his blood run cold because of *my* hands?

What if they forced me to do it immediately?

I couldn't do it. Not yet. I needed him too much.

To find my sisters, I reminded myself. *I need him to find my sisters. That's why.*

There was no other reason, though even as I thought it I felt a pinch of unease form in my chest and break up into my throat.

I swallowed and, as I bowed low to the ground, I thought of all the ways I'd lied in the past, and all the truths I kept secret.

I have to kill him, I thought. *But not today.*

Today I will save him.

I lifted my head up slowly, put my *leviti* over my heart, and said in a voice that could have broken glass, "I, Katherine Black, faithful Warrior to the Order only, present Calum Wade to the honorable Elder Council for trial against his life."

-CALUM-

DEATH.

I breathed it in, that acrid taste of lost life.

I felt it lingering close by, waiting.

Felt it shiver around me, wanting.

Even the bravest person would have imagined their death in this place, felt it close in, suffocating in its need to kill. The cavern pulsed with fear; its walls brown, rough jagged rock with blackened lines of water running down like dark blood bleeding from the ceiling. Pools of muted red formed on each side of us, the *drip drip drip* of rusted water falling in them from pointed stones above; teeth dripping saliva, hungry for my death.

Barely inside, Kate and I stopped on a slanted path that lead down to a raised table, both a strange yellow-white lit by candles.

"What's this floor made of?" I whispered to Kate after she introduced us. I kept my voice as quiet as possible, biting my lips to keep them still. I looked closer, and felt myself surrender to a chill that had been tickling my spine since I stepped through the Doors.

The candles burning alongside the path were pushed deep into human skulls, dripping wax as dark as blood down the sides of the forgotten, lifeless faces.

"Bones," she said through gritted teeth. "Dead Warriors. We honor them this way. It's sacred. *Shut up.*"

Thin red lines of wax flowed down toward the table, stopping where chalky bone erupted from the floor and climbed in a chaos of dead arms and legs and ribs before meeting a tangled table top of twisted fingers and toes and teeth.

The flickering light pulsed around the room like lost heartbeats of dead souls, illuminating the people sitting on white chairs around the table. Five pairs of inhuman eyes gazed up at me, all as black and vast as night - or death. Each Elder wore different colored robes that matched the color of swirling tattoos on their bodies: Red, yellow, blue, green, white. I recognized Marcus in red sitting in the middle of the group. His hands tapped against the bone impatiently, his lips spread apart in a grin. His eyes never left me, watching as though he was a burning flame and I a moth. The man to his right was doused in yellow, his golden tattoos alive with light, but had the same cold glint to his eyes as Marcus did. The only other man in the group was covered in white, from his robes to his curled hair to the silvery lines circling his body. The two women were different; they seemed to breathe a small amount of life into the room when I looked at them. The one with pale, blue-tinted skin swirling with tides of blue-green was draped in robes that seemed to shimmer and flow around her like ocean waves. The other woman though, with warm, blushing brown skin touched with intertwined emerald vine tattoos, seemed to sit as still as a tree in robes the color of spring.

Still, their eyes were all as dark as shadows in deep graves. And as the Elders sat there unmoving, their colored stones shone from each of their foreheads, shining as though the reflecting lights were secret deadly words between them.

"The Elder Council acknowledges your faithfulness, Warrior, and beckons you forward," Marcus said with a curt nod to Kate. And then to me, his eyes narrowing, he said, "You may come forth, Calum Wade, and see where fate has placed you."

Kate moved first, walking quickly ahead of me as I followed. She sat in a stone chair framed in crossed spines set to the right of the table, her eyes never leaving the Elders.

"Sit," Marcus commanded me.

I swallowed. "Where?"

His eyes blazed with candle fire. "Do not speak! Sit! There!" He pointed to a chair directly in front of where he sat, one covered in jawless, pale skulls.

I am not afraid. I am the Caeles, I thought, sitting down.

But I wasn't, not really. Until I found the key to unlocking my powers, I wasn't anything yet.

I remembered what Orion said:

It is closer than you think.

I had to get out of here.

"Calum Wade," Marcus said, drawing out my name so it hung heavy in the room. He closed his tattooed hands together. "Oh, Calum. Calum. Where to begin."

"The beginning might be nice," the woman in green muttered.

Marcus shot her a look. "Yes, the beginning. In all honesty, Calum, it appears that we should not even hold this formal trial for you. It has been foreseen by the first enchanter, the Great Myrddin, that you will be the one to destroy us all. We believe you are the Destroyer, and that you will do more damage to us than even our greatest enemy, the Orieno. You will take what is sacred and most honored to our people and kill it. You will destroy our hopes and dreams until they are nothing but deaths and bits of destruction and hopeless-"

"Get *on* with it, Marcus," the woman said rolling her eyes. "Stop trying to scare everything out of the boy and let's move this trial along. Some of us have places to be and people to save, if you remember why we're here in the first place."

"Not this again," the man in yellow said under his breath.

The same woman sighed. "Yes, *this* again, Lisander! This is ridiculous. We have much larger things to be focusing on that have already happened, but here we are worrying about things that haven't. We are supposed to be balancing good and evil in the world, yet here we sit letting the scales tip against us. How does that make sense?"

Marcus scowled. "It makes sense, Gae, because that's the way of the Order. Or have you gone rogue on us now?"

"You know that I will always have the Order's best interests at heart, Marcus!" she shouted. "Don't you dare put me in league with any of our enemies."

"As if you would know who those actually were."

"Enough!" Lisander shouted, his gold tattoos shining bright. "Silence, Gae. We have a trial to conduct and you're not helping anyone."

Gae looked like she wanted to scream, but her mouth stayed closed. Beside her, the woman with blue robes tilted her head down.

"I understand where you are coming from, Gae," Marcus said in a voice much too light for his dark eyes. "However, we do know that Calum is the Destroyer, and therefore we need to do everything in our power to stop him before he destroys us."

Gae shook her head. "With respect, Marcus, we do not know that for sure. You yourself know that the prophecy is inconclusive. Only the witches know the truth behind it."

He nodded and pointed to the man on his right. "Yes, and although we feel it irresponsible of our past Elders to leave the last half of the prophecy with the witches, Lisander and I have gone to the Woman of Prophecy to hear the *Legend of the Dreamer* in its entirety, and we are both certain that Calum is, in fact, the Destroyer."

"You did?" Gae asked, her lips curling in disbelief. "When was this?"

"While you were gone on one of your 'important missions.'"

"Do not belittle me, Marcus! They *are* important!"

"As is this."

"There is no doubt," Lisander agreed, frowning. "We saw the prophecy and Marcus is certain of its meaning."

"You don't understand," I started, feeling the skulls dig into my back. "I'm not the Destroyer. I'm the-"

"I agree!" Kate shouted, standing up.

Marcus looked livid. "You agree with what, Warrior?"

"I agree that the boy is the Destroyer, and that he should be taken care of like we agreed."

Like we...

I whispered, "Kate?"

"Silence!" Marcus yelled, standing up. "Quiet or I will slit both your throats right here and now!"

Gae leaned forward. "You agree, Warrior? Why?"

Kate blinked. "He is the Destroyer. I have seen the

evidence with my own eyes and agree with what Marcus has said. We should take care of him as we planned. That's what we discussed, and that's what should be done."

"What evidence?" a quivering voice next to Gae said. "Are you sure?"

"Oh shut it, Layla," Lisander barked. "Of course she is sure. Marcus is the one that brought her to us in the first place. He helped train her. Do you doubt him?"

Layla blanched. "No, of course not."

"I agree with the Warrior," Gae said, her voice definitive and darkly certain. "The boy should be taken care of."

"Agreed." Marcus focused on me. His black eyes were horrific fury against all I was, and I felt my throat close around terror unwilling to escape.

Lisander and Layla both said, "What?"

Marcus smiled. "I knew you would come around, Gae. I'm glad you finally made the right choice and saw the truth."

He licked his lips, wet and dark red. "It is decided. Calum Wade is the Destroyer, and he is sentenced to-"

"Wait," Gae interrupted. "I said, Marcus, that I agreed with the Warrior. I agree that the boy should be taken care of, but I never said I agree with your idea of sentencing."

Marcus turned to her. "Excuse me?"

"I don't think we need to kill the boy until we are *all* certain of what he is. It would be better to wait until he actually did anything that would lead us to believe we're right."

"Agreed," whispered Layla.

"Both of you are idiotic!" Lisander bellowed, standing up and throwing his hands in the air. "This is what we *believe*, don't you both understand that? Or do you not have faith in the Order anymore?"

Gae rose to her feet, her mound of curly black hair shaking like a storm. "I have faith in what is right for everyone, not what is believed by few without just cause. Here we are accusing this boy of things that might be true when there are still Orieno attacks happening in this very state. Two just over an hour ago when the boy was here!"

"He's in league with the Siblings!" Lisander shouted. "You know that, Gae. The boy lets them do his dirty work while he is working to defeat *us*! You are going against this Council and mocking our faith!"

"You are so willing to believe anything, Lisander, that I'm wondering if *you* are even on our side anymore," Gae said. Her tone was hushed, deadly. "If you even remember the difference between right and wrong, or if you simply submit yourself to power."

"How dare you! I will-"

"The boy is guilty!" Marcus yelled over everyone. He shot to his feet, his crimson robes billowing around him like runaway flames. "Calum Wade, the prophecy is clear to us. Our sacred words name you as a king among evil. You are the Destroyer! You are guilty! You are sentenced to death *now,* and I will kill you myself if I must!" He spoke quickly, every word a crescendo of anger until his eyes grew red with rage, as if the words were spilling out to make room for something more.

"No!" Kate jumped from her seat. "You can't kill him!"

Lisander exploded. "You dare speak again, Warrior?"

"The Warrior obviously understands that we should not kill the boy until we are absolutely certain who he is,"

Gae said calmly. She turned to the man in white. "Arthur, what do you think?"

Marcus was shaking in fury. "I have spoken! He has been sentenced!"

Gae waved a hand in the air. "Yes, you did, Marcus. But in order for the sentence to hold true, the entire Council needs to vote on the matter. We didn't. Now, Arthur, you are an enchanter of spirit and can see more than any of us. What do you think?"

There was silence for what seemed like hours, and then the man in white spoke in a voice that was a grating whisper. It was as though life had left him and he was nothing more than a shell, his spirit sucked dry for the sake of others. "The boy is more than he seems, but he is not yet who he should be."

"See," Lisander said. "He is the Destroyer. Kill him."

"Arthur was not clear." Gae shook her head. "Arthur? I apologize for asking twice, but can you be more descriptive in your detailing of the boy? Is he the Destroyer or something else?"

Arthur closed his eyes and breathed, "He is the lost one we seek. Soon he will be the Caeles."

Silence.

Then, "HOW DARE YOU!"

"Marcus!" Gae cried. "What are you doing?"

Fire burst around Marcus, the entire room hot from his element. "Lisander! Destroy them both! Lisander!"

Lisander began to run toward me, his eyes glowing with deep red fire that said this: *Kill, kill, kill.*

"Run!" Kate screamed at me.

I jumped off my seat and bolted toward the Doors.

I felt hands on me, gripping my shoulder so tightly I

felt blood.

"Hurry, boy. We must hurry." It was Gae. "I'm with you. Trust me."

Behind me I saw Lisander and Marcus throwing bolts of light and fire at Layla. Her hands were thrown out in front of her, shaking as pale blue light engulfed them. A wall of light blue water broke the room in two, protecting us.

Suddenly, Kate was beside me. "Run!" she yelled.

As my fingers touched the door, I heard Marcus howl with an undying rage. "Morphis! Hear my plea and fight beside me! It is time!"

I turned just as the wall of water crashed down in waves, shattering into white-hot flames as it fell around Layla.

Even from where I stood, I heard her cries burst from her throat, wet and lifeless, until she was engulfed in light and fire. Until she was nothing but ash and dust and death.

Beside me, Gae whispered, "Sister."

In a flash of darkness, gray smoke began to billow from behind Marcus. His body began to change, grow as he screamed. His teeth elongated, and his eyes grew as red as embers on a hot fire burning bright. His tongue reached out and licked at air and more flames burst from the smoke.

Lisander bowed to the thing that used to be Marcus.

"Lissssander," it hissed. "Kill the boy. Kill him!"

I knew that voice, knew the devil-eyes and the shape of the dark smoke that reached like fingers. It was the monster from my dream, the one that couldn't touch me.

Blood beat in my ears. Faster and faster.

"Morphis," Gae whispered from my side. "No..."

A hand found my own. Kate.

I couldn't speak.

"Run," Gae whispered, her voice so filled with fear it burned my throat. She turned up to the ceiling and clasped her hands together. "Emaline. Christopher. I'm sorry."

Her eyes were wide, and her lips white with fear. She reached into the folds of her robe and pulled out a small dagger, the hilt gleaming with emeralds. She thrust the knife into Kate's hands and closed her fingers around it. "Sweet Kate, forgive me for not protecting you, for not telling you the truth about what I could not stop; Marcus has become Morphis. Now you must run toward the truth kept from you, and don't look back until you've reached the outside. The morning sun has nearly risen, and Morphis will need the day to regain his strength; he will eat souls until the moon rises again. You both have until then to become what you must be. Run while you can. The Orieno are already here, and they will move as quickly as they can before the night leaves completely. The wards in the tunnel have already been broken. I can feel it. *Go!*"

We ran.

CHAPTER FOURTEEN
DARKNESS BURNING BRIGHT

-KATE-

INVISIBLE HANDS TOOK HOLD OF MY HEART, my lungs, and squeezed until I couldn't feel or breathe. Until my whole world melted in death and betrayal, and burned dark around me from the bright flames of one body on fire.

Gae's voice was a quake of power, surging through me so her words repeated furiously: *Go! Go! Go!*

I remembered Dad screaming.

Remembered being afraid.

Hiding.

"Go!"

"Move, Calum!" I shouted, the words barely slicing through the air in time. I shoved Gae's dagger up my sleeve. "Run!"

I heard a crunch behind me, bone against rock.

Someone else was gone. Dead.

Please let it be Marcus, I thought as my legs pushed me forward, away. I grabbed Calum's shirt and pulled. *Please let Morphis be gone.*

Marcus.

He had been my family when I had none, and my

world when mine unraveled. My father when I could look to no one else, trust no one else.

And now he stood as a man possessed by a demon; Morphis, the dream-eating demon banished from Hell itself. Now Marcus' soul was nothing but dust, a cold bundle of ash in his heart that beat as dark as death; that's what they did. Morphis wouldn't stop until he stole every soul in sight, eating the helpless dreams of innocents in the name of the Orieno. He wouldn't stop until he had an army of damned, lawless victims to control. Until the world was dark.

Marcus was gone. Dead.

Calum and I burst through the falls and out into the lost beauty of the open cave. The shine of the angel tears on the lake was too bright against the horrific screams behind us. The magic was gone, almost forgotten. Even the tears were falling more slowly.

A piercing siren shook the rocky walls of the cave, bursting through the air and rippling across the lake and falls as if alive; a cry for help to all those Warriors still alive. A cry for death.

A reason to hide.

Time was a beating drum, sounding faster and faster until it kept a driving rhythm with my speeding heart, and I knew we didn't have much left.

"The other Warriors will be here soon. They can't find us or we'll never leave; after what happened no one will be allowed to." My eyes darted left and right, searching. "Come on!" I ran toward a small stone storage house, yanked open the red-rusted door, pushed Calum inside, and locked us in.

Except for blood sounding loud in my ears, racing through my veins like fire eating a thousand lines of gasoline, there was nothing but quiet.

"Quiet," I whispered while I waited for the fire to reach my heart. To explode.

Calum jerked his head toward me. "I wasn't going to say anything."

"Yes, you were. So, shut up and sit still. If they know we're in here, we die."

He nodded. "Should we hide or do you have a plan?"

"Hide." I looked around. "Get behind those food boxes in the back. They should be big enough to hide us if someone comes in."

"You think that'll help?"

"No," I said. "Not at all. But hiding will give us the advantage in an attack if someone does find us."

We crouched down behind the boxes, our knees touching. This close, I could feel how warm his skin was.

I closed my eyes and tried to banish the beat of my heart so I could hear the outside. I listened and heard just this: A slow *beat beat beat* of a heart that wasn't mine.

Calum.

I opened my eyes and saw the sky-

saw my reflection in his deep blue eyes.

I saw him looking at me like I was someone else, like I was a girl made of sunlight, the only thing shining bright in a world of complete darkness. Hope in a place without.

Like I was someone more.

"Stop it," I said. "You said you'd stop looking at me like that."

"I never said that."

I turned away, curled my arms around myself and hugged my body. "Well, stop."

For a while, I was alone with my thoughts, my

heart. Alone, with Calum next to me.

"What *was* that?" he said breaking the silence. "What did Marcus turn into?"

I shuddered at the name, betrayal so thick in the sound of it that I felt it rattle my bones and crawl under my skin. I didn't dare speak loudly, so I moved closer to Calum and whispered, "Morphis. He turned into the most powerful demon sibling of the three banished from Hell, and the leader of the Orieno."

And then I realized, "Marcus had to be working for them all along."

"I saw him in my dreams," Calum said, his eyes darting back and forth. "He came to me. Spoke with me and tried to touch me but he couldn't."

"He should have been able to," I said. "He's so powerful. Maybe it's because of who you are."

Calum was quiet. His legs shook unsteadily against mine. "I'm sorry, Kate, but what do we do now?"

Remorse bit my tongue. *Why am I hiding? I'm a Warrior. I should be fighting with the others, not running away like a coward.*

I ground my teeth together. "I don't know. He's too powerful. Even if all the Warriors stood as one, we'd die instantly; we're trained to fight the Orieno, not the Siblings themselves. I've never done anything to prepare for this. No one has."

He put his hand on mine. I didn't push it away.

My sisters.

I'm not running away, I'm running to find them.

Truth will set me free.

I almost felt safe if not for the fear in my heart.

"We still need to find the key," Calum reminded me. He closed his eyes and leaned his head against a box. "It might be our only hope in stopping this war. With it I know we can win."

"You can't know that."

He said, "I believe we can."

"Why?"

He shrugged. "Because I believe in you."

"But why? Calum, you don't know me. You can't believe in someone you don't even know."

A shy grin played at the edges of his mouth and he said, "Maybe I don't know you as well as I should, but I know you better than you think. I know that you miss your parents even though you hate them. I know that you loved someone once, before you came to the Order, and that you regret not meeting him that night. I know you are loyal and smart and incredibly stubborn. I know that sometimes you second guess yourself, but always have the best intentions. And I know that you will do anything to find your sisters and make sure they're safe."

I swallowed. "You don't know me."

"Yes, I do, Kate."

"No," I said, my voice flat, "you don't."

Suddenly, the siren died. It sputtered and coughed like a bird shot down from the sky and, just before it crashed to nothing, exploded in one last ear-piercing roar.

Calum looked at me in that way I hated and, in a voice filled with quiet determination that resonated loudly in the aftermath of the siren, said, "I want to know you, Kate."

I was not afraid.

I was terrified.

-Calum-

My chest rose and fell, harboring a silent scream. If I let it out we would die in seconds.

I closed my eyes and leaned my head back. My hand was hot in Kate's, and I knew I needed it to stay there. I pulled them to my chest, holding tightly to their warmth. I felt better entwined with her like this, less afraid.

Filled with fear, but less afraid of what that meant.

Still, why didn't things just stay the same? I had been happy. I was happy with Tyler and Mom and my friends back in Lakewood Hollow.

I almost laughed.

No, I never was, I thought. I'd always known something was missing. I had never felt like myself.

Now, even though I'd lost so much, I felt alive and a different kind of anger began to erupt inside me, from a brave new place, and my heart filled with the urge to fight.

This was my time. Ours.

Beside me, Kate whispered, "Why is this happening?"

"What do you mean?"

She leaned close and pulled her hands from mine, balling them into fists. "I mean why now? You're the Caeles, the one born a thousand times before, so why are we just trying to figure all this out now? *You should have the answers, Calum!* Why didn't you stop this war a hundred years ago?" Her fists pounded against my chest, softly at first, then harder until I was numb to everything else but the feeling.

With every blow, I thought, *No one can have all the answers, no matter who they are.*

I grabbed both her hands, held them as tightly as I could, and shook them as I said, "Kate, be quiet! They'll hear us."

Her eyes blazed a furious violet in the dim room, and her teeth bared white. "I don't care! Why didn't you stop this! You could have saved us all! You could have saved my sisters!"

I whispered, "In all my past lives I don't think I've ever been in love. Orion said that love would be the only reason the Devil could find me; he said it would be the only way to free the Guard. So, I couldn't have been, otherwise they'd already be free. Orion said that in every past life, I've died before I even get the chance to live, to love."

"Calum, I-"

"Can you believe that, Kate? I've always died before I've loved. I don't remember why. Maybe I've never found a reason to fall in love, never let myself. I don't remember anything, other than a flash of purple light blinding me. Even in this life I've dreamed of it. Of *you*, Kate. I think I've been searching for you. I think I always want to remember you, find you."

Kate blinked and, for that one fleeting moment, I felt my heart drop as her eyes disappeared. "What do you mean? How?"

"Your eyes," I said, squeezing her hand. "I might not know that much about you in this life, Kate, but from the first moment I saw you, I've known your eyes as if I've seen them a million times before. I remember when I saw you back in Mr. Brandt's room, and all I could see was violet. It was as though I remembered that color from somewhere; as though I'd known you before."

She shook her head. "That can't be right, Calum. I'm not immortal. I'm just me. Nothing more."

Calum smiled. "That's where you're wrong. When I look in your eyes, I know I've seen them before. But you're right that you don't die over and over again like me. You are mortal, and this is your first life. But it isn't mine."

I breathed, "I think I've finally found a reason to fall in love, Kate. That's why this time is so different. You might be my reason. I think I've been searching for you for a thousand lifetimes."

-KATE-

Lies.

Calum's voice rang in my thoughts just as a cacophony of voices exploded outside the door; harsh shouts of power and courage and fear, and one scream filled with bloodlust. How many were out there? Thirty? Hundreds? Thousands? It sounded like more.

Calum tapped my knee. "Kate, what do we do when they find us?"

"Fight and run," I said, choking back words I didn't want to say. I bit down hard on my tongue, felt it pop, and swallowed my blood as though it were my secret.

I could swear I remember your eyes, too, Calum.

I closed my eyes against the sounds of Warriors dying, against the inhuman howl of Marcus changed, and breathed against my own fear. "Gae said that we need to run toward truth."

"What do you think she wants us to do?"

"Only the witches know the truth of the prophecy." My eyes blinked open. "We need to get to the Woman of Prophecy. No one, not even Marcus, is allowed to see her unless she summons them first. He lied during the trial; he couldn't have known the complete prophecy. I don't think anyone's actually seen her in the past century except for my parents. The witch must know something we don't about the prophecy."

"Maybe she has the key."

"Maybe."

I thought, *Maybe she has the answers I need.*

"Do you know how to get there?" he asked.

"Yes," I choked. "Gae showed me the way a long time ago. But we need to hurry. Once we get out of here we won't have long until the sun sets again. And Ashfall is miles away. If what Gae said is true, that's when Morphis will come back, stronger than ever."

"Do you trust what she said?"

"With my life." I breathed, in and out and in, and said, "Calum. If something happens to me, I want you to-"

"Don't, Kate. Don't even try to give me that speech. I meant what I said." His words were fierce and deliberate. "I trust you, and I will do everything in my power to save your sisters if you can only trust me. Believe me."

I nodded, but my words were lost to thoughts.

Marcus had been everything to me.

Adam had been everything.

My parents and sisters.

Everyone who once had been anything to me is gone.

"Trust me, please," Calum pleaded.

All these lies surrounded me; I could barely breathe in this thick, fetid wasteland of half-truths.

"Why would you help me when a war is happening right outside? There are so many other people to save. *We might die, Calum.* Why would you ignore all that to help me?"

"It's what you need, Kate." He sighed. "Both you and Orion have told me that I've died so many times before, it's impossible to count how many lives I've lived. And out of all those lives, this same war has persisted. But still, the only thing I remember is the way your eyes make me stop breathing, make me feel alive as if this was my first life all over again. And that's the thing: You don't let me forget.

I've tried so hard for the past few days to forget my father, the Bloodletter, my friends, my *past*, but you wouldn't let me. You make me remember that I have a future, and that maybe, some day, it might be good. Maybe my future is worth living for."

Calum looked into my eyes and I found myself lost in the blue once more. He leaned close, pressing his legs against mine, molding his warm hands to my shoulders and, just as a soft chill ran up my spine, he whispered, "I'm not ignoring the war, or the people that need saving, but you're worth fighting for too, Kate. In fact, I think I've been fighting to be with you, for this moment, forever. That's why."

I breathed in and in and in and couldn't find the air to breathe out.

Calum smiled. "Breathe, Kate." He touched my face, warm against warm, and reached behind my neck to pull me close. I felt his nose tickle my neck, felt him breathe in and out when I couldn't. In my ear, he said, "I've got you."

I closed my eyes, felt the walls Adam had trapped me inside close in and-

Adam.

"What are you doing?" I asked...
..."I'm holding you," he said.

~~*Adam.*~~
Black bits of ~~Adam~~ nothing.
found nothing but darkness there.
Adam was gone.

When I opened my eyes, there was only warmth and Calum and-an earsplitting crash against the door, sending cracks of ceiling rock falling down on us.

"Kate!" Calum shouted, grabbing my shoulders and pushing himself away from me as two shards of black rock fell between us.

I saw my *leviti* over Calum's shoulder, the red bright in the dim room. I heard voices outside, phantom feet pounding around us like sounds of thunder. Screams. I heard blood burst from Warrior mouths.

And I was in here. Hiding.

More rock fell. The entire house shook.

Then, as though all noise had been abandoned in wake of death, a sudden stillness possessed the house, and the world outside was silent.

In that second, everything changed once more.

I became who I had been, a Warrior. I felt my eyes slant down, growing hard and cold like two pieces of unbreakable stone. My lips pursed in fealty to the Code I was bound to.

I pledge my allegiance to the Order, the one and only truth.
I vow my life to thee, over sky above and ground below.
To kill, to die, or to bleed, my eyes only see one Order.

My heart dropped.

Calum's eyes found mine, and deep down I knew what he was seeing, knew why his eyes looked so sad.

But I needed to be this person now.

Calum nodded as if he understood. "I'm ready."

"Let's go." I didn't know any other way to survive. "I don't hear anything. It sounds like they've moved out of the cave."

I stepped quietly toward the door and Calum followed.

"On the count of three," I said.

Calum nodded, his eyes locked on the door.

"One," I whispered, grabbing the handle.

I held up my fingers. *Two.*

My heart raced.

Three.

I turned the handle and we burst out into the cave.

Silence.

Emptiness.

Nothing.

The entire cave seemed to be void of life; the sun must have risen, casting the Orieno away.

Then, "Calum."

I didn't try to hide my voice, and in this deserted place it rang like a hundred tiny, broken bells echoing off the walls.

He asked, "What is it?"

I pointed.

-Calum-

Bloody and torn, as though it had been ripped from its body by teeth, was a severed head dripping drop after drop of thick blood on Kate's foot. Loose, red film coated the jagged neckline, strips of flesh hanging at odd angles. The eyes, a pale mossy-green, were iced over with blue-tinted death, matching sickly lips crusted dry. Lips that were opened to a scream.

Gae.

"Kate," I started.

A voice like breaking glass cut through the silence between us. "She was the only one who cared..."

I started to speak, "Kate, I'm so sorry-"

"We can't stay here. We have to move." She jumped over the head and started running, her dark hair flying wildly behind her.

"Kate! Wait!" I yelled, but she had already slowed, slumped, and fell to her knees. I wasn't sure why until I saw her face etched red with lines of tears.

I bent down and touched her shoulder, but she turned her face away.

I said, "It's okay to cry."

Her voice was coarse, cracked. "No, Calum. It's not. Both Marcus and Gae are gone and I have nothing left here, but breaking down like this goes against everything I believe a Warrior should be. Against everything I want to be."

"Crying?"

Still the tears fell freely down her face. "Yes! It's weak. I can't afford to feel like this right now."

I dug my nails into her shirt so she couldn't brush me off and said, "Don't think for one second that you are weaker for crying. I've never met a stronger person than you, Kate."

"That's not true," she sniffed.

I shook my head. "This person you are right now, this is who a Warrior should be. Not that girl you were before, the one that was cold as ice and afraid to show me anything. You, Kate, crying right now for someone you just lost? Someone you loved? You look like you could take on the world. Don't you see that tears, *feelings*, make you stronger? Loving and losing and hating and caring: Feelings give you reason to fight. They destroy you and build you up again. They can kill you and then give you life. That's not weakness, Kate. It's strength."

She turned to me, violet to blue, and the tiny freckles on her face made me think of Orion, of the sky. Of possibilities.

"Calum?" she asked.

"Kate?"

"Thank you." Her lips curved in a crimson smile, and then down against before it stuck. "I don't believe you, but thanks."

"You're welcome," I said. "I don't really believe you either."

Her forehead creased. "Believe me about what?"

"People say we hide things in the most obvious places when we don't want anyone to find them. And with you, you've hidden a secret where no one has looked in a long time."

Her voice broke. "Where?"

I touched one finger to her cheek. "Your eyes. When I look in them it's like I know exactly how you feel. And right now I know you're stronger than you think. Your eyes tell the truth, Kate. They are your strength even when you cry." I brushed my finger down the golden lines of her face, rested it on her chin, and tilted her face up toward mine so all I saw was violet.

And it was though time had stopped-

as though there was no river rushing around us-

no quiet water brushing against the bank of the lake-

just her and me and one hopeful moment free from time.

My heart beat like a drum inside my chest, pounding and pleading to run rampant against it all. Cheeks on fire, I closed my eyes and my lips moved down and close and then-

quiet, softer than a breath. "Calum. I can't."

My eyes opened and I saw a sad smile.

"Not now," Kate said. "Not like this, when there's so much death around us and I have nothing."

"You have me. Don't you see that?"

"Not yet." She shook her head, turned, looked straight into my eyes, and said, "Not like this."

Again, before I could question it, her face became a canvas of unbreakable stone.

My lips burned, but still I clung to hope.

We ran.

"Wait. Where's Gae's body?" Kate said, stopping suddenly. "We have to find it!"

I looked around and, when I found it crumpled in a pile a few feet away spurting red into the air, my heart stopped.

There, scrawled beside Gae's twitching, fingerless body, were liquid words written in blood.

One, two, I'm coming for you.

"Calum."

Cold dread slit my throat and dripped down my chest.

The Bloodletter.

Dad.

"Calum?"

Those bloody words stuck in my throat, choking me as if the entire song was scratched from my mouth down to my stomach.

"You were right," I choked. "My Dad has to be working with the Orieno."

Her hand reached toward me, but she pulled it back before her fingers could brush my arm.

"Which means we really need to get out of here, Calum. If the Bloodletter is here along with Morphis, we don't stand a chance if they catch us."

I mouthed, "Okay," but didn't move.

"Calum?" she touched my arm.

"Let's go," I said and started to run.

CHAPTER FIFTEEN
HEAVY BLOOD IS FALLING

-CALUM-

THE MORNING WAS QUIET AS DEATH AND JUST as dark. Clouds covered the rising sun in shades of desolate gray and across the sky lay a blanket of shadowed mist that smelled like rain.

"A storm is coming," Kate said as we ran toward the Jeep and jumped inside. "It's too quiet."

"It just seems too easy," I muttered. "I know Gae said Morphis should be gone until sunset, but where is everyone else? Where are all the Warriors that we heard fighting?"

Nervous chills drizzled down my back.

I thought, *Where is my Dad?*

"The Orieno can only stand in darkness, but we should still watch for your Dad; he's something else entirely." Kate gripped the wheel tighter. "But you're right. Something's not right. If all the Warrior's are gone, I don't know what we'll do. And if Morphis has more Orieno on his side, it'll be just like before. Everyone dead. Gone."

I caught my reflection in the door's mirror: Lightly tanned skin, dark hair, eyes like moonlight reflected in a deep sea. Everything about me looked the same as it was days ago, yet I didn't recognize myself.

I thought of Mom and Tyler and didn't think they would either.

I turned to face Kate and found her already looking at me with eyes filled with sad memories and grave possibilities.

She said, "It's really just you and me now, isn't it?"

"Yeah," I said. "For now I think it is."

Dust clouded behind the Jeep, swirling in our wake like billowing dirt fingers trying to pull us back as we rocketed down the mountain toward Ashfall.

"The sun is already so high in the sky," Kate said. "We don't have much time."

"We'll find a way, Kate," I said, gazing up at the darkened, blue-kissed sky. Clouds rolled in from beyond the mountains, hiding the sun so it was mostly gone. "We have to."

~

The steep road fell past tall trees and sharp cliffs, and slowly began to open onto a town that looked as though ghosts lived in every foreboding crack. Beyond, the mountains rose in uneven peaks, dark silhouettes.

"It's been like this since my parents betrayed us," Kate said, slowing as we got closer to the place where green met gray and died in an instant. "Ashfall is where most of that blood was spilled. The Order has tried to restore it but nothing works. No amount of magic can restore something touched by so much death."

"Then why does the Woman of Prophecy still live here?" I asked.

Kate shrugged. "Witches are wildly different than enchanters, Calum. They are dark, unnaturally wicked creatures who use the blackest of blood magic, and find themselves in the darkest of places. Their magic is like a drug to them; they can't stop once they start, and eventually it becomes all they are. If they stop using, they die. Besides, the Woman of Prophecy probably likes it here, surrounded by a town unable to live. That, and she's bound by the Order - by an ancient, unbreakable spell - to stay in Ashfall."

"She can't leave?"

"Not unless she has a death wish *and* there's another witch to take her place. There always has to be a Woman of Prophecy. The duty is usually passed down through bloodlines from mother to daughter in death, but I don't think this one has any children."

"So will the Order find someone else?"

Kate nodded. "They'll try. If another witch is brought in then the current one will die as soon as the power is passed between them. But if they can't find another, this witch will be trapped here forever withering to nothing. And even then she'll be forced to protect our secrets."

"That's horrible."

Kate's bright, violet eyes glinted in a flash of moonlight. "That's the price of dark, blood magic."

Buildings rose before us in the brazen shine of the shy sun, like a handful of tombstones rising from the dirty brown grass of a desolate cemetery. Their windows shattered with tiny, webbed cracks; glass hanging down in sharp shards clinging to twisted vines. Trees, most a lifeless gray or sickly white, broke the deserted streets in two like skeletons dancing around the rusted cars.

Nothing moved.

Nothing lived.

When we reached the edge of the wasteland, past the heaps of broken, sunless images, Kate pulled into the parking lot of an old church.

"I remember when I used to follow Gae's flowers here," Kate said. "Nothing but lines and lines of red and yellow and blue and purple flowers from the lake all the way here."

I smiled and, against the church, it felt wrong.

I could see the block of stone that once supported it crumbling to pieces; black and gray bits surrounded the building, slivers of dead faith. On the roof, a large wooden cross tilted forward. Even from here, I could see deep holes decayed through, hollowed places where history spread disease. On the crossed beam of it, someone had spray painted "tonight the heavy earth is falling" in dark, dripping orange that looked like old, dried blood.

Kate said, "Calum, you're squeezing my hand."

"Oh, sorry." I let go but my eyes stay focused on the cross. Something about the church made my head spin. The shattered windows and the dead-looking wood made me want to keep running. "Are you sure this is where she lives?"

Kate leaned forward and pointed a finger at the front door of the church. "Right there is where the flowers always stopped. I never went in, Gae forbade it, but I always touched the black door, always only once and just for a second, before running back."

"Why?"

"I wanted to see if the stories were true. That if you came too close to the witch's house her magic would trap you inside so she could lick your bones, cook your flesh over a black-flamed candle, and eat your heart." Kate's eyes moved to the cross looming above. "I did it because it was forbidden. But no story is completely true, and here I am just the same as before, flesh and all."

"I doubt you're the same person as you were back then, Kate. No one ever stays the same for long."

"Maybe." She turned to me. "Ready to go inside?"

Palms against jeans, I rubbed until my hands felt raw and warm. My mouth dry and burning hot, I said, "Oh, *yeah*. Let's go. That story didn't freak me out at all."

Under our feet the dried gravel lawn crunched like teeth grinding hungrily together, each wooden step to the porch like creaking old bones. Long and winding, the porch was dotted with rusted-red nails and lines of thin silver webbing poked with spiders.

The scent found me quickly: Honey-sweet sulfur and the sickly tangy smell of rotting, burning things.

Death.

Fear punched me hard in the stomach, grinding a strong fist deep inside before pushing up at my heart and squeezing it until I could barely breathe.

Still, the smell of death was ruthless, screaming from the church like a chorus of rotting corpses singing blood songs into the night.

I opened my mouth-

"No!" Kate gasped, her hand covering her mouth. "It's a spell. Don't breathe."

But it was too late. I felt the poisoned air race through my veins like fire. I *burned* with it. Toxic flames licked inside me growing hotter until I was shivering cold with heat; I was death, frozen and still and lifeless.

I couldn't move.

Slowly, so that the creak echoed in the night like a hundred children softly crying, the black door opened.

I saw her fingers first; four thin sticks dark as

charred wood covered in gilded rings, red and black with shining stones. Poking through the dark slot of shadow, each fell to a hard, slow beat, drumming on the door frame one by one. I heard the scratch of long, crusted nails against decaying wood, soft then harsh, as if clawing through death was like breathing in the mountains for her. The lost hand pulled up from nowhere and gave the woman's stained lips a puff from a thin black stick. Her lips opened to cracked yellowed teeth, dotted brown and black, feathering in the wave of her smoky breath like dust in the wind.

In my mind, fearful words exploded.

Her face, half covered by darkness and twisted locks of thick brown hair, I could barely see. Only the light of her dangerously bright eyes shone through the shadows, brushes of gray smoke swirling around them, a savage violet in the wicked dark.

-KATE-

MY EYES LOOKED BACK-
at me-
at her.
Those are my eyes, I thought.
My eyes looked back, and I-
the me that loved Adam-
the one who had two sisters-
the girl who despised her parents-
the child who became a Warrior-
the fighter who wasn't-
was gone.
Cold and cruel violet killed it all.

Breathe.
Breathe, I told myself.
It means nothing.
And even though my heart choked me, like always-
I breathed.

Breathe.

It meant nothing.

-CALUM-

It was the first time all over again, but different than the last. This time: Eyes purple as dead lips and crazed with the sweetness of sin. Wild, as though reality was imagined through them, not before.

"You's here," the woman whispered blowing more wispy gray tendrils up around her eyes. Her coarse voice, like a train going too slow, was a twang of lost letters and reproach. Her lips moved deliberately, and the blackness of them seemed permanent as though only her lips had died and the rest of her was just holding on.

She breathed and I felt it in my chest.

"You's here and it's time. Get in." She snapped her fingers: Two bones breaking, rings grinding in song. The spell vanished. "Hurry, before it's not time no more. Before you's gone." She stepped back in shadow, pulling us forward with the motion of her hands.

The smell inside was worse than death. Hot and sticky with the scent of sulfur, the wet air stuck in my throat. The church was small, closed-in with stacks of thick books and tables riddled with massive white candles, thin black and red ones strewn randomly between, laying dormant against the golden flames. Bowls and tiny, brightly colored bags dotted the floor, spilling beads that looked like teeth in dirty rivers.

"Kate?" I asked. She was still behind me, her chest moving up and down rapidly, so I turned to the woman. "Are you the Woman of Prophecy?"

The woman clutched her throat and began muttering

strange words under her breath. "Hush, boy! Yes, that's who I am for now. My name is Magdaline, but you may call me Magda."

Kate stepped beside me and shoved her hand forward. "I'm Kate Black and this is Calum Wade. We're here-"

"Don't you think I know who you's all are?" Magda's eyes turned dark, tempestuous. She waved her hands through the smoke around her. Her voice faded low. She growled, "Coming here like this, who else would you's be? No'ne else woulda been able to come in through that door. Not without fallin' dead on the ground there first. No, I know exactly who you's are, girl and boy, and what you's came for."

Magda smoothed her dress, the deep brown folds as dirty as her hair. Her chest was rising and falling so fast it looked like a storm was brewing inside her, and her right hand clutched a small pouch hanging low from a twine rope around her neck.

"Bad," Magda said, her hand twisting the pouch. Her eyes locked with mine. "Bad, bad, bad, bad, bad, bad. Not good. No. Not good at all. You's brought the evil with you tonight, boy. Let it touch you, lick you so you stuck with it. You brought that devil out to play and they's comin' for you. Ain't no more time to run away."

"Who?" I whispered. "Who is coming for me?"

Magda's eyes met mine and I wanted to grip Kate's hand but she was too far away to reach.

Magda, her tongue against her teeth, said, "Why, they's *all* comin' for you, boy. Every last one."

Magda smiled.

She shrieked-

and lunged at me, her back arched so I could see the

outline of her spine poking against her dress. Both hands grabbed at my face, and I tasted dirt and rubbery flesh over hard bone inside my mouth, bitter and salty-sweet.

"No! My heart can't breathe no more! I can't!" Magda shouted. She ripped a crack in my lip.

Blood. I tasted blood.

"Get off him!" Kate ran at Magda.

"Blood," Magda said in a frenzy, licking her lips. "It's mine. I need it, I do. Red blood, blood, blood, *blood*!"

I tried to push Magda away but both her hands were stuck in my mouth, hooked against my teeth.

"Get! Off!" Kate shoved Magda. The witch staggered back looking dazed, shook her head once, and smiled.

"Sorry. *Sorry*," Magda said in a violent whisper. "I forgot. My gris-gris must be dead. It helps, but dies as fast as I make the charms inside it. No time for a new one. You..."

She looked up at me, a trace of sadness in her eyes, and when she spoke her voice was quiet, regretful. "You's *him*. The one who is more than they think. The one who I bound years ago. The one who makes the sky so lonely without him in it. I forgot. My memory, it ain't the same as it was. It tricks me every now and then, even when I tell it not to. It don't listen, my memory, without the blood, and in this dead place there ain't no more blood to take."

Him. She had said it as though I was a bad dream come to life. As if *I* had plagued her life with misery.

"You're kidding, right?" Kate asked. Her mouth twitched up and to the left. "You're sick. Are you using too much magic, or are you normally this messed up?"

"Don't you talk about things you don't know, girl! Not to me," Magda hissed at Kate, inches away from her face. Kate's eyes watered, and it was like looking at two sets of the same violet stones: Sad, dark, angry. "Dark magic does that to you. Makes you forget. Darkness seeps in and gets in the cracks and won't ever leave you. And I got years with it. I breathe it. I *live* it. And now, it's all I am. All I got. This is my burden still, you hear me? *Mine until I die.*"

A blink. A beat. "You want to talk about death, witch? Look at this." Kate raised her red-branded finger and let her *leviti* hang near Magda's face. Her voice acid, Kate said, "You know what this is? *This* is death. It's a mark on my soul, and when I look at it the only thing I can think is that I was the one who took life from these people. I killed. I know death, witch. Know it like the back of my own hand. I *am* death. So maybe it's you who shouldn't talk about things you don't know."

Magda stepped closer to Kate and I could smell the fetid odor of her breath like skin burning in the sun. "I know things that would make your pretty hair fall out, girl. Your caramel skin rot sweetly against your skull. I know things that would make your tongue fall back in your throat and your eyes ooze out your head slow like honey."

"If you know so much, tell us what we need to know about the prophecy. We were told to come find you; Gae sent us. Help us and we won't hurt you."

"Hurt *me*?" She laughed: Nails dragging down a headstone. "Oh, child, I ain't worried about that. Not when neither of you's know the truth. None in the Order ever did. None but four who weren't."

I asked, "What do you mean?"

Magda turned her head slowly, tilting it to the right and back so her eyes were more white than anything. "The truth, boy, is everything. There's power in truth, and power in keeping it secret. I know the truth and I hold the secrets. *Your* secrets."

I swallowed back the acrid air and said, "Tell me."

"There's a price."

"Name it," I said.

Kate said, "No, Calum. Wait-"

"Blood." Magda clasped both hands around her gris-gris. "Always, the price is blood. For anything. The question is this: How much blood will satisfy the heavy price for the answers you seek?"

I needed this. "Name the price and I'll pay it."

"Calum," Kate said grabbing my arm. "Seriously, don't. I don't think we should be bargaining with a witch. Gae wouldn't have wanted this."

"I don't care," I said turning to Kate. "We have to do this. It's the only way to find the real prophecy and the only chance at breaking the binding spell on me; the only chance we have at saving everyone. You know we need to do this."

I turned to Magda and held out my arm. "Name it."

"Truth or secrets?"

I turned to Kate, asking with my eyes.

"Truth," Kate said.

Magda grinned. "About you, girl? Or the boy?"

-Kate-

"What *about* me?" I asked against the swift undercurrent of doubt sweeping me away; those words betrayed me, washed away my confidence so all that was left was a desperate need for an answer.

"I know all truths, girl," Magda said. "Yours especially." She was so close I couldn't see anything else, just the black crust of her lips and the familiar violet of her eyes that meant nothing. "I can tell you the truth you seek. I can give you what you want most in this world, all in an instant. Just pay the price, and the truth will be yours."

"How can you know something like that?" I whispered, "You don't even know me. What do you think I want most?"

"Our blood holds our stories, our secrets." Magda said, her black tongue running across her lips. "It is with us always, our blood, and it flows wherever we go, soaking up everything we are. I don't have to know you to understand who you are and what you want. Give me your blood and I'll tell you what it says, girl."

I started, "I don't want-"

"Don't you?" Magda's voice was a shadow of what it once was, like a black, placid lake before a storm. "Don't you want to know about your parents? About why they betrayed what you believe in? About *you*? Pay the price in blood and I'll tell you its truth."

"Kate," Calum said. "You don't need to do this. We just need to find out the prophecy and let her unbind me then we can go. I'll pay the price. Let me do this. You know who you are already."

But I didn't.

Not ever.

Not really.

My heart weighing me down, I said, "I'll pay it."

"Kate!"

"I have to, Calum. I *have* to."

"Without even knowing the price?" Magda asked.

"Name it then," I sneered, but I knew the price meant nothing; I would do this if it meant my life. "How much blood will it cost for me to know the truth about my parents and me."

Magda's tongue ran across the stubs of her teeth, sliding against them like a black leech against jagged rock. She said, "Not how these spells work, child. To know the truth you must be willing to give everything you's got. Sometimes it's until your heart stops. Sometimes it's just a drop. The blood will know the price. All we need to do is let it flow."

I nodded. "Fine."

"Come then," she said and ran a finger down my arm. Cold. Cold. Cold skin against mine. She squeezed my hand and pointed to a broken brown leather chair in the corner. "Sit over there next to the table."

I walked forward. Cuts and tears split the chair like a puzzle, pieces of yellow foam poking out from distressed hide. I could see lines and lines of coarse rips where hands might rest. Red stains where wrists might lay. Beaded blood in the seat, dried and hard.

Against everything, I sat, the chair and the blood cracking beneath me.

Magda looked around the room as if she'd forgotten I was there. She muttered to herself, words like wind in a quiet storm, and walked over to the round table in the center of the room where she lit white candles to burn around a tan bowl, dripping wax down to the wood. She flipped through a book covered in deep brown leather; dust rose and blended with the glow from the candles.

"Kate." Calum came to stand beside me. He kneeled and said, "Are you sure about this? You don't even know how much blood she'll take."

"I have to," I said again.

He nodded. "I know." And then, "You could die."

I met his eyes. "So could you."

"I know."

"This is something good," I said. "We need to do this. I need to do this."

"Good is just another shade of evil," Magda chuckled. "No such thing as black and white, you know. Good or evil. We all bleed the same. In this world there's only life and death, and those in between. Soon the lines will blur for you's. Always do." She ran a crooked finger down a page, her rings bursting with light so close to the candles. Her lips puckered as she searched. Her hand moved toward a yellow bag on the table. She undid the neat twine holding it together and let a mountain of tiny teeth form on the table. Black fingers taking hold, she closed a fist around a pile and brought her hand to her mouth, crunching down on the teeth. Bones breaking in her mouth, she smiled.

"There you are," Magda whispered, her face so close to the book it blew more dust into the air; bits of teeth puffing out. A low hunger in her voice. "Been so long since I seen you. Forgot what you look like. What you sound like. Such beauty in this spell." She lifted the bowl into the air with both hands and turned to me, her eyes glinting madness. "You ready to know the truth?"

No, I thought. *No, I'm not ready.*
"You could die."
And then it would all be for nothing.
This is too much.
"Yes," I said. "I'm ready."

Magda, her crusted dress crinkling as she walked, stepped slowly over to where I sat, every step echoing in the unhallowed church.

"Put your arm over this bowl," she said, putting the tanned basin stained red on the table next to me.

My arm touched the gritty surface. This close, I could see the smiling skulls carved in the sides of the bowl, and I thought of the Order. Of the Warrior skulls leading down to the table where the Elder Council sat. Of Gae. Of Marcus. Of the blood we once shared so long ago, and if that ritual was like this one.

If that one had a price, too.

But as Magda pulled a white, bone knife from her sleeve, I knew that this time was not like the last.

"Is this like a blood oath?" I asked.

She raised an eyebrow. "It is not. You have experience in blood words, girl?"

"No," I lied.

She smiled. "Mmm."

I closed my eyes.

I felt the knife slide across my wrist: Fire on fire on fire. And then as soon as the blade cut me, it was gone, and there was nothing but a faint tingle of pain where a slice of it once was.

I turned.

I looked.

Red was born from the slit, flowing up like some living thing breathing. Tiny rivers of blood trailed down my palm to my fingers and dripped into the bowl.

Drip.

Magda dipped a shaking finger into the bowl of my blood. She touched a drop to my forehead, and then dotted the lids of her eyes with red, bloody circles.

She whispered, "Blood is my eyes."

Drip.

She ran a finger over the black of her lips, coating them in shining red. "Blood is my lips."

Drip.

Her tongue unraveled slowly from her mouth, black as her lips, and she made a line of red down it. "Blood is my tongue."

Drip

Drip.

Drip.

Drip.

Seven drops was my price.

Smiling, she picked up the bowl and touched the tip of it to her lips.

"Blood is my voice," she said.

She drank.

I watched as lines of my blood etched her chin in dark red.

She screamed.

Her whole body began to shake. I heard her bones rattle, quake beneath her flesh. Ripples of muscle began to run across her skin, moving like snakes beneath a dark sea. She threw her hands down on the table, her head jerking out, crying into the clouded air.

The dust seemed to swirl as though alive, making shapes in the dim light with bits of chewed teeth. I saw a scene begin to shape before me. The dust became a tornado.

It moved toward us, faster and faster. Magda's voice grasped the air on a crescendo until her voice began to sound like thousands.

Blood. All I could think of was blood.

Then, just as the candles blew out and the room went dark, Magda touched a bloody finger to my forehead and I found myself screaming as the blood dripped down.

"This is the only way, Christopher," she said. "We have to keep our daughter safe. You know this is the only way to protect Kate."

Christopher nodded, his lips a tight line. "I know, Ema. But I don't like it."

Her smile was sad, worn. "Neither do I, but Brigid and that young Warrior, Gae, promised us that Magdaline would protect her."

"I still hate that we have to trust a witch," he said. "It's insane."

"I trust her." She poked him in the stomach. Her brown eyes wild like her voice, she asked, "And what are you saying, Chris? My whole family is insane? That we'll all turn out like my mother?"

Christopher sighed, his full, deeply red lips pulling down to a frown. His pale face was beginning to look older than it was, as though time had taken him hostage and wasn't letting go without a price. "Ema, you know I didn't mean it like that. I won't deny I'm glad it was Magda who inherited the curse and not you. It's just that all that blood takes a toll on a person. I worry."

"Blood takes a toll on us, too, Chris. It has since we joined this cause. Since we met. We've been Warriors ten years too long."

"I know," he said. "I hate that this is your life, especially now."

"It's yours too."

"But you had a choice," he said as he ran a finger down her long brown hair. "I didn't. It's always been my fate to become a Warrior. My legacy."

Emaline touched his face. "And this is our legacy, Chris. Our daughter's. You saw her eyes. We can't just ignore what she is."

"I don't want to ignore it, Ema! But look at Magda. All that blood has made her crazy, and it drives me to the brink of insanity thinking about what might happen to our Kate."

Emaline was quiet for a minute, and then, "Magda's my sister, Christopher. I have to believe that she won't bring harm to our daughter. I have to trust her."

"You don't have to trust Magda just because she's your sister. That's not the way family works. Someone might be born into your family, but they have to earn the right to stay there. You know what that blood magic does to your sister. The burden she carries is too much. She can't control herself. Her mind was lost years ago."

Emaline said, "What about our daughter then? She's only seven, a child. If you think Magdaline is so lost, what about Kate?"

Christopher's eyes were stone. "Our daughter is different, Ema. Even Brigid says so, and Gae claims she's never seen a child so strong. Kate will be able to handle the curse, I promise you. That's why we agreed not to tell her about Magda, so she won't be tempted by any influence from your sister. Kate won't lose herself to the blood. She's strong."

Emaline asked, "How can you be so sure?"

"Because she has to be."

"Still," Emaline whispered, one hand touching Christopher's, the other moving slowly over her swollen stomach. "Do you think we're doing the right thing? Kate's so young, and we'll have two others any day now."

"It's right," Christopher said. "I can feel it. You know as well as I do that even without Kate's curse the Order would still be a problem. It's corrupt. It's dying. We need to do this to save it."

Emaline tilted her head. "You really think Brigid's right? That the Orieno have already taken control of the Warriors and the Elder council?"

Christopher was silent. And then, "I've seen it, Em. I've seen the fire in their eyes, all of them. I've seen the way Marcus has changed. He's not the Elder he was when we first started. Brigid thinks he's possessed by Morphis."

Emaline clasped a hand over her mouth. "No!"

"Worse," Christopher said, his voice low. "Brigid thinks that this is just the beginning. She doesn't have the power to heal what the Orieno can do. Both she and Gae are the only ones left unchanged amongst the damned."

"Then how can we stop them, Chris? Even if we destroy the Warriors and the Elders, we still can't defeat the Siblings. They're too powerful. The Order is already too small in numbers now. What do we do when we cut it down by more than half?"

"I don't know."

"Then why are we going to do it? We have children, Chris. We have lives already. Let's just stay where we are."

"We can't," Christopher said. "Don't you see that? If we let things stay the way they are, we will never get the chance to be happy. We'll never, ever have the family we want. Brigid has assured me of that. She told me the prophecy."

Emaline gripped his hand, her dark skin blending with his light. "She did? But that's impossible. How? Only Magda is allowed to know."

"Magda is on our side. She and Brigid have been planning this for years, since Magda moved to Ashfall."

"What did the prophecy say?" she asked. "Do we have a plan?"

"Yes, we do," Christopher said and turned his head away.

"Well, what is it? What did it say?"

"It's not important."

"Christopher. What did it say?"

"Nothing."

"Christopher."

"Emaline."

"Tell me!"

"No."

There was silence.

Nothing.

And then, "It's about Kate isn't it."

Christopher's eyes were red when he met Emaline's. He choked out, "Yes."

"Tell. Me."

Christopher swallowed. "Brigid says that she is destined to take Magda's place as Woman of Prophecy, that Kate will be one of two to stop this all. Brigid says that you and I are destined to carry out her plan. We are meant to take so many lives in order to protect our child's future. If we don't, they'll take her. Brigid says there's a plan to kidnap Kate and use her power against the remaining Order members. Gae has promised to keep her safe, but our daughter won't have a chance to live if we don't act soon."

"Okay. Okay." Emaline's hands were shaking. "What do you mean one of two?"

"That's why it's so important for us to follow Brigid's plan. There is a boy who will join Kate as part of her destiny. We must save him. He is the Dreamer. We can't let the corrupt find him, for that's when they will kill your sister and use Kate's powers against the world. We have to protect them both, and our plan is the only way to do it. We have to give them both those few years to live before everything changes. Magda will perform a binding spell on the boy so he won't be able use any of his powers until she undoes the spell. He should be safe until then."

"And what of Kate? What does she have to do with all of this?"

"There are two, Ema, always two: The Dreamer and the Destroyer. That's what the prophecy foretold. That's what Magda warned Brigid against."

"But... that means..."

"Emaline. Don't think about it, please."

"If... if the boy is the Dreamer then..."

Their hands together.

Eyes locked.

Hearts broken.

Emaline whispered, "Our daughter, Chris."

Christopher said, "If the boy is the Dreamer, then Kate is the Destroyer. She is the one who will end us all."

~

My eyes blinked open, and all I saw were Magda's looking back. And in that dark, violet fever I saw myself. My past and my future.

My beginning.

"Now you know they loved you," Magda said.

-CALUM-

MY WORDS DROPPED LIKE ROCKY CLIFFS breaking, falling into a still and quiet ocean, rippling waves out until they were nothing but tiny lifts against the horizon. Lost, hopeless words. I said, "That's not true. Kate, don't listen to her. It's not true."

The screaming still rang in my ears. Magda's voice painting pictures against Kate's wordless yells. Blood sliding down their faces, puddling just above their lips before falling further. Eyes white and wild, spinning madly.

"It can't be true," I said.

Magda licked her bloodstained lips, and her tongue raced over the black and red. She fell to her back, fingers dancing across her body where blood was splattered, writhing on the floor moaning for more.

Shaking, she said, "It is, boy. It's all true. Blood never lies."

-KATE-

ADAM.

"You know they love you," I told him, my hand stretching against his.

He said, "Maybe. But there are a thousand different kinds of love, Kate, and my parents don't love me like yours love you."

"What do you mean?" I asked.

"Your parents would do anything for you," he said. He ran a hand down my spine, tickling me. "They love you more than you know. Mine, on the other hand, just want me to follow in their footsteps. Be a fighter. Be someone I don't want to be."

"But they'd understand if you told them, right? I mean, they wouldn't want you to be someone you're not. They're your parents."

He laughed, sad and high like a dove shot from the sky. "I love how you are sometimes, Kate. Filled with hope, just waiting for good to happen. The world needs more people like you."

"I'm serious!" I said. "I bet your parents would understand."

"They wouldn't," he said. "You've never met them, Kate. They wouldn't understand at all."

"How can you be so sure?" I asked.

He was quiet, and there was no sound between us except for the soft brush of his nails against my dress.

And then, his voice like a secret, he whispered, *"I know, Kate, because they said if I don't become who they want, they'll kill me. I don't have a choice when it comes to destiny. I don't know if anyone really does. My life has been decided for me and there's nothing I can do to change it. Just wait and see."*

I moved closer to him, hugging my body against his warmth. *"They wouldn't kill you, Adam."*

"They would, Kate. You don't know." His chest fell with his words, rising only in between. *"The people they work for are ruthless. Savages. They would kill me in a heartbeat if I didn't become one of them."*

"Become one of what? A savage? I might not know your parents but I've known you for almost a year, Adam. You could never be a savage."

"We're all savages, Kate. All of us. Just like love, people come in all different shades, but deep down we're all the same: Savage and brutal and heartless. And I love that you think I'm different but I'm not. Soon, I won't even have a choice. We can't stay the same forever; I'm just waiting for the moment when my life changes."

"You won't change. I can't believe that," I said. *"What exactly do your parents do, anyway? Who are they?"*

"I can't tell you," he said. *"I can't tell you what I'll become."*

"Why?"

"I just can't. I'm sorry, Kate. Be happy your parents are different. They love you. Just be happy you can be anything you want."

~

When I opened my mouth, a drop of my blood slid down my throat and stole my voice, my words. It sank to

the bottom of my chest where my heart beat and waited.
    I waited. The blood waited.

Chapter Sixteen
Truth Like Poison

-Calum-

"The blood," Magda said, her voice shaking with one word that fell in whispers: *Blood.*

Blood.

Blood.

Her body twisted.

Blood.

Violent shudders moved down her spine and back again. Her smile danced from pain to glory, need to loss, as though she missed the taste of blood on her lips. As though it was the one thing that kept her alive, her tongue frantically searched for more.

Blood.

As her eyes found mine, her lips became a half-smile and she said, "You next, boy?"

"Kate?" I turned to her, trying to meet her eyes, but even when I did they were blank and lost. And, as the blood cut her face down the middle with a red line, it looked like she was wearing a mask, hiding behind someone I didn't know.

Magda stuck a finger in her mouth and sucked until

her lips disappeared. She said, "It does things to a person, the blood. Can show us truths we can't take back. The girl knows that and she's paid her price. Let her be while you take your turn."

"No," I said. "Not if it's like this. Look at her! It's not worth it."

Magda's smile slithered at the edges. "No? Not worth it to know the truth about the prophecy? To know the secrets you hold deep in your blood? This is the only way you's both will ever know what is real and what is not. You don't think that's worth it?"

I shook my head, but said, "Okay. I'll do it."

Magda crawled slowly to her feet. "Truth or secrets? Which one would you like to know?"

"Both," I answered. "I need to know what the prophecy says. And I need you to unbind me from the spell you cast."

"Truth, then," she said. "You want to know the true you, find out who he is. Truth takes the most blood, they say. Cuts through the veins like poison. Hurts the most, too. You ready for that?"

"Yes."

"Give me your hand then," she said, grabbing it and pulling me toward the round table. She snapped her fingers and the candles flamed again. When she let go of me, she moved in front of the leather book, flipping the pages like wind. "Take that candle, boy."

"Which one?"

"The black one there," she said raising a finger toward a tiny, unlit candle, blacker and smaller than the rest, and wrapped with a blue twine ribbon. "That's the one I used on you so long ago. It's made of your blood, boy. It's the only thing in this world that can free you from what I did."

She smiled, as though I should be proud. "Now, let me see your right hand."

I stuck my hand out, palm up. Before I could pull it back, I felt the cool blade of a knife cut across it, coaxing warm blood up and out.

"Now hold the candle in that hand just over your heart," Magda told me. "Hurry, boy. Do as I say."

I moved my hand to my heart, clutching the black candle tightly, and I felt a sudden pull from within me, as though I had been here before.

Magda leaned forward and lit the candle.

Suddenly, helplessly, I felt myself falling back, lost to a world I couldn't see.

Leaves falling.

No, *they seemed to scream as if they were dying. All were red, as deep and crimson as fresh blood, falling from the sky like tears, or tiny angels.*

When the first one touched the ground, I felt the earth move. My entire body vibrated with the pain of its death. I shook, terrified. Each brought an earthquake. Each brought a tear and soon my face was flooded. Another, and then another came crashing down, until I realized that these weren't falling leaves dying at all.

They were people.
They were like me.
Falling stars.
"Save us," they said. "Save us."

-Kate-

Blood.
Blood.
Blood.
Blood.
Blood.
Blood-
pulling at me-
dragging me under-
calling me.
All I wanted was the blood.
More of that sweet blood.
Blood.
Blood.
Blood.

-Calum-

I remembered.

The mist crawling through the forest, shivering. The wolves howling, and the wind whispering. The red leaves as they fell.

I remembered my wish. Just that one.

A hand brushed my shoulder. A smell like rancid bodies burning filled the air around me. "Do you feel it, boy? What you must do? Do you understand your true gift now that you're free?"

"My gift? What do you mean?" I asked.

Magda waved her fingers at me, coughed, frowned. She rolled her eyes, and instead of white all around her pupils I could see lines of red, blood. "Since the beginning, the Women have passed down a story that tells of a boy, the Dreamer, the Caeles. His soul, *yours*, is different. Your *ti bon anges*, your soul, has the power to step through the lines of time. Unlike humans, the Caeles's *ti bon anges* belongs to the stars; it's how you are born time and time again. Your spirit lives in your *ti bon ange* and knows nothing of rules, of death. It can be killed in ways, but it is not trapped like the others, not bonded to the earth, and cannot be taken by the likes of the Orieno. This is how Morphis has possessed the damned; he has taken control of their *ti bon anges*. Without their souls, they are empty vessels."

"Is that why Morphis couldn't touch me in my dreams?"

She nodded. "And it's why you need to fight back.

Your *ti bon ange* can touch the future. You've seen it, boy. You can change it."

"All those people..."

"Dead," she said. "If you's don't get their *ti bon anges* back to them, all they'd be is dead."

I asked, "What will happen if we can't return their souls? To the world, I mean."

Her voice was no more than a whisper. "Been said that when there is no more room in the deepest depths of Hell, then the damned will forever walk the earth. Without a *ti bon ange*, people have nowhere to go but bad. This is only the beginning, Caeles. Only you can stop the Siblings. Only you and the girl. Remember, you are not the Caeles yet. Almost, but not yet. You still need a key to unlock your full power. You's need each other to finish this."

"But how?" I asked. "I don't understand! Don't you get that? This whole time people have been telling me little details about myself, but never the whole story. Always what to do without showing me how to do it. And it doesn't help. It never does."

Magda walked over to table that had fallen, picking up the tan bowl on the way. She stepped in the red liquid that covered the floor, leaving bloody footprints as she walked around the room. Setting the bowl on the larger table, she went to search a cabinet that was against the far wall. Smiling, she pulled out a black velvet pouch and went back to the table.

"Then it's time for you to know the true prophecy. The Order has always known of the prophecy you seek, though they have never known how it ends," Magda said. She waved her hands over the bowl, muttering something in a language I didn't understand. Then, without warning, she pulled a dagger out of the folds of the velvet pouch and drew it across her wrist. Blood flowed freely from the cut to the bowl, filling the bottom of it crimson.

Magda said, "Blood does not have the power to hide anything. It tells the truth, even when it shouldn't."

After what seemed like too long, she put the knife away and tied a piece of cloth to her wrist. Her hands moved like the tongues of serpents, licking the air as if it were tangible. Magda touched her forehead, then her left and right shoulders, and finally her heart, making a cross on her body.

"Give me your finger," she said.

"Why?"

"Your blood holds the words of the prophecy, but mine is what gives them a voice."

I held out my finger and, before I could register the pain, her knife slid across it and my own blood dripped into the bowl. Red against red, the two were indistinguishable.

"We must drink to know the truth," she said. She brought the bowl of blood up to her lips and drank deeply. When she turned to me, her lips were crimson. I felt my stomach drop as she licked them, her black tongue searching for every last drop of blood.

She lifted the bowl, tilting it toward me. "Drink."

The church was quiet, so her voice echoed. Her breath sounded painful. Or was that mine?

"Drink, boy," Magda whispered.

I took the bowl from Magda, brought it to my lips and tasted the metallic liquid as it flowed down my throat. At once I felt warm, and wondered if it wasn't so much blood as it was poison.

"We are now connected," Magda said, taking back the bowl. "A part of you is me, and I you. It is with this lifeblood that we will see the truth of the prophecy and hear its ageless voice of reason."

Magda set the bowl on the table and started to flip through the old book.

"*Light, light, light,*" she spoke, each time a flame on the tall white candles flared bright. The words blended together like a hiss. "The blood binds our souls. With it our *ti bon anges* have become one. *Light.*"

Turning to face the book she raised her hands. I felt her blood inside me start to ignite, burn. My chest grew hot. My heart felt like it was about to burst.

The witch screamed. "*Blood of my sisters. Blood of the fallen. Light. Light. Burn. Burn. Turn my eyes to see the truth, and break the bond of life and death. Light. Light. Burn. Burn...*"

I felt my heart slow-

and then almost stop.

Magda's voice slammed into me from all sides. It was all I could hear. "*Turn my eyes to see the truth, and break the bond of life and death.*"

My vision grew white, then black. I tried to speak, but words failed. I could hear the blood bubble in Magda's throat, and I felt it in my own. I realized, terrified, that I was screaming, too. My mouth was moving, the words flooding out just like Magda's. My throat burned with pressure.

But still, no sound came.

There was only Magda screaming, and words dancing in the air like leaves in an autumn wind.

"Light floods over all,
Stars of the dream filled minds
Smile like white pearls above-

Until- They come,
Three kin with hearts so black,
Weaved tightly within dark.

Stars twinkle and fade,
So lost in the rising darkness,
Sun too weak to rise.

Then is hope, the time of the Dreamer.
The one who is lost but will be found.
The soldier who once was and will be always again.

Hope is dangerous.
Darkness will rise to meet it,
Wild and burning and cruel.

A commander will fall in blackness,
Leaving behind a ruling of false order.
They will be deceived and deceiving.

One will be two,
Heavy mind torn between those of truth,
And those of savage trickery.

Truth will be found for two,
Destroying all that was before,
And the heart of thieves will be clear.

Hope will come by two:
Two souls born as one,
Two hearts beating as one.

For one of two, shadowed heat of red will wage,
A future angered by the dwindled fire storms,
Vast as the Destroyer.

For two of one, a path not found will be taken,
Lost in dark places,
Found in light escapes.

Then, when all is lost, the time of hope is near.
One action will save them all.
One action to save the world."

I heard her body collapse, bones crack. I moved my hand around the floor and felt a wet, sticky liquid.

The world seemed darker than before, less clear. Dim light cut through the dust in the church at odd angles.

My eyes searched the room until they found Magda. My breath caught in my throat. She lay on the floor. Bones, white and red, were sticking out of her arms and legs. Her eyes, once such a bright violet, were completely white and glazed over. Blood dripped from her mouth and down her chin, forming a puddle on the wood floor. Her tongue lapped in and out, reaching for the blood.

Always for the blood.

A bone moved. Magda's hand tried to reach forward, but it was caught against the bone that was protruding from her leg. Her hand fell.

"Boy..."

I wasn't sure if the witch had really spoken, or if it was the wind against the church. I wanted to put my hand against Magda's face, but I couldn't. What was left of it was nothing more than hanging flesh upon old bone.

"Boy..." she whispered again. "Come... close."

I had no choice. With my stomach in my throat I crawled towards Magda, not daring to stand. I didn't trust any part of me.

Her hand twitched, or her foot. Bone. It was the bone that twitched. Bone grinding against bone.

"You must... *run*. Nothing... will protect... you now. Find the key. Do not be afraid of it, boy. Your soul might be yours now... but you need the power of another to keep it. Do not be afraid. Be brave... *Run!*"

-Kate-

"Girl," Magda whispered. Her breath bubbled out of her. Thick blood crawling up through her throat and out. "Kate..."

I ripped myself from the need for blood, away from the desire to do nothing but suck and lick and drink it. I felt myself break in two: Me and the blood.

For a moment, I was destroyed, and I knew what it meant to be what I was. This pain ran through my family's veins; the blood would be my burden, just like it had been Magda's.

"Magda," I said stepping slowly toward her. One foot followed by one foot, always wanting to go back. "What can I do?"

She blinked, her eyes once more violet than mine now shone a dull, faded blue. "Nothing, child. This is what must happen now that you's know the truth. I'm almost gone, but you still have time. You must run now before it's too late. You must ignore the blood. *Run*. It's not your time just yet. Destroy Morphis before you can't leave this place no more. *Run*."

I touched her, my fingers feeling dense, bloody bone, and said, "I can't."

"The blood calls to you," she said. "I know. But you have a different path than I. Follow it now, and come back to this later."

I felt a bone break in my hand.

Magda smiled, fresh blood covered her chin red, and said, "Girl?"

"What?" I asked.

"Drip the blood into my mouth. I need to taste it one last time."

I dragged my palms across the floor, scooping up everything red, and cupped them before Magda's face. Slowly, I dripped her own blood into her mouth and watched her eyes flash violet once again.

This was life, the blood.

Soon, it would be mine.

But not now.

Not yet.

Kate put her hand on my shoulder, then slowly moved it down in a line of red so she held my wrist.

"Your birthmark is glowing, Calum," she whispered.

I looked to my arm and saw the softened light of my mark. Even through my sweater, it twinkled like the stars I knew it stood for.

Why was it glowing?

Kate's voice drew me away, the quiet timbre of it too heavy inside the church. "We can't run anymore, Calum. You're the Dreamer. I'm the Destroyer. We don't have a choice. We have to fight this. I have to while I can, before the blood takes over."

I stepped closer to Kate and felt the room buzz with heat. I took her hand in mine and held it tight, hoping that somehow it would always be there. "I don't know if we can save them all, Kate."

"But we have to try," she said against teeth so gritted her full red lips fell together and turned white. When she looked at me and her lips opened, I could feel her breath hit my face, so sweet in this stale room. "What if today's the day you die? Don't you want to fight? Don't you want to live a little louder, just for this moment when you're so close to the end?"

I squeezed her hand.

Just for a moment, I forgot all about the war, that I was the Caeles and Kate was a deadly Warrior. Dreamer and Destroyer. The lost and the found.

Again, just for a moment, all was well.

I was just a boy. Kate, just a girl.

And then without warning, like so many of the worst things, normality was lost to silence; one so quiet even the lack of noise echoed in my head like an explosion as the church fell around us.

Chapter Seventeen
A Dark and Savage Light

-Calum-

The light was luminous, seeping through every crack of the old church, slowly at first, then faster until all I saw was a frenzy of blinding white.

Silence. *Silence.*

I held Kate's hand as our bodies tossed against the church wall and through it; limp dolls in a hurricane. Our bodies never touched the ground, but flew in the storm. At first, I felt nothing when we collided with the falling pieces of old glory. Then, all at once just as our hands broke apart, the pain and the sounds fell forever.

The white light exploded. The sound of wood cracking, walls crashing down. Glass shattering and falling like rain against my face.

I hit the ground hard.

I couldn't breathe.

Sharp pain stuck in my chest. I looked around but the world was a mixture of blurred vision and dust. Still, I heard screaming.

I tasted blood.

"Kate?" I called. Felt slivers of church in my throat,

choking.

I pushed myself up, splinters poking through my skin. I touched a finger to my lip and felt the wet stick of blood. "Kate?"

A voice made its way through the sky still falling, "Calum..."

"Kate!"

Against the fallen cross, she was broken. Both arms stiff, flayed out on the beams. Blood drenched her hands, dripping down and covering the words on the cross so they meant nothing.

She whispered, "I'm sorry."

My hands grabbed her wrist. Her pulse was slow and nearly silent. Her eyes flickered open and then closed again.

She was barely alive.

"Don't give up," I breathed frantically. My heart jumped around beats, skipping some altogether, forgetting how to drum. "I need you for this. I can't do it alone."

A word bubbled from her mouth, red and sticky and silent.

I knew it then.

"Kate..."

There were so many different kinds of love in the world, but just one that lasted forever: This love, ours.

It had always been love.

Kate lay in front of me, bruised, beaten and bloody. Her once soft brown hair was now a dark rust color, damp with sticky blood. Her once golden face the color of a deep morning sky was black and blue and I could barely see the girl underneath.

Against it all, I felt lost.

In this I felt so cold: Love changing. Hearts beating.

People dying. And in the dark of the evening, just before day passed to night, I felt the tug of regret against my heart.

"Stay," I said as I closed my eyes. "There's so much I want to tell you still."

I imagined the stars above, the way they blinked in time to my heart as if they were keeping it alive, and wondered if they would beat for Kate's as well. If there was anything I could do to save her.

I could not lose her.

I leaned forward and brushed my lips to hers and felt my heart cry. It was heat and fire when we kissed, as if our entire world was burning. The air around us seemed to spark and shine, with her and I breathing in the heat like oxygen.

It was only us.

And, I thought, *Only this*.

I opened my eyes and saw a bright light surrounding us like falling snow, whiting out the world.

Silence.

"Kate?" I breathed, my voice echoing in the blank time.

Nothing.

Already, I missed her eyes. The way they held the truth she could not say. The way the violet glinted and sparked with strength.

They reminded me of stars, her eyes, and in them I knew I had found my heart.

"Please, Kate."

There was nothing.

Nothing but my breathing.

My heart, lost.

Nothing.

Until-

"Calum...?" she whispered, opening her eyes.

I smiled down at her. "You're alive."

"What's going on, Calum? Your skin!" she gasped.

"My skin?"

Blackness. My skin was as black as the night sky and dotted with thousands of tiny, shining stars like diamonds. On my upper arm, in the place it had always been, was my birthmark. It shone the brightest of all, twenty-five glittering stars emblazed in a night sky.

I did it, I thought.

I stepped forward. I felt like flying. "This is it, Kate. I've done it. *We've* done it. We've unlocked my powers. I am the Caeles."

A voice to my left broke like thunder. "Now and for always, Caeles."

Kate and I both jumped as Orion emerged from nothing. Next to him stood a beautiful woman, the same midnight skin and starry-night freckles covering her body. What looked like a 'W' was marked on her neck in tiny, flickering dots. Unlike Orion, her hair fell down past her shoulders in waves of curled silver.

"Orion!" I said and moved to meet him. "How did I do it? What can I do now? What *is* this?"

He chuckled. "You found the key, Caeles. With that you unlocked the power inside you. You've become one of us again, the last constellation to rise from the ashes. We are free again, because of you. Heaven's Guard can protect the innocent once more."

Before I could speak, he turned to the woman and said, "This is Cassiopeia."

She nodded, and I did the same. She looked at me as though she could see my soul. Her eyes were colder than Orions, two graves digging deep. I wondered what she had seen that made them look like that. And then I knew. Death. And life. She had killed.

Kate had the same eyes.

Cassiopeia's voice was like ice. It burned me when she spoke, every word like frostbite. "Young Caeles, you have much to learn if you are to continue this journey. Listen. If not, we are doomed."

Orion smiled at her. His eyes, when he looked at her, were filled with something I couldn't have placed days ago.

Love, I realized. He loved her.

"What happens now, Orion?" I asked. I ran my fingers down my arms. "What is this?"

"You are a piece of hope torn from the sky, Caeles." He spoke quickly. "Your powers will allow you to call upon the stars of your constellation for help, guidance. With the stars you can control fire. Burn as bright as the stars you come from. You can become the night if you wish, blending into the shadows like a ghost."

He smiled at me. "You'll discover much more, too. You only have to wait until you are ready. But for now you must act quickly. We don't have much time before the Devil senses your curse has lifted, and we have one demon to destroy before that."

Kate stood away from us.

Though I had many, I needed one question answered more than the rest. "What was the key?"

Orion looked from me to Kate and back again. His smile widened. I saw his chest move up and down. The stars against his black skin moved slowly, and then quickly. A shooting star.

As he spoke, Orion gently followed the patterns of stars on Cassiopeia's arm. I felt like I should turn away, but his voice wouldn't let me. "Life, or the idea of it, is funny sometimes. We walk our days as hollow men, never truly realizing this day might be our last. This day might change everything. Too often it is forgotten that the truth can set us free. Today you felt that, Caeles. Willing to give your life, your soul and heart, to save another is a truth many are afraid to find. But that, truly, is the only way to find the truth of love. Real love is boundless. It is brave. Sometimes being brave just means falling in love, and to find it, we must surrender every fear we have until we are left with the irrevocable desire to believe in forever."

Orion stepped forward and put his hand on my shoulder. His body was disappearing. "Love," he said as both he and Cassiopeia vanished like a memory. "The key was love, Caeles. True love."

~

Fragments of the church still fell around us. Nothing more than ash and the lighter pieces of wood were still aloft, but the sounds of the smoldering building were enough to fill what silence was left.

"Are you okay?" Kate said. "What just happened?"

I turned to look at her. With her hair wild and filled with pieces of wood, her skin blotted with ash, burned, and blood dripping down her face from a cut on her forehead, she never looked more beautiful.

She was alive.

I reached to brush a stray hair from her face. It stuck, covered in blood, to her cheek. I brushed it behind her ear and moved my hand down her jaw, a line of red following, to her shoulder and finally her hand.

"You look like I feel," she said.

I tried to smile. I could feel my lips crack and my cheeks moan in torment. Every part of me was bruised except one.

"Does that mean you love me, too?" I asked.

-Kate-

No.

My heart said one thing-
my mind another.
Did I love him?
Yes.
But it went against everything I believed in.

As I thought about it, I felt lines of red run through
the Warrior Code and mark me free. Still, there were places
where the blood could not reach, where the vow was
unbreakable. Where a part of me would forever be a Warrior
girl caught between.

Soldier by soldier, side by side,
Never shall I break these words, or Death will reap the
victor.

Would this be worth it?

-Calum-

I saw something change in her eyes. The violet in them flashed blue. I could feel her pulse from her hand as it raced ever faster.

After a moment she spoke. "We are already dead, aren't we?"

"What do you mean?"

Her eyes never left mine. "I mean that there's no going back to what we were before. This is it. You are the Caeles. You walked into your destiny and have no way of going back. I was a Warrior but now... "

I pressed my thumb gently against her hand, felt the warmth of her skin flush in mine, and said, "There's this side to you I never knew, Kate. That Warrior you were before, well, you're still her, but now you're something more. You're dark and bright and savage. You're everything to me."

"I think I love you," she said in a breath. "But I still need to find my sisters. They come first right now, Calum. They have to. I can't run away from them. Even if the world ends tonight, even if we die, my heart needs to keep looking for them. I need to die trying."

I squeezed her shoulders. "I know."

When our lips met again I felt my heart explode even more than the church had, felt my skin burn. The world faded and became our own secret place. I couldn't breathe, or think, but somehow I went on living even more so than before.

For now, it was enough.

-Kate-

His skin was still the color of night with stars blinking slowly and, as darkness fell, he nearly faded away. "Calum, I don't know if I can be who you want me to be. I can't be that girl who falls in love and forgets everything but you."

He sighed and closed his eyes, but didn't let me go. "I don't want you to be anyone but you, Kate. And I know what that means. But you can't be afraid of this. Of us."

When Calum opened his eyes, I saw galaxies. Millions of tiny stars shone in the blue; a vast sky filled with hope. He said, "I don't want you to change who you are, but you can't be afraid to open your heart a little."

"I'm not afraid," I lied. "It's just that there are things about me you don't understand. Even if I do save my sisters, I'm cursed. This thing that I am? This witch? It's not going away anytime soon. You saw Magda. One day I'm going to be exactly like that."

"You won't. We're all a little cursed, I think, but we can still love as if we weren't. When I was little," Calum said, a smile curving into his lips, "I used to count the freckles in my birthmark and pretend they were wishing stars. I used to wish for so many things: More birthdays, better parents, a car, a dinosaur. And love."

He looked down at his arms and, still holding my hand, twisted them around so he could see the way the stars shot from his fingers up to his elbow and around to his shoulder. "Now I'm covered in shooting stars and my only wish is the one I already have; you, Kate. *I love you.* And I promise I'll love you until the end no matter what."

"You can't know that," I said and closed my eyes. My heart felt like it would rise up and choke me at any second.

"Kate," Calum whispered. "Look down."

I opened my eyes and gasped.

We were flying.

Calum hugged me close. "So this is how love feels." His voice sounded completely at ease, as if flying was the most natural thing in the world. White folds of tiny clouds floated around us, and stars lit up my face.

I closed my eyes again and felt the air run around me, felt it breathe against my skin as if it were telling a story.

I was free. *Free.*

When I opened my eyes, the night was not as dark.

From a distance I could see a soft glowing light near where the Order's entrance should be.

"Calum," I said. "Look."

Below us, hidden in the shards of the church, were words written in the dust. The reason the unhallowed place was nothing more than splinters in the wind:

I'm coming for you.
I'll destroy the world until I have you.
You can't hide.

-CALUM-

FROM A DISTANCE, THE LIGHT LOOKED LIKE hope, a hollowed sphere of light rising from the mountains. But my mind kept floating back to what was really there, what I remembered. The words written in blood. Bodies covered in blood.

Always blood.

The light wasn't hope. But then, what was it?

True night would fall in minutes; the sky was tinged with eerie silver, and faint, thin beams of dark were poking through what light was left.

The darkest hour, I thought, *is just before light takes over, but what of the moment before the light goes out? What then?*

And then, *I'm coming for you, too, Dad.*

"Hurry," Kate shouted, her voice muffled by the sky. I felt her entire body tense, growing more compact as we flew. Her voice grew delirious as I moved through the air toward the field, away from the blood in Ashfall.

I could not see her eyes, but I knew they were open.

Violet, always.

We flew against the stars, the wind.

"Faster," she shouted. "Let's go!"

CHAPTER EIGHTEEN
THOSE THAT KILL

-CALUM-

MIST COVERED THE FIELD; A SEA OF FOG rising in waves of gray and white. Shadows danced in the dust that rose from the mountains; with night came the fog of darkness; cold mixed with colder. Rancid smells hit my nose when we landed.

Cold and a lingering heat that didn't belong.

And then-

one.

My heartbeat, pounding.

Two.

My pulse, racing.

Three.

My fear, rising.

Out of the shadows came everything I wanted to stay hidden. Morphis, the heartbeat of it all, was in the middle. A smile set firmly on his face, his pointed teeth touching his bottom lip making blood drip down. A boy stood to his right, skin puckered with wounds, pale blue eyes fixed forward in something like hopeless, sorrowful conviction.

And my blood-covered parents stood at the edge of

it all. Mom was walking blindly forward and Dad was smiling. His eyes found mine and locked and held. In his eyes fire raged, burning madly as if the flames were eating his soul.

In their arms were two small girls with dark brown hair, gagged and bound with black swirls of shadow.

-KATE-

I WAS WRONG BEFORE.

It's not loving that makes people weak. It's when you love someone too much that you get hurt. Sometimes love burns with a fire so fierce it kills you like this:

Adam.

His smile.

Karen and Kelly.

Kelly's head fell back as the Bloodletter moved, smiled. A noise escaped her. A sigh? A breath?

But she was alive.

They were alive.

"Kate," Adam said stepping forward. His eyes were darker than I remembered. "You've grown since that night I took you and your sisters. I can smell the blood all over you, see it in those pretty violet eyes of yours. Didn't I tell you this would happen? We all become savages after a while. Give it time and we all destroy the people we love the most. Now it's your turn." His lips twisted into a sad smile. He tilted his head. "So, tell me, little witch, are you ready to die? Or would you like your sisters to go first?"

My mind reeled in this: *Adam.*

Adam.

Adam.

Why are you doing this?

Adam.

Adam.

Adam.

I thought you were gone.

I don't know you anymore.

Anger rippled across a scream that started deep in my stomach, ran across my *leviti* and ended in my Warrior's heart. The urge to kill was blinding, ripping through my veins like poison destroying everything but this: Adam was a boy that I once loved. Now, he was someone entirely different. He had taken my sisters, ruined everything I'd ever loved.

He had broken my heart.

Now, I would break his.

-Calum-

"You have something I want," Morphis said, sucking on two fingers covered in twining vine tattoos.

Kate's voice sliced through the mist like knives. "What do you want? Tell me!"

"Silence, little Warrior," Morphis said and waved his hand through her words. "This doesn't concern you at the moment."

Kate's entire body shuddered. Her fists were tight at her sides, shaking. Anger seemed to be rippling under her skin, moving through her veins until it reached her mouth. Teeth gritted, she said, "Those are my sisters. Tell me what you want or I will rip your throat out and send you back to Hell where you belong."

Morphis' lips tugged slowly up. "Marcus liked you, Warrior. Did you know that? I can still hear his thoughts sometimes if I listen closely enough. He loved you once a long time ago. Wanted to protect you just like that pitiful, earthy woman I killed. But you were no match for the power I could give him. Really, you're no match for anything are you, little Destroyer?"

Mutilated and dripping red, his body was bone and muscle poking out of ripped flesh, as though the possession was too much for a human to survive, even Marcus. He flicked his hands down his robes. I could see the red of his tattoos gleaming from underneath his shredded garments. When Marcus had been in control his eyes had been black, his gem had glittered menacingly on his forehead. Now, as Morphis, his eyes were a red so filled with blood they were on fire. His tongue lashed out at his lips, raking rapidly on his pointed teeth. I could see that he kept cutting his tongue on the sharpness of them, but that didn't stop him. He seemed to like it, the taste of blood.

"Look, Destroyer." A trickle of red ran halfway down his chin. "Look at what your pitiful leader Marcus has become." He ran his eyes down his body. "But still, you both have something I want. And so we will make a trade. If you do not agree with my terms, death will come for everyone you see before you, and everyone you don't."

"Tell me," Kate demanded.

Morphis laughed. "I want you both to kill each other."

"What?" I asked.

"Death, Dreamer," Morphis said. "You both must die for everyone else to live."

"Take me!" Kate shouted.

"No," I said. "You can have my life but no one else's."

Morphis said, "Both or nothing."

"Then nothing."

"So be it," he said. "Death becomes you."

Deep within my skin my blood became ice. My heart stopped. It seemed like forever until it started again.

His words pulsed with fire.

Hate.

In that I knew what Hell sounded like.

The redness of Morphis' tattoos deepened, looking like blood flowing freely; snakes of evil slithering across his joker smile. They moved faster and faster until his entire body was on fire with a crimson light. Then, almost instantly, the crimson drained from his face and crawled across his body. His arms raised high above him, the color jumped from his hands in flashes of blinding blood-light toward the sky.

The sky turned a brilliant, shining red-

then cracked to black. The moon faded briefly and all was night.

Thunder crashed as burnt-red clouds raced toward us from the heavens, lightning clearing their way. Fire erupted from lightning strikes. Everywhere, random trees were burning, their branches falling with leaves to the ground in flames.

His hands revolted from his body and, in a spasm Morphis threw them down, palms to the ground, and shouted, "Come forth my fledgling demons. Come forth! Walk within your dreams to me! It is time for you to do my bidding. Rise. Rise! *Rise!*" His held tilted up toward the sky, his mouth open.

Suddenly a massive crack erupted in the earth where his hands pressed, revealing red light. Above, the circling of trees began to die, burn. Morphis howled, roared. I could see his veins, blue with blood expanding beneath his skin. They would burst at any second.

My tongue felt large, catching the back of my throat.

People.

People crawled out of the broken earth, moving like zombies. They were possessed with red eyes, just like Morphis.

I knew. These were the missing people. This was where they had gone. *Hell.*

"*No!*" I shouted, my voice breaking and my hands reaching out to save them, useless. Kate held me back, her grip on my arm hot and firm.

Pale. They were all so pale, their souls gone. The

only life left was in their eyes. Red. They wanted to kill.

There was Kendra Little, skin turned whiter than snow. Her blood-red eyes seemed to look right through me, hunting for something. I could see her sharpened teeth and... blood. There was blood all over her mouth, dripping from her glossy lips. Brett, Justin, and Charlie were there, all covered in red. Falling leaves stuck to their faces. They didn't bother brushing them off.

They were all there, all my friends, pale and changed like all the others.

Knight.

He was unrecognizable. A rip in his skin ran down his right cheek, making him a monster. His tongue lashed out and licked the wound. Every few seconds his face would twitch to the right; he wanted more.

I wondered if they felt, if when they were possessed they were still human. Could I kill them if they were still human?

My heart stuck in my throat. I was choking.

The world stopped spinning, blackness threatened to take over the scene.

There was a moment of nothing, a second before the battle, the calm before the storm.

And then Morphis raised his eyes and met my gaze. In them there was only black and red flames. His lips rose into a sly, wicked smile. He muttered under his breath something low and deep, chanting faster and faster. His head twitched left, then right.

As his neck cracked, Hell broke forth.

Bodies lunged forward, the possessed grabbing fallen tree branches and jagged stones to use as weapons.

They were closing in, running now, moving fast like bloodthirsty dogs.

A cry. That Warrior from the cave. Zack's voice: "For the Order! The one and only truth! Let us fight and let death reap the lives of those against us!"

With Zack leading, his eyes like dark, crushing oceans, gray-covered Warriors exploded from the tunnel hidden in the mountain behind us. Their *levitis* pointed forward, the silver blades in their hands caught the moon's light and, even in the dark fog, glinted with hope. They screamed, eyes mad and hungry for the sight of death, and charged against the Orieno.

Then: A familiar scent. Old raisins, with a metallic note hidden at the end. A body stopped me and I felt as though I had hit a brick wall. Ghostly hands seemed to find my lungs and squeeze. *Squeeze* until my eyes were too wet to see clearly.

My mother.

She was leaning against a tree, her shirt and pants stained red with blood and tinted with what looked like bits of flesh. She was smiling, laughing, and swinging a broken arm in circles. The limb's hand, red and fleshy and bitten, glinted against the dim light shining on the field, and I saw something that made my heart fall.

A wedding ring.

Even covered in blood, it glittered in the moon's light, its yellow diamonds pieces of lost hope in the night.

Lost memories.

Lost families.

Next to her was my father.

Their two smiles hit me the hardest, so red. Both thrust broken arms and legs like weapons deep into those that passed them, whether they were against them or not.

Then my mother reached down with one finger and stroked the phantom arm she held, gathering a glint of crimson blood on her finger. And, with a smile on her face, she brought her finger up to her mouth and licked it. Her cheeks sucked in, and her eyes flew back into her head, relishing the taste of death.

The Bloodletter turned to me.

"Son," he said. "This will all end with you."

-KATE-

I FELT A FIRE START IN MY HEART, KINDLING, burning and exploding in a burst of rage. Morphis was smiling against Warrior attacks, fire shooting from his hands like bullets. Karen and Kelly were crying, their shrieks like knives cutting me over and over again. Love poured from my heart.

I turned to run for them-

and then suddenly Adam was standing in front of me and everything else blurred and was gone. Only him and me, alone in a shadow-filled world.

"Adam." I pulled my hand back and closed my fist, ready.

His eyes found mine. "Run."

My fist dropped. I breathed, "What?"

"Run," he said again. "I'm going to hit you, and then you're going to run like hell. Don't look back. This is the only way you'll escape alive. Got it?"

"No," I said. "I won't leave without my sisters."

"I'll take care of them, I promise."

I shook my head. "I can't trust you, Adam."

"I know. But can't you trust that I still love you? That I wouldn't let anything bad happen to you or anyone you care about because I know it would destroy you and make you hate me forever?"

"Adam," I said, "I don't trust love, and I don't trust you."

"Then let me help you. Let me prove myself."

"Why are you doing this, Adam?" I asked. I felt my

shoulders fall. "What happened to you? Why are you on the wrong side?"

He shook his head. "There is no wrong side, Kate, just people doing wrong things for good reasons. After everything you've been through, don't you see that?" he asked. "Even though you don't trust in love, I still do, and there are things I need to make up for. You are my good reason. So I'm going to hit you, Kate, and you're going to run. Ready?"

I stopped.

I breathed.

I thought of Adam's eyes, the way they had made me feel so happy before. Thought of the way his touch had made me lighter than air. How everything about him had made my heart soar.

How everything had changed.

"No," I said, and it was though a part of me that had been waiting to die finally did. "I'm not going to run, especially not from you."

His eyes wet, he said, "Then this might go a little differently than I hoped."

"Maybe not," I said. "You were right about one thing."

He stepped forward, hopeful. "You love me?"

"I did love you once, Adam, but not anymore." I ran a finger over my *leviti*. I thought of my parents, of the sacrifices they gave so that I could live. Of the images from the blood spell: Mom's hands on her stomach, Dad's hands on hers. Of what Adam had said so long ago. "You were right about this: I am a savage, and I am brutal. But I am not heartless and I won't sacrifice the lives of so many others so that only I can live."

"Then you're an idiot," he spat. "You'd let yourself

die just for two people you haven't even seen in five years? How can you be so blind and so stupid?"

"We all have a choice, Adam," I said. "We can be anyone we want. Love anyone we want. It's crazy, isn't it, how love is kind of like war? People get hurt. Some even die because of it. But it's worth it if we fight for the right reasons. And Adam? This is my reason: I'm the kind of girl that fights for the people I love even if it kills me."

I took Gae's dagger from my sleeve and plunged it into Adam's chest. His eyes gleamed with betrayal, with the loss of love I didn't have to give him.

"Kate, I lo-" he started, but blood took his words away.

I didn't take the knife out until I heard his heart pop and break.

I reached a hand up and closed his eyes.

I said goodbye.

-Calum-

He said, "As if that means anything to us. You're our son, and that's all you'll ever be."

"To '*us*'?" I asked. "You and Mom are suddenly some perfectly happy couple?"

"Not at all," he laughed, and as if he were trying to prove a point, he leaned over, ripped my mother's arm off and drove the sharp, pointed bone straight through her heart.

She fell with a soft thud, twitching until she was dead.

Mom, my heart cried in a beat.

No.

"She meant nothing to me," he said. "This has always been about you, son. About what you are to me."

I choked. "What am I to you?"

"My reckoning. My means to an end." He stepped towards me, slowly putting one foot in front of the other.

"I tried," he said, his words as blood-filled as his mouth. "I tried to be better once I found out the truth, but I couldn't control it."

"What?"

"It happened when you were small," he said. "Since the day you were born I would get these pounding headaches, like fire in my skull, and they would get worse whenever I was around you. Always. I hated it. I hated you because of it."

I stepped back. "You never told me."

"I shouldn't have had to. Look at you! It's your fault I'm like this. I didn't know what was happening, until one day I realized this wasn't me. It couldn't be. I would wake up and find myself standing over your crib, a knife in my hand. And the thing is, Calum, I wanted to kill you. I still do. But I know they're not my thoughts. They're his. That demon's. He's in my head all the time. Controlling me. You are the reason he did this to me. He is part of me now, and we both want you dead. I don't think I can live with him inside my head anymore. It's too much."

His lips twitched. His tongue ran across them as he said, "I tried to run away to protect you, but I couldn't. I want your blood too badly. I tried to taste others but they were never enough."

"But-"

"You have to kill me if you want to live. That's the only way I can protect you now. Kill me and you'll be free of me, son. You'll be free."

"I can't," I said.

"Then I have to kill you."

He ran at me, the mask of the Bloodletter stuck on his face with a wide, malicious grin. His fist connected with my stomach and, as I fell to the ground, I wished once more.

I am not my father's son, I thought.

I am the Caeles.

I am the Dreamer.

But, no.

I was just a boy who loved a girl. A boy who needed her to live.

I would die for that, for her.

For all these people that didn't have a choice.

So I wished.

CHAPTER NINETEEN
RISING HEARTS

-CALUM-

THE SKY WAS ON FIRE.

The high trees burned, lighting the field in a cage of danger.

The Orieno crawled across the field, rising and falling in waves of dead-gray, moving as if one large breath of darkness.

My Dad's cold fingers grabbed at me, tearing bits of my flesh away until I felt the warmth of my blood drip down.

A cry broke through the moaning of the Orieno, a scream in the night so dark. Morphis: "Die, Dreamer! Die like you should have years ago!"

My head fell back and I saw the stars above, saw the moon shining full and bright in the otherwise darkened sky. I saw the leaves fall from the trees like drops of blood bleeding down from the stars.

My dream, I thought. *This is my dream.*

This is the future, the past come true.

And then the sky exploded in a light so blinding white it seemed almost black.

They fell from the burning sky like red leaves drifting down from autumn trees; broken constellations turned fallen stars. They were hundreds, covering all but a lone patch of moonlight next to me that shone red with blood.

"Caeles!" a voice called from above.

The Bloodletter snarled and fell back, rolling until he was feet from where Morphis stood with Kate's sisters still bound and gagged.

"Orion!" I cried as a gust of wind hit my face.

The clouds around his body swirled menacingly in the night. He landed next to me and said, "Caeles, it's come to this: You must choose a path. Life or death."

His hand reached out and touched my neck, a cold moment in a dark night, and I felt better.

"I don't want to die," I said. "But I don't want to be the only one left living, either."

"A difficult choice."

"I want to save who I can."

Orion nodded. "You always have. You've dreamed it haven't you?"

"Yes," I said. "But what does that have to do with anything? I already know the prophecy. I have to die."

Around us, the Orieno demons and those possessed shouted and my heart exploded in fury. It was as it always had been: Death on death on bloody death.

"Please, Orion," I pleaded. My throat exploded in pain. "How do I stop this?"

Orion's hand fell to my birthmark. His skin matched mine exactly. Brilliant stars fell fast down his arm and shot through his hand to meet my own version of a night sky. Clouds swirled around my wounds and I felt myself heal. "The prophecy you heard was nothing more than words strung together by a witch who liked the taste of blood. Remember, Caeles, that you are the Dreamer, and the true prophecy was just a dream you had long ago. Anything can become true if we allow it, but what do you think dreams are if not the moments we step through time to see what could be? You can step through this. You can stop this, too, if that is what you want. Perhaps that is what the prophecy meant all along."

"I can stop this?"

He nodded. "You are the Caeles. Use your power."

"How?" I asked, my heart beating fast.

"Feel it in your heart, Caeles. Love is the key to everything. Let desire burn through your veins and explode out your hands in fiery glory." His voice grew beyond the cries of the Orieno and the Order. Bold and fearless, he shouted, "Use your love to rid the world of everything against it, until the only thing left is your heart bursting, rising in love!"

I closed my eyes, squeezed them shut, and thought of the girl I met days before who I had known forever.

Kate.

My heart boomed against my ribs until I could barely breathe and all I could think about were her eyes. So violet in a shadowed world. Our eyes meeting and that one moment lingering forever, shining a bright light in my life so dark.

You're my reason to fall in love.

I thought of leaning forward, brushing my lips to hers and feeling the heat and the fire and the entire world burning around us in love.

Kate.

It had always been about love.

I opened my eyes and saw Orion smiling in the

center of a mad world tinted red with blood. When I looked down, my hands were on fire, bursting with bright flames flickering blue-violet in the dark, red night.

-Kate-

I RAN AGAINST STARS AND WARRIORS FALLING dead.

Move, I told myself.

Faster.

Run faster.

Almost there.

I pulled my hand back in a tight fist-

felt the rush of anger feed into my *leviti* as I gripped the dagger.

Five more feet, I thought.

Four.

Kill.

Three.

Just kill him.

Two.

Kill Morphis!

One.

"You've taken nearly everyone I've ever loved!" I yelled as I let my fist fly. "I will die before I let you take my sisters from me too!"

-Calum-

AMONG THE FALLING STARS, I COULD NOT find my heart.

And then, I saw her jump toward Morphis, saw him smile and grab Kate and sink his teeth deep into her neck. Saw the look of pleasure on his face as he sucked and swallowed her life.

I saw her fall.

"Kate!" I shouted. "No!"

Against everything, I ran.

My heart flew in front of me, carrying me forward so fast it was like I was flying through the air. Wind ripped my hair back and stuck in my eyes like needles.

In a second, I was there.

I slammed into Morphis, grabbed him by the waist and threw him against a tree. He stood, but I shot a blast of fire that hit him in the chest.

"Kate?" I leaned down and wrapped my arms around her body. I shook her.

Nothing.

"Kate!" I cried. "Be alive! Please, Kate! Please!"

"She's dead, Dreamer."

Morphis moved like a ghost across the field until he was standing before me.

He grinned and blood spilled down his chin. Kate's blood. "Pity, though. She tasted so good."

Rage like I never felt before shot through my veins and beat my heart until it was all I could feel, until the world turned so blue it burned for the one thing I missed.

I gripped the fire in my hand, pulled Morphis against me, and shoved a fiery burst into his stomach.

He stumbled back. "You'll need to do better than that if you want to defeat me."

I turned my head up to face the moon, thought of my Dad and Mom and Tyler and Kate and everything I'd ever lost, and felt the light of the moon shine down on me like hope.

I closed my hands tighter, turned to Morphis, and let out an explosion of blue-violet.

He raised his hands in a shield of burning red.

"Your dreams are nothing," he said. "You have no-"

He stopped, and put a hand against his throat.

"What is-" he choked.

His body started to glow, shine as though a fire had started inside of him. Slowly, the fire broke through his skin and erupted in violet flames over his entire body.

"The blood oath," a voice from below whispered.

I looked down. "Kate! You're alive!"

"It wasn't for you." Weak, she tried to smile.

I slid my hand under her head. "What wasn't for me?"

"Before I knew you, Marcus forced me to make a blood oath with him. To kill you." Her breathing came slowly. "I... I think the blood oath I made with Marcus was meant for Morphis, not you, Calum. Marcus knew all along that Morphis couldn't have my blood. It was cursed to poison him. Marcus was protecting me."

And, as Morphis exploded in a burning violet light, I leaned down and rested my lips against Kate's.

-Kate-

"Kate!"

As I pulled my lips away from Calum's, I heard a voice I had not heard for years.

"Kelly?" I shouted.

I felt a burst of happy energy.

All around us the Orieno were slowly falling back to sleep, and I knew they would wake as the people they once were. The Guard were rising back to the sky, and Calum was next to me.

I opened my mouth. "Karen?"

I looked and saw them walking slowly towards me. Shadows still covered their arms and legs, but they were smiling with tears in their eyes, calling me.

I smiled and, for that moment, my heart felt like it was bursting out of my chest.

I grabbed at Calum's arm and pulled myself up. I didn't feel the burn in my legs, or the pain in my neck. I just ran.

And then a man came out from the shadows, walking towards my sisters with a knife in his hand.

The Bloodletter.

"No!" I screamed and ran as fast as I could.

"Kate! Wait!" Calum shouted behind me, but there was no time.

Feet from them, I pulled Gae's knife out and shoved it deep into the Bloodletters skull.

He fell.

Dead.

I flung my arms around my sisters, finally.

"I missed you both so much," I cried.

"We love you," they said with their faces buried in my sides.

I turned to find Calum, but when I saw his face I didn't recognize him.

"He couldn't have been the Bloodletter anymore. Morphis is gone," he whispered. "He couldn't have been possessed anymore. He wasn't the Bloodletter."

CHAPTER TWENTY
BLOOD CALLS BACK

-CALUM-

I HEARD HER VOICE AS THOUGH SHE WERE miles away. She kept calling my name, saying words I couldn't understand, her eyes pleading with me to forgive.

I looked at her through eyes streaked with tears. She didn't look the same. Her hair was just as wild, her eyes just as violet as they had always been. Her freckles, the same. I searched still, but couldn't find the girl I loved beneath everything she had become.

"Calum?" Kate asked, her voice breaking. "I had to. I thought I had to."

Just then the sun broke through the clouds, streaking in jagged lines through the dust. The light played against my skin. A new day was starting. The sun rose higher and higher in the sky until it became a beacon.

"Calum?"

The sun hit her body from behind. Standing a few feet away from Kate, I was trapped in her shadow. There, in that gray and cold limbo, I felt something inside me change. The fingers of the sun trailed across my hands, my arms, and then my neck. A disembodied soul. It seemed the hands focused there, each finger like a burn. Like sweet betrayal choking me.

Who did I blame for this?

"Calum, please. I had to."

"I know, Kate," I said, caught in the darkness she had made. "I forgive you."

-Kate-

Blood.

I heard it singing my name-

calling to me louder than before, and I knew Magda was gone.

Dead and gone.

I reached out to touch Karen's fingers, to brush my hand against Kelly's, but I felt a dark shadow inside me pulling me back, away. My body flung back.

I heard my sister's screams.

I said, "Keep them safe."

Calum nodded but said nothing.

I met his eyes, deep and blue and wild as an untamed sky, and said goodbye.

The blood called me back to a place already dead.

CHAPTER TWENTYONE
THOSE FOUND AND LOST

-CALUM-

TWO BODIES CLUNG TO ME AND, ALTHOUGH I didn't know them, I hugged them back just as desperately as if I did. I ran my fingers through their hair, squeezed their shoulders, and told them not to worry.

"Where did she go?"

"Where did our sister go?"

I pulled them closer.

"She'll be back," I said against their screams.

In this first light of morning, the world looked darker than it should have. Bodies littered the ground in pools of blood, pieces of misshapen lost lives, and severed heads stuck in odd places like headstones looking up at the sky.

This place was a graveyard for the lost-

My father laying crumpled in a dead heap with my mother's blood still stuck to his lips. Knight, pale white and shaking, holding Kendra Little in his arms, sobbing quietly until both were silent again-

and the found.

My shirt was wet with tears and warm from two little girls holding on tightly to the only person still standing. Against their paled, golden skin, mine looked burnt and blotched with faded stars.

Still, I pulled them closer.

"It's okay," I said. "It will be okay."

And then, as I remembered the place where I began and the people that once lived, I closed my eyes and whispered a simple melody into the air; a slow, sad song for a sad day; a few words to remember:

When the moon's away
And our tears fall down
And our fears fall down
And our hopes fall down-

Our hearts beat on,
Our hearts beat on,
Our hearts beat on.

When the sun comes up
And the girl is gone
And the night is gone
And the world is gone-

Our hearts beat on,
Our hearts beat on,
Out hearts beat on.

"I'll keep you safe," I said.
I hoped.

Author's Note

There are many facts woven into this story, but only some of them are completely true. I've taken liberties with the idea of Morpheus, Greek god of dreams and leader of the Oneiroi "Dreams" triplets. There are many interpretations of the Oneiroi, but I have molded the idea that Latin poet Ovid presented when he named them as Morpheus, Phobetor, and Phantasos. I also played around with the Arthurian legend of Merlin, and the idea that Myrddin Wyllt was his modern image. There have been several claims that a prophet named Lailoken was truly Myrddin Wyllt, and therefore Merlin, so I thought it interesting to incorporate that as well. And, as with everything else, I chose to bend and break some of the constellations and star patterns in the sky to better fit the story. Any differences in the reality of astrology were intended. For Calum's constellation, I focused on the latin word "Caeles" (pronounced "KAI-leyss") which means "divinity/dweller in heaven" and used that name as a model for both his character and his power.

Acknowledgments

To my Mom because she was the first reader, and the first believer. And to my Dad for always being there. I won't thank you for all the things you both have done for me over the years because that list would be another novel entirely, but I will say this: Thank you both for letting me run after my dreams with my whole heart, and for giving me the courage to believe. To you both, I am forever thankful.

Thanks to my sisters, Kara and Kelsey, who would fight for me even harder than Kate fought for her siblings. Rest easy, because I would do the same. Thank you both for being there no matter what, and for being the only two people in my world that never asked me when I was getting a job.

Many thanks to Amy, Jean, Toby, Gordon, and the many people that helped me learn about myself at Hazel Park High School.

A special thanks to Abby, Lindsay, and Brandon who know me better than anyone in the world. You three were, and continue to be, my lifelines to the real world, and my closest friends.

A big thanks to early readers, Will and Rachel and Matt, who asked me repeatedly if they could read this story until I caved. And to Donna, who read this story years ago when it was a completely different story.

To my whole extended family, both blood related and not, who have given me endless amounts of happy memories.

A big thanks to Keary Taylor for designing such an amazing cover and for her early enthusiasm. To Helen Boswell, the Queen, for her support and superb editing skills, and for her friendship. And to you, the reader, and to all those I've forgotten, my thanks is yours. Always.

DAVID JAMES lives in Michigan. He has worked as an editor and a teacher, and still dreams to one day be a Power Ranger. He lives for cool autumn days, gummy worms, bad movies, popcorn, and books.

Learn more about David's writing process at
http://djamesauthor.blogspot.com

LIGHT OF THE MOON
DISCUSSION QUESTIONS

1) Describe the relationship Calum has with his mother and how it differs from Tyler's relationship with Mrs. Little. Are they fundamentally different, or are they both faulted?

2) Kate's *leviti* marks her kills. As a Warrior for the Order, she had no choice in getting it. Do you think she still would have chosen to get her *leviti* if there was a choice? Why or why not?

3) Calum chooses to believe in what Kate told him about the Order before he is shown proof, though his mind is assured soon after. Do you think a person can choose what they believe even if they can't see it? Or do they need some kind of affirmation to be sure?

4) On page 183, Calum says, "I was afraid of death." He's explaining that he is afraid to die when he is sure there is more to the life he has been living. What do you think of this? Is there a part of your life you would want to change if you were in Calum's place?

5) When did you first realize that there were romantic feelings between Kate and Calum? Why?

6) On page 188, Kate says that "Words have power when they have purpose." Do you agree? Why or why not? Do you have any examples from your own life?

7) On page 213, Kate says that "There's always a choice." Do you believe that? Why?

8) On page 216, Kate and Calum stand in a "place where things came back." What do you think this means, exactly? Do you think this same idea applies to real life as well?

9) As we see through her parent's flashback, Kate is racially mixed. Does this make a difference to you as a reader? Because her skin is so light in coloring, were you even aware of this fact? Did it make a difference to you when it was stated in the flashback scene?

10) On page 229, Orion says that "War is very rarely the answer to anything, and never so when the ultimate goal is power." Do you agree with this statement? Why or why not, and what real life circumstances made you think so?

11) On page 236, Orion says that "Sometimes bravery comes from letting your heart make choices your mind cannot." Do you agree with his statement on love? Why or why not?

12) When Calum is being judged by the Elder Council, he is placed in a seat comprised of jawless skulls. What is the significance of this? How do you feel about the Order's judgment system, and do you see any similarities to their system in our lives today?

13) We see that Kate, along with many others, is beginning to question her faith and belief in many things. Do you think that faith or belief in something can change over time? If you agree, why do you think so? If you don't, why not?

14) On page 274, after Gae is killed, we see Calum tell Kate that "feelings make you stronger." Do you believe this, or do you think that Kate was right to believe that a strong person should be devoid of emotion?

15) The town of Ashfall is based on the poem "The Waste Land" by T.S. Eliot. Do you note any similarities between that poem and the city itself?

16) The graffiti on the cross that sits on the church in Ashfall says "tonight the heavy earth is falling." This is loosely taken from a translation of the poem "Autumn" by Rainer Maria Rilke. What things about the poem and LIGHT OF THE MOON do you find are similar?

17) Do you believe there is a price to pay when finding out the truth of things?

18) On page 291, Magda says that "Good is just another shade of evil." Do you agree?

19) On page 301, Adam tells Kate that "There are a thousand different kinds of love." Do you agree? What instances have you seen in real life that suggest this? In this story?

20) Do you think loving someone makes you weak? Explain.

21) The legend of Myrddin Lailoken tells us that he fell in love with a witch while trying to find his sister. Now that the story has ended, do you see any similarities between his story and Kate or Calum's?

22) During the final battle scene, Calum's original dream at the beginning of the story comes full circle. Can you see the similarities between the two?

23) Throughout the entire story, Calum and Kate struggle to trust each other. Why do you think this is? Do they ever truly trust each other? How have you felt like this in your own life?

24) Kate decides to go against the Warrior Code to risk saving her sisters, and eventually, Calum. How is this similar to what happened to her parents?

25) The idea of fate, or the idea that life is a circle, plays a large part in this story. What are some instances that you found in the story that suggest this?

26) Throughout the entire book, the subject of avoidance is brought up. In what ways do you think Calum and Kate and the rest of the characters in this story avoid things, or fail to deal with difficult situation until they absolutely have to?

27) Many times, Kate claims that she does not believe in or trust love. Why do you think this is? Even so, does she still love Calum? Her sisters?

28) At the end of the novel, do you think Calum still loves his parents? Why or why not?

29) How does the idea that hope is essential to life play out in this novel?

Watch out for

The Warrior's Code: Zack's Short Story

And find out what life was like for Kate and Zack on their journey to become Warriors.

Available in e-format
Early 2013

Find out what happens next in
Book two

Shadow of The Sun

With Kate bound to live in
Ashfall, Calum is left to
Protect her sisters and help
bring the Order back to grace.
With more blood, more magic,
and more romance on every page
this second chapter will
leave you breathless.

To be released Late 2013

Made in the USA
Lexington, KY
14 November 2012